CAPTURING HER HIGHLAND KEEPER

Time to Love a Highlander Series
Book Four

by Maeve Greyson

ARE YOU SIGNED UP FOR DRAGONBLADE'S BLOG?

You'll get the latest news and information on exclusive giveaways, exclusive excerpts, coming releases, sales, free books, cover reveals and more.

Check out our complete list of authors, too!

No spam, no junk. That's a promise!

Sign Up Here

www.dragonbladepublishing.com

Dearest Reader;

Thank you for your support of a small press. At Dragonblade Publishing, we strive to bring you the highest quality Historical Romance from some of the best authors in the business. Without your support, there is no 'us', so we sincerely hope you adore these stories and find some new favorite authors along the way.

Happy Reading!

CEO, Dragonblade Publishing

Additional Dragonblade books by Author Maeve Greyson

Once Upon a Scot Series
A Scot of Her Own
A Scot to Have and to Hold

Time to Love a Highlander Series
Loving Her Highland Thief
Taming Her Highland Legend
Winning Her Highland Warrior
Capturing Her Highland Keeper

Highland Heroes Series
The Guardian
The Warrior
The Judge
The Dreamer
The Bard
The Ghost
A Yuletide Yearning (Novella)

Chapter One

Edinburgh, Scotland
May 2019

KEYS RATTLING ON the other side of the door jarred Lyla Smythe from her search for candles. That was Abby. Time to convince her twin they could manage just fine without electricity. At least for a little while during the longer days of summer. But she needed to find those blasted candles.

"Where did I put them?" She pawed through yet another of her many junk drawers, spilling out an assortment of odds and ends to the floor. Knobs, screws, and various bits of whatnot that might be useful someday bounced everywhere. *Throw away nothing.* That was her motto.

As the creaky door whined open, Lyla scooped up the mess and shoved it back in the bureau drawer. Then, with the speed and grace of an Olympic athlete, she vaulted to the window and pushed the curtains open wider in a last-ditch effort at coaxing a little more light into the room. Sunset was not her friend. She braced herself for another of her sister's entirely unnecessary lectures.

"Why are you sitting in the dark?" Abby tossed her keys into the bowl on the bookshelf beside the door and flipped the light switch. It clicked but nothing happened. "Lyla."

How her twin could infuse so much disappointment, accusation, and condescension into one word had always amazed Lyla. "I hate it when you say my name like that." With the winning smile that always worked on everyone else, she crossed the small flat to the kitchenette. "Ready for tea, dear sister?"

"The rest of the building has power."

"Yes, it does." No sense arguing the facts. She lit one of the two burners that still managed a decent flame on the decrepit stove. Thankfully, both water and gas came with the flat, so the stove worked. Or at least, parts of it did. Pity the lease didn't include the pesky electricity. She filled a dented kettle with water and set it to heating. "Do you want tea or not?" She retrieved the squat brown ceramic teapot from its shelf inside the oven, which also didn't function but made a handy extra cabinet. With her fingertips curled into the cups stored on the same oven shelf, she glanced back and waited for Abby's answer. "Well?"

"You said you had the money to cover all the utilities this month."

"I did." Lyla pulled both cups from the oven and hooked the metal door closed with some artfully engineered baling wire. She opened the tin of tea and added enough of the rich black blend for a stout pot. Abby didn't look at life the way she did. They might be fraternal twins, but their parents were the only thing they had in common. "Mrs. McCleary had no food at all, and Mr. Culpepper didn't have enough to last him to his next check. By the way, you'll have to use powdered creamer. I stopped stocking perishables." This was not her first time without electricity. "I concluded perishables are quite the waste of money because they perish." She chuckled at her own play on words.

Abby sagged down into the overstuffed chair Lyla had rescued from the curb before the trash collectors carted it away. "You cannot keep doing this."

"Of course I can, and I fully intend to." She squinted at the containers in the cabinet above the stove. One box held biscuits for humans, and one held treats for the dogs she walked every day. Both metal canisters were the same size and color, and she couldn't remember which was which. The deepening shadows hid the descriptions she'd written on them in black marker. Bloody hell, she wished she could remember where she put those candles. She opted for the box on the left, popped off the lid, and sniffed. Dog biscuits. Perhaps one of these would put Abby in a better mood. They always made Herschel the bulldog happier.

"This is exactly why I left London and came here." Abby wrestled her way free of the chair's threadbare yet overstuffed cushions and stormed toward her. "You take care of everyone at the expense of your own needs. It is not sane, Lyla. You deserve better. Why won't you let me help you?"

This again. Lyla returned the pet treats to the shelf and closed the cabinet. "I did not ask you to leave your posh flat or successful practice on Harley Street. I get along just fine here in Edinburgh. You and Mother are the ones with issues. Not me."

"We are worried about you. Ever since your miscarriage—"

Lyla turned and shut that conversation off with a look. "Not another word. When you showed up here, uninvited I might add, I was happy to see you, but I thought I made it clear I would tolerate no psychobabble. Save it for your patients." She pulled in a deep breath and centered herself as much as she could. She didn't need this right now. Not with her intuitiveness nettling the bloody hell out of her for reasons she had yet to discover. "The pub pays me tomorrow, and the coffee shop the day after that. I'll get the power back on then."

"I will pay it." Abby snatched up her purse. "I should be paying my share anyway."

Lyla grabbed hold of the expensive designer bag and stopped her. "You will not." She locked eyes with the sister who looked nothing like her. Auburn hair. Puppy brown eyes. Big boobs and at times, what seemed like a small heart. So different in both mind and body; she always wondered if the hospital had sent one of them home with the wrong parents.

A soft pecking on the door interrupted their standoff.

Lyla yanked the purse out of her sister's grip and carried it with her to the door.

Before she could open it, Abby stopped her. "Aren't you going to ask who it is or check the peephole?"

"'Tis Mrs. McCleary," said a wavering, high-pitched voice from the other side.

"There. Are you happy?" Lyla rolled her eyes. If there had been any danger, she would have known it. Instincts hadn't failed her yet. Or at least, they didn't whenever she listened to them—and understood what they were trying to tell her. She opened the door and beamed down at the kindly old soul who grandmothered everyone she met. "Come in, Mrs. McCleary." She ushered the gray-haired lady inside. "I just put on the kettle. Would you like some tea and biscuits?"

Peering through her smudged, wire-rimmed spectacles, the widow toddled forward. Her confused squint deepened as she looked around. "Since when do ye take yer tea in the dark, lass?"

Lyla waved away the tiny woman's wonderings, not wishing her to know what really happened to the money earmarked to pay for the electricity. "Power's off. Probably just a blown fuse. I was just headed down to the boiler room to check."

"Ah well, I'm glad I caught ye then." Her clenched hands trembling, Mrs. McCleary lifted two brightly colored cloth shopping bags higher. "I promised ye some when it came ready. Remember?"

Lyla didn't remember but wasn't about to let on that she didn't have a clue. "Let's take these over by the window. Abby, where are your manners? You've met Mrs. McCleary. Say hello."

"How are you today, Mrs. McCleary?" Abby offered a polite smile.

The elder responded with a sniff and a curt dip of her chin.

Lyla chuckled to herself. Mrs. McCleary might be poor, but she was proud. She had labeled poor Abby a snob early on and refused to change her opinion. "Now, what have we here?" As soon as she touched the bottles inside the first bag, she remembered her neighbor's promise. "Your homemade wine!"

The sweet woman beamed with pride, nodding and clapping. "Aye, lass, and the best batch I have ever made if I do say so m'self." She pointed at the other bag. "Brought ye four good-sized bottles." After a side-eyed glare at Abby, she continued, "I thought ye might wish to share some with that nice lad who always comes by the shop when he knows ye're walking Murphy for me."

"Now, now, Mrs. McCleary—we agreed. No matchmaking, remember?" Lyla held two of the bottles up to the window to catch the last of the sun's rays in the green glass of one and the brown glass of the other. "Do the flavors differ between the green and the brown?"

With a dismissive clucking, the matron shook her head. "Nay, lass. The green are olive oil bottles. The brown used to hold liniment, but dinna fash yerself. I clean'm all good and proper afore I reuse them."

"Who knows?" Lyla held the brown bottle higher and winked. "Maybe this one'll be a good pain reliever for muscle aches."

The amateur winemaker tittered with a delighted chortling as she wobbled her way back to the door. "I must go now. Murphy must have his tea and biscuits or he'll mope about like a spoiled bairn."

"Tell Murphy I shall see him tomorrow at our regular time." Lyla loved the little old woman and her floppy-eared hound. They were more like family than friends.

As soon as the door clicked shut, Abby started in—just as Lyla knew she would. "You sacrifice your own necessities to feed that woman who is somehow resourceful enough to not only make her own wine but serves her dog afternoon tea and biscuits?" She marched over to the flat-topped trunk that also served as a coffee table, flipped it open, and snatched out several pillar candles.

"So that's where I put them." The trunk. Lyla remembered now.

After lighting the candles, Abby continued her rant. "She is using you. How can you not see that?"

"She and Murphy had not eaten since Sunday. Two whole days, Abby. Almost three." Lyla resettled her stance, barely holding herself back. The urge to shake her twin was strong. "And do you know how I found out they were starving and needed food?"

Her sister opened her mouth as though to speak, then closed it and shook her head, looking more sheepish by the minute. She slowly lowered herself to perch on the edge of the couch.

Lyla stabbed the air with a judgmental finger, then pointed at the door. "She was crying to her dog and apologizing. Even though it wasn't her fault her pension check got nicked when that maggot stole her purse." She bore down on her sister who always jumped to the wrong conclusions. "If I had paid my light bill rather than buy her and Mr. Culpepper a few staples for their pantries, I couldn't stand to look at myself in the mirror. I'll take the temporary darkness of compassion over the convenience of light every time. Do you not agree?"

"I am sorry. I didn't know."

"You never care enough to find out. That's your problem." Lyla didn't soften the attack. "I know you consider me an uneducated, soft-hearted, karmic-believing twit, but if you can't accept me the way I am, then go back to London. Tonight." She took a step closer and poked the air to stress the final ultimatum. "I didn't ask you to come here and don't need you mucking around in my life."

Abby's bottom lip quivered, and her big brown eyes went even wider. "I really am sorry. And I don't think all those things about you. I love you. You're my sister."

Lyla allowed herself a groan and turned away. "Do not start with the puppy dog eyes. It works on Mother. Not me."

"You are my only sister, and I worry. I promise that's what's always at the heart of everything I do."

Before Lyla could reply, the lamps flickered and then flooded the flat with light. She frowned and rubbed at the eerie tingling across the back of her neck. While she believed in many things, magic was not one of them. "I wonder if we won a drawing or something," she said.

Her landlord's trademark rapid-fire knocking shook the door, rattling the hinges. "Miss Lyla," he boomed out loud enough to be heard across Old Town. "It is Mr. Bulgari."

"And Mrs. Bulgari," his wife shrilled, sounding like she always did—irritated and ready to wage war. Poor Mr. Bulgari must be in trouble. Again.

"Busy place tonight." Abby settled deeper into the couch pillows, appearing relieved by the interruption.

Lyla opened the door and invited them inside. "Mr. and Mrs. Bulgari. How are you?"

Once tall but now stoop-shouldered and covered in tattoos, the older man scrubbed a burly hand across the top of his bald head. He gnawed on the end of what Lyla believed was the same unlit cigar stub he'd had when she met him over a year ago. "We do not wish to trouble you, Miss Lyla, but my wife insisted." He grunted as his wife's plump elbow caught him in the ribs. "And I agree with her," he hurried to add.

"It is the right thing to do." Mrs. Bulgari bumped him out of the way with her sturdy girth made even wider by the cardboard box she carried on one hip. "Mr. Culpepper told us how you help him with food. And how you help nice old Mrs. McCleary and her dog." With a huffing grunt, she slid the box of foil-covered containers onto the table. Her bright red fingernails flashed and clicked as she flamboyantly flitted her hands, accenting every word. "It shamed us that people in our building, good people who always pay rent, did not feel they could come to us with their troubles."

Bracelets rattling, she dramatically clasped both hands to her well-endowed chest. "I always cook too much." Her overly teased and lacquered hair didn't budge as she jerked her head from side to side. "I think my boys will come to eat with their mother, but they never do. Inconsiderate sons, I have. Too busy, they say." Her scowl melted into a trembling smile. "But it is a shaming thing that some under my own roof should go to their beds hungry, while food goes uneaten in my kitchen."

She offloaded two covered dishes, hefted the box back onto her hip, then nodded toward her husband. "Mr. Bulgari paid your light bill this month, and as long as you live here, he will pay it. You help us much and fix things he can't." Her heels clacked across the hardwood floors as she marched back to the door. "Is that not so, Mr. Bulgari?" She arched a painted brow in his direction.

"It is so." Mr. Bulgari gave his wife a genuinely loving smile and bowed. "I am proud to have such a caring woman who thinks of everything I forget."

"Come. We have meals to give out." Mrs. Bulgari tapped a toe, then blessed Lyla with a smile. "You are a good girl. Thank you for reminding us to be better." Before Lyla could respond, she jerked her head toward the hall. "Come, Mr. Bulgari. Why do you doddle when we have so much to do?"

Her obedient husband hurried after her, pausing long enough to give Lyla and Abby a smiling bob of his head before he gently closed the door.

"That poor man," Abby observed.

"He would be lost without her," Lyla countered. Over the past year, she had witnessed their byplay and recognized the pair as having the sort of romance found in fairy tales. Browbeating and food were Mrs. Bulgari's love language, and Mr. Bulgari fully understood and enjoyed it.

She lifted the foil off one of the deep platters. "We dine like royalty tonight, Abby. Mrs. Bulgari's carbonara is the absolute best."

Abby appeared at her side. "All that for just the two of us?"

"She's been trying to fatten me up since we met," Lyla said.

"And marry me off to her youngest son."

"Is he handsome?" Abby's teasing tone made Lyla smile. Their arguments might be heated at times, but neither ever held a grudge. Peace between them almost always resumed quickly.

"Tall like his father or short and sturdy like his mother?" Abby continued as she gathered their dinnertime necessities from the cabinets. "I might be interested."

"Mama's boy to the nth degree. Poor bloke was the last to move out on his own and nearly didn't escape." Lyla checked the other plate. "Oh, and she brought homemade garlic bread, too. Yum!"

"If we eat all this, we'll go into a food coma and be in no condition for our hike to watch the stars." Abby set mismatched silverware on the table and added a couple of tattered cloth napkins and a pair of glasses. "You know…we could go to the shops on Saturday. A few new tea towels. Napkins. Dinnerware. I've been here since March. Two months and you've yet to let me pitch in."

"If I let you pitch in, you might stay forever." Lyla forced a careful lightheartedness into her tone. She loved Abby dearly and enjoyed having her around. Especially since she had felt so out of sorts of late. But her dearest sister could also be a royal pain in the ass. Even though they were twins, sometimes a few hundred kilometers between them was a good thing. She lifted a bottle of the homemade wine to change the subject. "Shall we open a couple of these now or keep them all for while we're waiting for the meteor shower?" Bless Mrs. McCleary's heart. The bottles only held about a pint each.

"Water now. Alcohol once we reach the summit of Arthur's Seat. Agreed?" Abby filled the glasses, then frowned at the kettle still steaming on the sputtering stove. "We haven't had our tea yet. Shall we combine teatime and supper?"

"If there's enough water left. It's surely all boiled away by now." Lyla loaded their plates with the creamy, parmesan-coated pasta littered with mouth-watering bits of crispy guanciale. Or maybe pancetta. Or rashers. She didn't know or care. All she knew was that the fried bits of cured pork were delicious.

"Kettle's empty," Abby announced as she seated herself, then leaned over and sniffed her plate. Bliss filled her face as she picked up her fork. "Water for now. Carbs. Then off to Arthur's Seat to enjoy the stars with Mrs. McCleary's wine. Yes?"

Mouth already full of food, Lyla nodded and lifted her glass in a silent toast. Finally. Something they could agree on.

LYLA REALIZED SHE had been wrong. She and Abby had more in common than the same set of parents. They shared a love for the stars. Always had. For as far back as either of them could remember.

"You know," Abby called out from behind her, struggling to walk, talk, and breathe at the same time. "We could have taken the trail that's a gentle stroll along Salisbury Crags."

"You're out of shape." Lyla tossed a grin back at her sister. Too much time behind a desk had made her soft. "This way has the best view. Just look down there at Edinburgh. All lit up like a Christmas tree. And you can enjoy the Crags from this route, too."

"If you say so." Abby panted and wheezed, stumbling along, the beam from the headlamp strapped to her cap bobbing with every step.

Lyla adjusted her cap's beam to better light the dirt trail and prevent stumbling. She didn't want to risk breaking the wine bottles stowed in her backpack. Out of mercy for Abby's less-than-athletic state, she carried all four of them, plus two canisters of water, a blanket, and the brass monocular she had borrowed from Mr. Culpepper, who had once been quite the seafarer. Abby's backpack only held two bags of chips—basically crunchy, potato-flavored air. The distractions of cell phones and pagers stayed back at the apartment. Nothing tonight but pure relaxation.

Clear skies and a refreshing summer breeze accompanied them. It was the perfect evening for the nearly two-hour hike to the summit of the extinct volcano. Arthur's Seat. Overlooking Edinburgh. She paused and let her gaze sweep across the vista below. The city's nightlife made it sparkle and gleam like a blazing crystal chandelier. But man-made lighting couldn't compare with the blanket of stars filling the sky. The serene beauty floating above her lifted her spirits, appeasing the elusive unknown that had been nagging at her for the past few months. It was glorious, like a dark sea carrying endless points of light to the edges of eternity and beyond.

The closer they came to the summit, the stronger the wind gusted, pushing against their backs as if to hurry them along. Lyla loved it. She'd worked up a bit of sweat. But thanks to her daily walk with her four-legged patrons, breathing came easy as they reached their destination.

"Bloody hell." Abby sagged forward and propped her hands on her knees, sucking in as much air as she could. "I have to find a gym here in Edinburgh." She reached up and flicked off her headlamp. "No need for this now. Plenty of light from the moon."

Lyla slid her pack to the ground and started unpacking. "Here's the blanket. Over there looks nice and grassy. Pat around to make sure we don't end up with rocks up our bums."

"Now, who's the bossy one?" Abby shook out the wool plaid, spread it across the ground, then crawled back and forth over it, smoothing the wrinkles and patting it down for stones.

"We'll weigh it down with these." Lyla placed a pack on the corners of the dark green and blue Blackwatch tartan, then took out a pint of wine for each of them. "Liniment or olive oil?" She held up a green bottle in one hand and a brown in the other.

"Olive oil, thank you." Abby accepted the pint, pulled out the cork, and sniffed. "Wow. What proof is this?"

"Knowing Mrs. McCleary, stout as she can get it. It'll probably peel paint." Lyla settled down beside her and uncorked hers with her teeth. Fumes wafted up into her face, making her nose tingle and her eyes water. "Wow is right. I wonder if it's safe to drink?"

"You go first," Abby said with a sisterly nudge.

"Coward."

"No, just cautious. That's why you're seven minutes older than I am." Abby beamed a wicked grin as she clicked the neck of her bottle against Lyla's. "I toast your fearlessness, Lyla Louella."

"Call me that again and I'll roll you back down that trail." After another sniff of the possibly volatile beverage, Lyla tossed caution to the wind and took a hearty swig. Big mistake. Liquid fire. It burned her mouth. Her throat. Every inhale sizzled hotter than the one before. She fully expected to spew flames at any moment. But the sensation finally abated and settled into a pleasant, blood-warming mulberryness that seemed to increase the capacity of her lungs and charge her energy to full capacity. Amazed, she stared at the bottle. "She should sell this as a health tonic. I can breathe better, and everything's brighter and more focused."

"I think that's called being stoned." Abby hazarded a sip, immediately choked, and succumbed to a coughing fit.

"Don't panic." Lyla thumped her on the back. "Ride out that first wave. Soon you'll be breathing better than you have in years."

"Bless my soul, you're right." Abby pulled in a deep breath, her eyes widening in amazement. "I wonder how she makes this stuff?"

"A secret she'll take to her grave, I'm sure." Lyla hazarded another taste, bracing herself for the initial burn. It wasn't as bad, making her wonder if she'd seared off a few nerve endings the first time. She took a deeper drink, noticing more of a sweet grape flavor than the mulberry tanginess this time. "And it changes with every sip." She nudged Abby. "Give it another go.

You'll see what I mean."

Abby took a deeper swig, then giggled. "Keep this up and we'll be too rat-arsed to make it back down the trail."

A blaze of brilliant white streaked across the sky.

"Look! It's starting!" Lyla set the bottle aside and plopped onto her back. She snagged hold of Abby's shirt and tugged. "Lay back like this. The stars wash across you."

On their backs, shoulder to shoulder, the sisters stared up at the radiating points of light shooting across the backdrop of star-studded, velvety darkness.

"They remind me of a pod of dolphins jumping through the waves," Abby whispered.

"Nature's fireworks." Lyla reached up and stretched her fingers toward the sky. "What if we could catch hold and ride along with them? Wouldn't that be wonderful?"

Abby didn't answer.

Lyla let her hands drop and turned to her twin. "Abby? You all right?"

"I'm a bit unwell, actually." Eyes squeezed shut, Abby held the sides of her head as though she feared it would split in two.

"Probably the wine." Lyla pushed up to a sitting position. Or tried to. A nauseating, spinning sensation shoved her back down. "Bloody hell. It's hit me now."

"Do you think it poisoned us?"

"I don't know the symptoms of alcohol poisoning." Lyla risked opening an eye. The whirling didn't seem quite so bad as long as she kept still and didn't open both eyes at the same time. "You're the one with all the degrees. Are nausea and head-spinning symptoms?"

Abby started crying. Not sedate adult tears, but the high-pitched, whiny blubbering of a child with hurt feelings. "Don't make fun of me for being smart. I just wanted to help people. That's why I went to University."

"God help me," Lyla muttered to herself. She wasn't well enough to deal with a crying drunk right now. Especially not when that drunk was Abby. "We'll just rest here until we feel better. I'm sure we'll be fine." She forced open both eyes, determined not to miss the rest of the meteor shower. Big mistake. Unseen pressure rushed in from all sides, squeezing against her and somehow making it seem as though the land itself was about to shoot her upward. She swore the ground trembled as if preparing to heave. "Abby—did you feel that?"

Still holding her head, Abby groaned, rolled to her knees, and barely made it off the blanket before she started retching.

"Believe I'll join you." Lyla rolled the other way and rid herself of everything she'd eaten for the past month. "Bloody hell, I think I just turned myself inside out." She collapsed back on the blanket, curled into a ball, and prayed to die so she would feel better.

THE SICK CHURNING in her head and stomach finally abated. The weird squeezing-in from every direction stopped, too. Thank heaven for that. Lyla cracked open an eye the barest slit then fully opened them both. Daylight? How in blazes had it gotten to be daytime already? She hadn't passed out. If she had, she would know it. Maybe.

Her sister huddled beside her on the blanket, kneeling, hunched over with her arms hugging her head and her nose touching her knees. Turtle-in-the-shell mode. She had done that since they were little any time she got overwhelmed.

Lyla poked her. "Abby. It's morning. Wake up."

"I am not asleep," came the muffled response, but her twin didn't move.

Lyla nudged her again. "Come on. It's morning. We must've passed out after we got sick. Let's have some water, then head down for a proper cup of tea to sort us for the day." She pushed herself to her feet, squinting against the day's sunny brilliance.

Gorgeous sky—lightest blue with brushstrokes of wispy white clouds. Birds singing. Warm summer breeze rustling across the grassy hillside. She turned to take in Edinburgh's grandeur in the morning light, then froze in place and almost choked. That was not her Edinburgh, her precious adopted city. That was a…a village. "Abby, get up! Now!"

"I feel like pure shit this morning! Stop yelling at me." Abby uncurled from her panic position and wobbled to her feet. Hands clutching her head, eyes squeezed shut, she swayed in place. "My noggin is splitting. Do you still keep aspirin in your pack?"

"Your headache is the least of our worries." Lyla rubbed her chest in a futile attempt at slowing the rapid pounding of her heart. Something was terribly wrong here, and she had no logical reason to explain it. "Look at the city. Look at it."

"Why? Is it on fire or something?" Abby stepped forward and squinted at the town below. The longer she stared, the more her scowl turned to one of bewilderment. "What is that place?" she finally whispered. "And where the hell is Edinburgh?"

"I don't know." Gone were the paved roads. The neat tenements of reddish-brown brick closest to Holyrood Park had disappeared, too. No tall business buildings. No fancy, glass-ceilinged observatories. Edinburgh Castle was still perched on its mighty rock in the distance. But even it looked different somehow. And then it hit Lyla. There wasn't a car, truck, or bus in sight. Not even so much as a motorbike. Only horses. Wagons. Carriages like she had seen on exhibit at the Kelvingrove Museum in Glasgow.

"We have company," Abby whispered, tugging her around. "And they do not appear to be friendly."

"We will *make* them friendly." Determined not to panic, mainly because she knew Abby would take care of that part in spades, Lyla adopted her friendliest smile and lifted a hand in greeting to the two men riding toward them. "If this goes bad," she warned under her breath, "shimmy over the edge and work your way down the far side of the peak. It's a little dodgy, but you can do it. Just be careful."

"What do you mean, *if this goes bad?*"

"Shh…" Lyla stepped forward, stoking her courage. "Excuse me, but my sister and I seem to have gotten rather turned around. Could we bother you for some directions?"

Both men halted their mounts and studied her, their scowling glares so cold and hard she shivered. Neither spoke. Even their monstrous horses seemed to be sizing her up for…whatever. The two were obviously Scots by their dress. And while they didn't favor each other—one being all burly and reddish-brown as if his parentage included a man-eating bear and the other a hulking, flinty-eyed Viking type come to pillage—she guessed them to be kin since they wore the same tartan.

Their kilts differed from those she usually saw around town. Not neatly pleated knee-length things. These were great sweeping swaths of belted yardage like she had most often seen in movies. Half tempted to address them as Mr. Viking and Mr. Bear, she decided to try again. "We came up here to enjoy the meteor shower last night and must've drifted off to sleep." She tossed a glance toward the town below. "And now, this morning, we are…confused." She pointed at the castle in the distance. "Could you tell me the name of that fine-looking fortress?"

"Who are ye?" The blonde mountain with the steely eyes edged his horse closer. "And what business do ye have in Edinburgh?"

"Lyla," Abby said in a trembling whisper. "Lyla—where are we? That cannot be—"

Lyla caught her twin by the shoulders, gave her a hard shake, then locked eyes with her. "Panicking. Will not. Help."

"But—"

"Who are ye?" the scowling Highlander repeated in a tone that dared her not to answer.

With an arm around her sister, Lyla forced a smile. "You must forgive my manners." She flipped a hand as if shooing away her rudeness. "It's our confusion, you see. I promise we are never this rude. I'm Lyla Smythe and this is my sister, Abby Cornwalt. It's a pleasure to meet you, Mr.—"

"Chieftain Grant Reddoch."

The way the man bit out the words reminded Lyla of rumbling thunder. An exciting tingle rippled up her spine and ordered the tiny hairs on the back of her neck to stand at attention. She swallowed hard and nodded at the other man. "And you, sir?"

"Malcolm Cransie. War Chief to Clan Reddoch."

The burly man spoke with an odd, hitching rhythm as though he struggled to get out the words. Before she could respond, he brought his horse up even with Chieftain Reddoch's. "Prisoners, my chief?"

Prisoners? Lyla shoved Abby back toward the ledge. "Run, while I stall them."

"But—"

"I said run!"

CHAPTER TWO

"WHO ARE YE and what brings ye to Edinburgh?" Grant pointed his sword at the one who talked so much yet said so little. The one calling herself Lyla. Both women appeared to be English. Or at least they spoke with an English accent. Nothing about the two made sense. Their clothing. Their feigned confusion. Had to be spies for certain. But for whom?

He moved closer, caught the sun with his polished blade, and glinted it in the stubborn one's lovely hazel eyes. He noted they shifted to a deeper green depending on what she said. A sure sign she lied. "Answer me, m'lady. What brings ye this far north? Why are ye skulking about here above the city?"

"We are not skulking, and I already told you." She squinted against the bright reflection, turned her face aside, then whispered something over her shoulder to her softly weeping sister. Bound back to back, the two sat on their blanket, and there they would stay until he had some answers.

The woeful sister keened out a high-pitched yowl, drew up her knees, and rocked forward.

"Abby! Stop! When you do that, the ropes cut off the circulation in my hands. Now, sit up and get hold of yourself. Panicking helps no one." Lyla shot him a fierce scowl that stirred a wee bit of admiration in him. "Will you please at least bind us side by side so I can help her? She doesn't handle things as well as I do."

"I dinna believe ye are in any position to make demands, m'lady."

"I am not demanding. I'm asking. Nicely." She tossed her head and huffed a golden-brown curl out of her face. "Please," she repeated. "She is not well, and I'm worried about her."

"The crying one does look a mite peely-wally," Malcolm murmured for his ears alone.

"If I could give her some water, it might help calm her." She aimed a pointed glance at one of the strange bags on the plaid whose pattern he didn't recognize. "And something for her headache."

So, the fetching Englishwoman wanted her bag? Probably had a weapon inside. Did she think him a fool? He snatched it up, then frowned down at the curiosity in his hands. What looked to be the entry point of the heavy canvas sack was sealed tight with strange-looking bits of metal. Not hooks and loops but tiny toothlike things. Something clinked and sloshed inside. Glass bottles. "Are ye a smuggler, then?"

She rolled her pretty eyes as if he was some sort of eedjit. "No. I am not a smuggler. My neighbor shared some of her homemade wine with us. All I want is that water canister on the side there and the bottle of aspirin from the front pocket. If you want to go through the pack, go through it. I have nothing to hide."

He turned the bag and studied the odd container she called the *water canister*. It was some sort of large metal bottle coated in an oddly textured paint as blue as the sky and capped with a lid shinier than his steel. He tapped on it. "This is the water?"

"Yes." She tipped her head toward her sister. "If you will untie us both so I can take care of her, we won't try to run again. I promise. She is in no condition, and I would never leave her behind. Then I'll empty both bags, and you can go through everything. Deal?"

Here on the peak, it was doubtful the women could get far if they decided to go back on their word. At least here, Malcolm could stand lookout until they decided whether to return to Edinburgh or head back to the keep. "Untie them," he ordered.

As soon as Malcolm freed the one called Abby, she rocked forward and balled up on the blanket. Lyla shushed and patted her, bending to whisper into her sister's coal-black hair. The pair looked nothing alike, even though they claimed to be sisters. Must have different fathers. Either that or it was all part of their poorly contrived lie.

With a heavy sigh, Lyla rose and held out her hand for the bag.

He relinquished it, curious to see how she opened the thing.

She pulled the water canister out of the cloth loop that lashed it to the side of the bag and handed it to him. "Here. Hold this while I get her an aspirin."

"Do ye not fear me?" He felt mildly insulted.

"I do not cower. It solves nothing—especially where you're concerned, I think. Do you not agree?" She ran her fingers along one of the outer pockets. The metal teeth made a soft hissing sound, then the flap sagged open. She retrieved a small vial full of amazingly identical white pebbles, then plopped the bag on the ground and took the water container back from him. "Thank you."

Without another word, she knelt beside her sister, offering the hysterical woman the water she poured into the lid of the canister. "Come on, Abby. You've got to pull it together. Have some water and aspirin, then I need you to try and tap into that strength I know you have. Can you do that for me? I can't get us out of whatever this is without your help. You get that chin up and keep it there. I know you have it in you."

Instinct told Grant what he witnessed now was the truth.

"I dinna think they are dangerous," Malcolm whispered from behind him. "The wee upset one seems truly distraught."

While Grant agreed, he still believed they should proceed

with caution with these two. After all, it had been but two days since his uncle had been hanged, drawn, and quartered in the town below. All from trusting the wrong ally. It was a dangerous time. He trusted few without solid proof of their loyalties.

Still snuffling and jerking with an occasional hiccupping sob, the dark-haired sister hugged the water cup to her chest but at least remained upright. Lyla, the fearless one, seemed pleased with the progress. She rose to her feet and turned to him. "I honestly don't know what else to tell you about us. As I said, I am Lyla Smythe, jack of all trades and master of none." She cast a glance back at her sister. "Abby is the brains of the family. A psychiatrist, in fact. Helps people sort out their problems."

"Hard to believe," he said. "The woman canna even *sort* herself."

Hands tightening into fists, Lyla jutted her chin higher. "There is no need to be rude. It has been a very trying morning for her."

The slight quiver in her voice made him peer closer. Protectiveness flashed in her eyes, illuminating the flecks of gold. Even though the top of her head barely made it to his shoulder, she carried herself with the ferocity of a fearless guardian. Or a courageous warrior queen who was so much more than she appeared. The clinginess of her strange trews and tunic both shocked and inflamed him. While not as amply curved as her sister, her lean tautness did not leave him wanting. Well, actually it did. Her appearance left him wanting her. The rattled sister might not be a danger, but this one definitely was.

"Where do ye live, Mistress Lyla?" He pulled in a deep breath, then leaned a hair closer and drew in another. An air of intoxicating sweetness came from her. Like a garden filled with newly bloomed roses. Nay, more like fresh honeysuckle. A clean, beguiling scent—not the nauseating stench of a cheap brothel and its overly perfumed whores. For certain, this Lyla was a lady. Or perhaps an expensive mistress. By no means was she a common harlot. He indulged himself with another deep inhale of her pleasing essence.

"I live in Edinburgh. And please call me Lyla." Eying him with a perplexed look, she tried to give herself an inconspicuous sniff, then seemed even more befuddled. After a glance back at the city, she chewed the corner of her lip for a moment, then shook her head. "But that place doesn't look like where I am from."

"That is Edinburgh," he said. Her confusion seemed genuine. And neither did she flirt or play with words like he expected from a spy. Either she was very good at whatever game she played or was as disoriented as she acted.

"The date?" Abby rasped in a quivering whisper.

With a concerned frown, Lyla turned and squatted down beside her. "What's that?"

Stricken with uncontrollable shivering, the dark-eyed lass lifted her gaze and fixed it on him. "Today's date. What is the date?"

"Twenty-three of May. Why?"

"The year?" Abby urged, her whisper becoming more strained.

"Year of our Lord, 1650."

The cup of water fell from her shaking hands, and she rocked back and forth, muttering.

Lyla rolled back on her heels and plopped onto the ground. Mouth ajar, she stared downward as though dumbstruck.

He studied them closer. For whatever reason, the date sorely troubled them. "What is wrong?"

Abby didn't answer, just rocked faster, mumbling under her breath. He fully expected her to wail at any moment. Either that or throw herself over the cliff. He motioned for Malcolm to stand between the women and the ledge. Crouching beside Lyla, he shifted his full focus to her. "Tell me. Why does the date trouble ye both so?"

"Uhm…" Her unblinking stare was still locked on the ground, and she trembled a weak shrug. "It's a…it was…" She stopped, swallowed hard, then wet her lips. With a jerk, she straightened and finally looked him in the eyes. "A year ago today, our father was murdered. We swore to dress as the sons he always wanted until we avenged his death."

"I see."

She was lying. Her eyes betrayed her again. Their greenish-gold hue shifted to a more vibrant green than a Highland glen in spring. The golden tint to them all but disappeared. But for now, he would act as though he believed her. "My condolences, mistress." He nodded at Abby. "To the both of ye."

"Even though we are twins," Lyla continued her voice strengthening. "Abby was always closest to him." With a sad shake of her head, she lowered her voice. "She hasn't been the same since that terrible day." She hugged an arm around her sister and yanked her close. "Isn't that right? You were always Father's favorite."

Abby stared at Lyla, blinking fast as though waking from a dream. "What?"

"You were always the favorite," Lyla repeated, then shifted her attention back to him and winked. "She never admits it. Mother and Father always liked her best."

Abby pressed the heel of her hand against the end of her nose. "I need a tissue. Badly."

"She needs what?" Grant preferred to communicate solely with Lyla. Even though he knew she was lying, at least she behaved with more sanity than her sister. "What is a *tissue*?"

"Uhm…it's French for handkerchief," Lyla explained as she pulled a wadded bit of whiteness from her pocket and shoved it into her sister's hands.

"*Mouchoir* is French for handkerchief."

The sly minx recovered well. She gave her sister a fond nudge. "You told me *tissue* was French! Shame on you." With an apologetic shrug, she gifted him with a smile he didn't trust in the least. "She always does that. Makes up words to fool me. It's a sister thing. She likes to tease me because she has schooling and I do not."

Abby gawked at her as though she thought her mad. "I do not—"

Lyla cut her off with a hard shake. "Of course, she always denies it. She's the teasing one of us both. Always has been."

Grant stood and raked a hand across his eyes. These two made his thoughts knot so hard that his head ached. He did not need this distraction right now.

"Yer orders, my chief?" Malcolm squinted down at the two women, appearing just as perplexed.

"Gather yer things, ladies. Ye will come with us." He turned to Malcolm. "We can ill afford to leave them here. Our enemies must not notice our presence until we have accomplished Lady Napier's request."

On her feet and attempting to get her sister to stand, Lyla shook her head. "I assure you we won't tell anyone we saw you." With a dismissive shrug and flip of a hand, she peered into her sister's face as if trying to communicate without speaking. "I don't even remember their names. Do you?"

"Chieftain Grant Reddoch and War Chief Malcom Cransie," Abby supplied in a tremulous voice.

Lyla flinched as though struck, her mouth tightening into a hard line. After a frustrated huff, she lifted her chin. "We won't tell anyone we met you. You have my word."

"I fear *yer word* gives little reassurance, m'lady." He scooped up both their bags and handed them to Malcolm. "Lash these behind the saddles, aye?"

"Wait! At least let me pack the rest of our things." She picked up the water canteen by the loop on its side.

Something about the way she held it told Grant exactly what she intended. He grinned. This should prove interesting. He lifted his hand and halted Malcolm. "Let Mistress Lyla and her sister pack their blanket and water."

As Malcolm lumbered forward and set the bags in front of them, Lyla swung the canteen, aiming for Malcolm's head.

Malcolm easily dodged the blow, caught hold of her wrist, and flipped her to the ground.

"Run, Abby!" Back on her feet, she snatched up the blanket and threw it at Malcolm.

Abby remained rooted where she stood, as lost as she had been since they found them.

Grant strode forward, grabbed hold of Lyla by the shoulders, and stilled her with a firm shake. "Enough!" He turned her toward Abby. "As ye can see, yer sister is in no condition to *run* anywhere. She will ride with Malcolm. Ye will ride with me. I have wasted all the time here I intend to waste. Now, ye can either ride like a civilized woman or I'll throw ye across my horse like a sack of grain. The choice is yers."

She glared at him. He fully expected her to spit in his face, but she didn't. "Where are you taking us?"

"My keep."

"Why?"

"For reasons of my own. Consider yerself a prisoner of Clan Reddoch. If ye behave, we will treat ye kindly."

She tried to yank away. "Liar! I know what happens to prisoners here. I've watched…I mean…I've heard stories."

"What have ye watched?" He yanked her back and leaned in until his nose nearly touched hers. "And the truth this time, m'lady."

"I have watched man's inhumanity and cruelty firsthand." She bared her clenched teeth. "Let me and my sister go. We are nothing here and won't make any trouble for you."

"Explain what ye mean when ye say ye are nothing here."

Defeat flickered in her eyes. "We are not from here," she said.

"Ye said ye lived in Edinburgh."

She scowled at him, her light brows knotting as though she suffered from unspeakable grief. With a toss of her head toward the town below, she huffed out a sad laugh. "I lied. I have never lived there."

The golden hue of her eyes had returned, muting the telltale green sign of lies poorly told. She spoke the truth this time. He squeezed her shoulders one last time before releasing her. "Ye are still my prisoner, but rest assured ye will not experience cruelty at Eadar Keep. Now, gather yer things and give me no more trouble, or ye force me to keep my word about binding ye and tossing ye over my horse."

Without another word, she yanked up the blanket, wadded it into a ball, and shoved it into a bag. She retrieved the water, took a hearty drink, then shoved it in the bag as well. After handing both to Malcolm, she went to her sister and spoke too low for him to hear.

Abby's head snapped up, and she stared first at Grant then Malcolm with terror in her eyes. She shook her head and backed up a few steps before Lyla caught hold of her and gave her a shake while leaning in close and whispering so hard and fast, she hissed like an angry goose.

"We have no choice!" she finally said loud enough for him to overhear.

At least she realized it. That would make the trip to Eadar easier. If they left now, they would arrive before nightfall. He cleared his throat to get their attention. "Come, ladies. It is time."

Lyla half-led, half-dragged her sister to Malcolm's horse. "She has never ridden before. So be patient with her. All right?"

"She has never ridden?" Malcolm cut a disbelieving look over at Grant.

These two must be poor spies indeed if they only ever walked or paid a carriage to get them where they needed to be. "And what about ye? Do ye ride?" Grant asked Lyla.

"In theory," she said while helping Malcolm hoist her sister up into the saddle in front of him. She threatened him with a pointing finger. "Be patient with her or I won't miss the next time I try to knock you out. Understand?"

Malcolm's cheeks flared a bright red. A sure sign he liked both the women. "I willna let her fall, Mistress Lyla. I assure ye."

Once her sister appeared to be as settled as she was going to get, Lyla eyed his horse as if trying to decide the best way to attack it.

"And what does *in theory* mean, Mistress Lyla?" He sauntered over and stood beside her.

"It's Lyla, remember? And it means that I have always wanted to ride but never had the opportunity." She squared her shoulders and glared at him, daring any challenge he might fire back.

"So, ye've never ridden either?"

"No, but I'm not scared like Abby. She's rather stressed right now." Her gaze swept from the ground up to the saddle. "Are they all this big?"

"Only the finest ones." He took her by the waist and hoisted her into the saddle before launching himself up behind her.

She latched on to the hard leather lip at the front, clenching it so tightly her knuckles shone white. "Bloody hell, that's a long way down."

"But ye are nay afraid, aye?" He couldn't resist teasing the defiant minx. Her courage and fire demanded it.

"Of course, I'm not afraid." She wiggled a bit, resettled her grip, and sat with every muscle tensed. "I'll just hold on tight and if I slip, I'll make sure I roll away from the horse so I don't get stepped on."

He snaked an arm around her waist and tugged her back against him. "I willna let ye fall, m'lady. After all, I would hate to lose a prisoner."

"I am sure you would." Sarcasm dripped from her tone, making him smile.

"We willna reach Eadar until late in the day. Ye will weather the ride better if ye relax." Her shoulder-length curls fluttered back into his face, treating him to a silky, rose-scented caress. That paired with her warm softness hardened him immediately. He had denied himself the company of a woman for too long, and his cock was not about to let him forget it. If he did not get his urges under control, the day's ride would be miserable for him, as well. Best try to find out more about the two strange women to take his mind off his aching manparts. "How is it that neither yerself nor yer sister has ever ridden?"

"Not everyone can afford a horse."

While that excuse could be quite true, it still made no sense that neither of them had even sat a horse. "Since ye admitted ye lied about living in Edinburgh, where are ye from?"

"Abby and I were born in Manchester, but our mother moved us to London when we were…older."

"How much older?" She was trying to come up with a lie. Her difficulty in choosing the words betrayed her as surely as her eyes.

"Twelve, I think. Maybe thirteen."

"Is that when yer father was killed?"

She didn't answer. Either the subject overcame her with emotion or she was struggling to keep her lies straight.

"Uhm…no. He wasn't killed until later. Our mother left him because she caught him with another woman."

While plausible enough, he still wondered how much of it was true. "I am sorry. It could nay have been easy for a woman alone with two nearly grown daughters in London."

"Life is never easy," she said. "That's what keeps it interesting."

"Well put." He veered the mount to the west, selecting a route along the Firth of Forth. While rocky in places along the shoreline, the way was smoother than taking the path through the woods. It also provided better visibility should anyone choose to follow them. Once they drew far enough from Edinburgh to grant him a bit of ease, they would hie to the cover of the woods.

"And where exactly is your keep?" She raked her hair out of her eyes, but the wind set the wild curls dancing back in her face as soon as she released them. "Bloody hell. Hold tight to me, will you?"

"Gladly, m'lady." He hugged her waist tighter, noting the lean, muscular strength beneath her softness. This lass was no idle soul who spent her days lounging.

She rummaged in her pockets and pulled out a strange circular blue ribbon that stretched like a strand of raw gut. After wrestling her hair back into a thick ponytail, she secured it with the bit of blue oddness, hitting his chin in the process. Twice. "Sorry. Didn't mean to pop you, but I had to get this mess under control. It makes me daft sometimes, but I always regret it when I cut it."

"A woman's long hair is her glory."

"A woman's long hair is sometimes a royal pain in her ass." She twitched a shrug, looking from side to side and taking in their surroundings. "But I think short hair is more of a bother because you have to muck with it in the mornings or it looks like a rat's nest." A hawk's cry split the air, drawing her gaze skyward. "Where exactly is your keep again?" she asked, squinting as she watched the bird floating on the wind.

"Northwest of Stirling a ways." A protectiveness for his home kept his answer vague. Besides, she would see it soon enough.

"I see." She went quiet for a while, then twisted, searching for Malcolm and her sister. "I wish he would ride closer so I could keep an eye on Abby."

"Malcolm will see that she comes to no harm." He glanced back, noting the man kept a slower pace than usual. His protective war chief and trusted friend always preferred riding abreast or taking the lead, claiming it was his duty to shield his chieftain. But not today. Apparently, his priorities had shifted to his passenger's comfort.

"You know—you could let us go once we're far enough from Edinburgh to suit you." When he didn't answer, she glanced back at him and offered a smile. "Did you hear me?"

"Aye, m'lady. There is naught wrong with my hearing." He had to admit she impressed him. Rather than greet and whine or try to turn him with seduction, she charged in head-on with whatever she wanted. "I will nay be releasing ye until I know the truth about ye and yer sister."

"I already told you the truth."

"And also admitted you told me a lie or two along with it. Did ye not?"

"Well…yes. But wouldn't you lie if someone you didn't know was asking entirely too many questions and acting all bullish?"

"Bullish?"

"Yes—bullish. All I did was ask for directions, and you and your bodyguard announced you were taking us prisoner. We didn't do a thing to threaten either of you. Fine way to treat a fellow countryman, I do say. Especially a pair of helpless females." She huffed out the same disgusted snort his mother always used when he did something that displeased her.

"In case it missed yer observation, ye are in Scotland now, m'lady. Not England. I am not yer fellow countryman." At least not yet, he added to himself, knowing it was the political intentions of some. Sharing a monarch with separate parliaments for England and Scotland was one thing. Invasion, subjugation, and placement under an English military governor was another matter entirely. "And I dare say, while I might indeed define yer sister as helpless, you are not."

"Your accent slips when you're trying to sound superior. You know that, right?"

"I am a Scot. That makes me superior. And I will thank ye to know I always speak the same."

She hissed out another snort.

He chuckled at the ease of irritating her, which made her huff again.

"Could you at least slow this beast so I can check on Abby?"

"Aye, m'lady." He did as she bade. The day's ride would prove to be a long one if this kept up. A word with Malcolm about increasing his pace and riding abreast whenever possible was definitely in order.

"Is aught wrong, my chieftain?" Malcolm called out as he drew up even with them.

"That is for Mistress Lyla to decide." He halted the horse. "Would ye care to get down and speak with yer sister?"

"I most certainly would." Her sulking tone reminded him of his four-year-old daughter when she'd been scolded for fighting with her twin brother.

"Help Mistress Abby down, Malcolm, so they might walk a bit and discuss their first horse ride." He dismounted and held up his hands. "M'lady?"

"Do not drop me just to be spiteful," she warned while narrowing her eyes in what he assumed she meant as a threatening look.

"Spitefulness is for petty women. Now, come. I willna drop ye." He caught her close and slid her slowly down his front before allowing her feet to touch the ground. Poor judgment on his part, considering his cock roared to attention with insatiable hopefulness.

She glared at him. "Very mature." Without another word, she turned to storm around the back of the horse.

He caught her arm, yanked her back, and turned her toward the front. "Dinna walk behind the beast. Could get ye kicked. He doesna ken yer scent, and ye could startle him."

"Oh. Sorry." She headed in the other direction, then paused and looked back at him. "And thank you."

With a chivalrous nod, he waved Malcolm over, while Lyla saw to her sister. "If we dinna keep them so they can see each other, we shall never reach Eadar."

Malcolm arched a bushy brow. "I had wondered about that. What with us stopping right after starting." He turned and frowned at the sisters. "She stopped her crying, but hasna said a word. Not even when I managed a question or two."

Poor Malcolm never stuttered or stalled in his speech whenever talking to men. But put the man in front of a female and it nearly rendered him mute. He had been that way for as long as Grant could remember.

Grant clapped him on the shoulder. "Sounds as though ye are the verra man Mistress Abby needs. Perhaps a quiet ride where she doesna have to talk will help calm her even more."

"What are we going to do with them once we reach the keep?" Malcolm studied the women with a befuddled scowl. "Surely, ye dinna mean to put them in the dungeon?"

"Depends on how the remainder of our journey goes." He nodded at Lyla. "My traveling companion is nay as quiet as yers."

CHAPTER THREE

THE SEVENTEENTH CENTURY. Lyla eyed the impressive fortress of weathered stone looming up ahead and didn't know whether to laugh, cry, or chunder out the oatcake and water she had choked down at midday. She wasn't accustomed to seeing castles authentically intact. Restored? Yes. Original and teeming with real people rather than historically dressed reenactors? No.

A glance at Abby took her mind off her own queasiness. Poor Abby. Left-brained and logical to a fault, this new, unbelievable reality might very well break her. And this was not the era in which to lose one's sanity. Didn't they lock them away or chain them out in the woods to starve to death or get eaten by wild animals?

"Could Abby and I walk the rest of the way?" The urge to talk her sister off the proverbial ledge was strong. Her poor twin needed her. She could feel it. "Please?"

Grant reined in the horse and halted. "Why?"

She turned in the saddle, hoping if she looked him in the eyes he might understand. Communicating with the hard-headed, epically alpha Highlander was difficult, even if her sixth sense did keep tingling across the back of her neck every time he looked her way. Her not-so-subtle instincts about him were probably off, anyway. Dislodged by the catapult back through time. "She is not well. Emotionally. I'm hoping I can help her before we get—" She tipped her head toward the castle. "There."

He didn't answer. Just studied her with those flinty gray eyes that looked straight inside her and sorted through all the rubbish in search of the truth. His gaze finally shifted to Abby who had started sniveling again. "Aye. Perhaps a walk will give her some ease."

"Thank you. I appreciate your understanding." And she did. It didn't escape her how lucky she and her sister were that Grant and Malcolm were the first ones they encountered in this mind-numbing adventure. Things could have gone a great deal worse. She didn't remember the exact dates or names of all the upheavals, but she knew this was not the most stable or safest time in Scotland's history. "I really do thank you," she stressed as he lowered her to the ground.

"Ye are welcome, m'lady. I hope it helps."

The deep gentleness in his tone touched her. Thank goodness Chieftain Grant Reddoch appeared to be a kind man. Remembering his advice, she crossed over in front of the horses and held her hands up to Abby. "Come. We'll walk the rest of the way. A good stretch of our legs will do us both good."

Malcolm nodded in complete agreement, relief written all over him as he lowered the teary-eyed woman down to the ground. "Straight beside the burn. Smoothest way," he advised with enough difficulty to make Lyla inwardly cringe. Poor man. She noticed his speech improved to almost normal whenever he spoke to Grant. It was only when he spoke to her or Abby that he struggled.

Abby hiccupped and sniffed between stolen glances at the stronghold up ahead. Otherwise, she stared at the ground, doggedly plodding at a snail's pace. Lyla took hold of her and tugged as she had done so many times when they were children. "Come on now. Pick up the pace. Time for a heart-to-heart chat."

"They are going to kill us."

"If they were going to kill us, they would have done it back at Edinburgh. Why would they go to the trouble to feed us, stop so we could pee a hundred times, or ride slower to keep you from going over the edge just to kill us now?"

"I am already over the edge and sinking deeper into the abyss." Abby hiccupped again and dabbed the bedraggled tissue to the corners of her eyes.

"Well, it's time you untwist those knickers of yours and put that mind to work on how we can get back to our time." Lyla slowed to Abby's pace. They trudged along the grassy ledge beside the gurgling waters of a stream so clean and clear the sight of it made her thirsty. "You are the genius. Remember?"

"I know nothing of quantum physics, alternate dimensions, or time travel." Abby's voice shrilled to the squeaking pitch it always hit whenever she was frustrated. "I know the human mind. Or at least I did. Currently, even that is debatable."

"There's my brilliant sister. Welcome back." Lyla looped an arm around her shoulders and squeezed. "Until we figure a way back, we have to act like we belong in this time. You remember what I told them about why we are dressed this way?"

"Yes." Abby rolled her eyes. "I cannot believe they swallowed that load of rubbish."

"Well, whether they did or not, we're sticking with it. I am not the best liar in the world. I don't seem to have the memory for it or the talent for keeping everything straight. However, I'm not all that keen on getting executed for being a witch or something. It's amazing how that improves my memory."

Abby halted, stared straight ahead, and started trembling.

Lyla followed Abby's line of sight to see what had triggered a sudden relapse. People. Not hordes, but several. Headed straight for them. Men. Women. Children. Three dogs and even some sheep. Without taking her gaze off the mixed lot headed their way, Lyla squeezed her sister's hand. "In all your studies, I am sure you covered the history of how they treated the insane. Did you not?"

"Of course," Abby replied in a quivering whisper.

"And what did they do to the mentally ill in this era?"

Abby gratified her with a shocked look, then hitched in a sniffing gasp.

"Now you understand why you must try and pull yourself together. Repress it like I do. We can break down when no one else is around." She squeezed Abby's hand again. "Our lives depend on it."

"I will do my best."

"That is all I ask."

Grant rode up beside them. "I prefer we ride the rest of the way." While his expression seemed aloof and unreadable, Lyla swore she caught a glimmer of worry in his eyes.

"Let me help Abby up with Malcolm." She led her to the horse, bent and laced her fingers together to give her a boost, then hurried back and held up a hand for Grant to pull her up.

"I thought ye said ye had never ridden before," he said as he lifted her up and settled her back in front of him.

"I haven't. Why?"

"How did ye know to give yer sister a place to step up?"

She couldn't very well tell him she had seen it done on television or in the movies, but the closer she could keep her lies to the truth, the less she would have to remember. She shrugged. "I saw it once, and I guess it stuck with me because it made sense."

"Did the walking help her?"

The closer they drew to the barking dogs, shouting children, and waving adults, the tighter his hold around her waist became, making it difficult to focus. "What did you say?"

"Is yer sister better?"

"Yes. I think so." Only time would tell. Dogs and children swarmed them, bouncing entirely too close to the horses. "Aren't you going to tell them to get back so they won't get kicked?"

"The horses willna kick them."

"You said they would kick me."

"Ye're English."

She twisted in the saddle and glared at him. "You're telling me your horses can not only tell a person's country of origin but are also prejudiced against the English?"

"Aye," he said with all seriousness, but she spotted a teasing twitch of his mouth. Not a mischievous grin exactly, but close.

"What a load of tosh." She turned back and immediately tensed. The sea of greeters had grown.

He pressed his mouth close to her ear, eliciting a shiver when his warm breath tickled across her flesh. "Steady, m'lady. Even though ye be a prisoner, no ill shall come to ye without my word to prompt it."

"Then don't prompt it," she said through clenched teeth.

His rumbling chuckle tickled up her spine. "Then dinna force my hand, ye ken?"

"Da! Da!"

"Ah, there are my precious wee ones." Love and pride changed Grant's tone from that of a stern chieftain to a doting father. He reined to a stop just outside the skirting wall, dismounted, and snatched up the pair as they charged into him. One in the crook of each arm, he hugged them tight, then tickled their necks with squeaking kisses. "And did ye behave whilst I was gone?"

"Rory nay behaved," chirped the little girl with the silvery-white ringlets. She pointed at her brother. "Set loose a mousie under Cook's skirts and made her scream."

"'Twas yer mousie and ye said to." An equally silvery-haired Rory dove toward his sister.

"Did not!" She wadded up a fist and swung at him.

"Enough!" Grant set them both on the ground and pulled them farther apart. "I am verra disappointed in the both of ye and will speak to Mrs. Fintrie and Grandmam about yer behavior."

"Now ye gone and done it, Fawna." Rory stuck out his tongue at his sister.

Not to be outdone, Fawna not only stuck out her tongue but stuck her thumbs in her ears and waggled her fingers at her brother.

Lyla snickered so loud, Grant turned and glared at her.

"Sorry. I couldn't help it. Your children are delightful. You and your wife are very blessed."

"Mam's in Heaven wif the angels," Fawna said. "Who are ye?" Without waiting for Lyla's response, she turned to her father. "Who is her, Da?"

"*She* is one of the prisoners Uncle Malcolm and I captured in Edinburgh." He took hold of the children and turned them toward a young maid waiting a few strides away. "Go with Greer now. We will discuss yer punishment after I talk with Cook, Mrs. Fintrie, and Grandmam."

"When will ye learn to hold yer tongue, Fawna?" Rory growled loud enough to be overheard.

Fawna shoved him hard enough to make him stumble. "Shut it, ye big baby."

Greer rushed forward, took them by the hand, and separated them. "Come along now. Ye should be ashamed. The both of ye. Is this any way to great yer father after his long journey? Shame. Shame. Shame."

So, their mother was deceased. Lyla studied Grant as he watched who she presumed was the nanny hurry his offspring back to the keep. A lonely wistfulness filled his face. And love. The man adored his children, even though they fought like a pair of territorial alley cats. She wondered if his wife had died in childbirth. The tots appeared to be fraternal twins, and in this era of poor hygiene and no medical care, bringing one baby into the world could be deadly. Two increased the dangers.

Then she noticed the rest of the adults drawing near, eyeing her as if she was the most recent addition to the zoo. She clasped her hands tightly and prayed she and Abby could navigate whatever lay ahead.

Grant reached for her. "Come."

One simple word, and yet it churned the bile higher in the back of her throat. She swallowed hard. Vomiting on him would not impress him or his clan. As soon as her feet touched the ground, she turned to fetch Abby, but Grant stopped her.

"Nay. Stand here and dinna speak, ye ken?"

Under normal circumstances, such an order would twist her knickers into a knot and spur a heated comeback. But this was a different time and place. For once in her life, she would do as she was told—at least, for now.

"Bring the other one over here." He motioned to Malcolm who escorted Abby to stand beside her. At least he was gentle with her. When it came to Abby, she would tolerate nothing less. She allowed no one to pick on her sister but her.

"They're going to put us in front of a firing squad," Abby whispered out the side of her mouth.

"Wrong century." Lyla took her hand and squeezed. "Steadfast now. Hysterical later. Remember?"

Abby managed a jerking nod.

A lad came and led the horses inside the imposing stone wall surrounding a tall, square tower that, from a distance, looked to be the center of the fortress. A blackened portcullis hung partially down in the arched entrance. It made Lyla swallow hard again. The sharpened points of the thing made the archway look like the gaping maw of some sort of multi-fanged monster.

"Tie them together so we might lead them easier," Grant instructed quietly.

"You don't have to—"

His hard scowl killed the rest of her words in her throat. Perhaps Chieftain Reddoch wasn't nearly as kind as she had first thought.

Malcolm bound their wrists and tethered them together, then gently tugged to get them moving.

Abby sniffled with every step. Lyla prayed her sister could hold it together, at least until they got some privacy. Something told her the curious onlookers would enjoy a show. Not that they seemed cruel or threatening, but it was just human nature. Like watching a train wreck and not being able to look away.

The high, protective outer wall not only surrounded the multi-level, squared tower of a building in the middle, but also several other structures of varying heights, shapes, and sizes. A smithy, stable, and compact dwellings about the size of her place back home. Several of them, in fact. The fortress was a walled-in village. A small one. But still, a busy settlement teeming with life. She couldn't remember if any type of housing or farms were on the outside. She had been too caught up in Abby's welfare to notice.

Abby stumbled into her. "I wonder if they have a dungeon," she whispered as Lyla helped her regain her footing.

"I guess we will find out soon enough." Malcolm was leading them up the steps to the main building's entrance. The tower's tall narrow windows scowled down at them. They appeared to be glazed. She couldn't remember what century glass windows became commonplace in castles. They must have covered that subject after she dropped out of school.

"My son." A smiling, gray-haired woman swept out from the grand double doors with both hands outstretched.

"Mother." Grant clasped her hands and kissed her cheek. "What is this I hear about ye letting the bairns terrorize Cook again?"

She made a huffing sound and tossed her head. "'Twas a wee mouse. All Cook needed to do was ignore it." Her cheeks blushed to a livelier pink and mischief sparkled in her eyes. "Or sit on the tiny beastie. The woman doesna realize how her girth protects her."

Grant's face tightened, and he briefly closed his eyes. "Mother—"

"And who are these two, and why are they bound?" She moved closer, her long, full skirts swishing with every step.

Lyla controlled the urge to back up, but Abby didn't and nearly stumbled back down the steps. "Abby! Take care." She caught her sister in time and steadied her back in place.

"English?" The matron eyed them with sharpened curiosity,

giving them a critical up and down perusal. "As far north as Edinburgh?" She cast an arched brow back at Grant.

"Aye. Exactly what I thought, so I took them prisoner."

His mother stepped closer still, studied Abby with a furrowed brow, then shifted her attention to Lyla. "Yer name?"

"Lyla Smythe, mum." She wondered if she should curtsy, then decided against it.

"Ye may address me as *m'lady*."

Lyla revisited her first inclination and curtseyed. "M'lady."

The woman's scowl softened to a kindly smile. "Ye manage yer fear well, Lyla Smythe."

"Thank you, m'lady."

"I am Lady Katherine." She rested a hand on Grant's forearm. "His mother." She tipped her head toward Abby who stood staring at the ground and shaking. "And who is this one?"

"My sister, Abby Cornwalt." Instinct urged her to take a leap of faith. "She is unwell and needs a quiet place to sit and have a cup of water…or something."

"Or something," Lady Katherine repeated, her head tilting to the side as she watched Abby. "Poor lamb is beside herself." She turned and frowned at Grant. "Do ye believe them dangerous?"

He fixed her with a pensive look, then slowly shook his head. "I have yet to decide."

She stepped closer to him and lowered her voice, but Lyla overheard every word. "I ken well enough they be yer prisoners, but can we not untie them? Seems almost cruel. Especially with the one as upset as she is. I dinna believe her a danger to anyone but herself."

Lyla strained to keep all emotion hidden. If she smiled now, something told her she would end up penned in with the sheep.

"Once secured inside, Malcolm will untie them." Grant cast a glance across the crowd, squinting as though deep in thought. The cobblestone courtyard had filled to standing room only.

"Secured inside," his mother repeated, then turned her back on those gathered and lowered her voice again. "Surely, ye dinna mean to chain them in the dungeon? I know they be oddly dressed for certain, but not dangerous enough to toss down there?"

He met Lyla's gaze, and the furrow in his brow deepened. "Not dangerous, but not truthful, either. I fear they are spies."

"Spies." Lady Katherine's sparse brows shot to her immaculate silvery hairline. "For whom, do ye think?" She cast another lingering look at their clothing. Her mouth quirked with an odd smile. A smile that made Lyla swallow hard. Was this woman not as kind as she seemed?

"Never mind, Mother." Grant jerked his head toward the door, directing Malcolm to take them inside. "To the second floor. Lock them in the chambers at the end of the hall."

Malcolm's mouth went ajar, and he didn't budge.

Lyla squeezed Abby's hand, silently warning her sister not to comment, react, or even breathe the wrong way. Something was not quite right here, and if she could discover what it was, perhaps, she could use it to their advantage.

"Is there a problem, man?" Grant glared at Malcolm with a sternness that made Lyla feel for the quiet giant.

"No, my chieftain." He cleared his throat. "But the second-floor chambers. That is where—"

"I ken verra well the history of my own keep," Grant said. "If ye feel unable to complete yer duties, I shall find another who can."

Malcolm bowed his head. "That willna be necessary." He held the door and wound the rope in his hands to lead them through it.

As they followed the quietly grumbling man up the steep stone staircase, Lyla couldn't resist trying to find out more. "Where are you taking us?"

"Second…floor."

"Those rooms." Lyla struggled to keep up as Malcolm increased his pace and started taking the steps two at a time. "Who did they belong to, Malcolm? Why were you so surprised when he told you to put us there?"

He didn't comment. Just snorted and climbed the steps faster. Once he reached the landing he sought, he shouldered the door open and held it.

Lyla shooed Abby through first, then turned back to Malcolm. He refused to look her in the eyes. Instead, he kept his focus locked on a spot above her head. "I won't tell Grant you said anything. Please."

He still didn't respond, just lumbered down the dim corridor.

Maybe if she played the frightened female. Even while following orders, he had been particularly gentle and attentive with Abby. Maybe damsels in distress were his weakness.

"Malcolm, please. You don't plan to kill us or torture us, do you?" She allowed her voice to quiver and added a sniffling gasp, praying that wasn't what he really intended.

It was as though she hadn't said a word. He kept walking. Stoic. Silent. His gaze locked on the door at the end of the hall. When they reached it, he stretched and ran his fingertips across the top of the ornate ledge above the entrance. His mouth tightened, making his reddish-brown mustache twitch. With a frustrated huff, he retrieved the large key and shoved it into the lock. He pushed the door open and pointed.

Lyla held up her bound wrists. "Grant said you would untie us once you put us wherever you were going to put us."

His bushy brows knotted, looking like a pair of wrestling woolly worms. "Untie…yers-s-selves."

The man's speech had become labored almost to the point of being unintelligible. Lyla felt for him. Poor thing must be sorely distressed. But so was she. And Abby. He was in good company. "We are not going in there until you tell me why you seem so afraid of these rooms."

"Are there spiders or rats?" Abby whispered, already scanning the ground and looking ready to climb the door facing.

"Himself's wife." He worked his mouth, his mustache and beard quivering with his efforts.

Lyla couldn't stand much more. "Grant's wife—the mother of the twins. Were these her chambers?"

He shook his head.

"No?"

He shook his head again, then shot a nervous glance all around and gently pushed them inside. Before they could turn around, he shut the door. Metal clinked against metal, then his hurried footsteps faded off into the distance.

"He locked us in," Abby whispered, huddling close.

"Well, of course, he locked us in. What did you think he was going to do?"

"Don't snap at me! This is not *my* fault."

Lyla clenched her teeth. "I am not assigning blame." She moved to the nearest window, yanking her twin along with her. Enough sunlight peeped in through the dingy panes to reveal which strand of rope needed to be pulled to untie the knot. She found it, sank her teeth into it, and jerked. The rope fell away, granting her freedom.

"How did you do that?" Abby stared down at her hands, which were still bound.

She eyed the knot imprisoning Abby's wrists, then tugged on the loop in question. The bindings fell to the floor.

Abby rubbed her arms and smiled. "Much better. Thank you." She stepped back, eyeing the room. "Do you see any sign of rats? Or giant spiders?"

"You watch too much television." Lyla meandered around the room and peeped under a few of the sheets covering furniture fine enough for the queen's sitting room. Well, at least as far as she was concerned, the upholstered chairs, couches, and mahogany tables were fine enough for the palace. Clan Reddoch must do all right. She ripped the sheets off one of the couches and sank into the pillows. Then it hit her. Their unbelievable dilemma. The weight of all that implied squeezed the air from her chest. She clapped a hand over her wildly thumping heart. "I can't breathe."

Abby rushed to her. "Oh, God. Since we're alone, are you going to have your breakdown now?"

"Highly likely." Lyla wheezed for air. "Open the bloody window. I cannot breathe."

Abby hurried to shove the tall panes as wide open as they would go. Their hinges creaked, and the casings rattled. "Crap on a cracker, these blessed things haven't opened in an age."

Lyla slumped over onto her side and curled into the fetal position among the musty pillows. She did not feel well at all. Emotionally. Physically, she was fine, but emotionally, she had lost the plot. "Do be a good sister and study the data while I have a little breakdown. Yes?"

Abby perched beside her. "The way I see it, it was Arthur's Seat, the meteor shower, or that noxious wine that sent us back."

"Or fate. Or destiny. Or some malevolent demon with a twisted sense of humor." Lyla closed her eyes and rubbed her throbbing temples, wishing their backpacks had accompanied them to their accommodations.

"Maybe they'll bring us our things so you can have an aspirin, too." Abby rubbed her shoulder. "Have a good cry. Sometimes it helps to get it all out."

"If I cry now, I might never stop." That's how it had been when she lost the baby no one wanted but her. The miscarriage had been a painful lesson on how best to control her exterior, while her interior shattered to bits. Now, as then, the best thing she could do was stay so busy she didn't have time to think about anything other than the task at hand. First order of business was to get back to Edinburgh and Arthur's Seat. "We have two choices."

"And they are?"

"We either wait 'til dark and make our escape or lull them into a false sense of security and make a dash for it then."

"This is not some spy movie where we possess innumerable gadgets that will assist us in getting our freedom." Abby jumped up and started pacing the length of the elaborate sitting room, hugging herself tighter with every lap.

"We are modern capable women. All we need do is put our minds to it." Lyla pushed up from the couch and returned to the window. She leaned out and studied the area below.

"Just because we're from the twenty-first century does not mean we are smarter than these people." Abby joined her at the window. "If anything, they're more intelligent than we are because they have the home-court advantage."

"Since when do you use sports analogies?"

"One of my patients was a retired basketball player from the U.S."

Lyla went back to studying the outside wall and what lay directly below the window. While they were on the second floor, a structure with a soft enough looking thatched roof sat wedged between the skirting wall and them. In fact, the roof of tightly bound grass bundles rose high enough to make a well-aimed drop out the window not only possible but successful. Only problem was, what then? Roll off that roof and make a dash for the gate in the hopes the iron portcullis wasn't down? Their discarded bindings caught her eye. "Do you think this rope is long enough to get us over the wall and close enough to the ground to drop without breaking our legs?"

"Are you mad?" Abby leaned out the window, scanned the area, then drew back in. "You mean to jump out this window, cross that roof, then hang off the skirting wall and drop on the other side? In the dark?"

"You don't have to use that tone." Lyla wound the rope into a neat coil and dropped it to the floor. "Do you have a better idea?"

Abby opened her mouth to speak, but a light pecking on the door cut her off. Her eyes rounded wide and filled with fear.

"We do not panic—remember?" Lyla shook a warning finger at her sister as she went to the door. "I don't know who you are, but we cannot let you in. The door is locked, and we weren't left with a key."

"We have the key, mistress," said a young female.

"We didna wish to barge in and catch ye unawares," explained a second. Another female that sounded about the same age as the first.

"Well, at least our keepers are thoughtful," Lyla said to Abby who still cowered by the window. "Do come in." She backed up a few steps and readied herself. To do what, she had no idea, but at least it made her feel better.

The key rattled in the door, then it slowly opened, revealing two very young women. Lyla wondered if they were even in their twenties. The one with reddish-blonde curls peeping out from her white linen coif carried their backpacks, one in each hand. The other girl, a dark-eyed lass with freckles across her small, upturned nose, held a large, cloth-covered serving tray.

The maid with the tray gave a hesitant smile and entered first. "Good day to ye, mistress. I be Eufamie, and this here is Besseta. Lady Katherine bid us bring ye food and yer things."

"We'll be setting the room up proper, too," Besseta said, her face twisting in dismay as she looked around. "What a feckin' mess. I thought Lorna was 'posed to be keeping this floor in order? Lazy cow."

"Besseta!" Eufamie stomped a foot, then nodded toward a table still covered with a drop cloth. "Clear that one so's they can eat whilst we work." She fixed a worried glance on Lyla and lowered her voice. "Please dinna try and run, ye ken? Master Malcolm's got two men at the top of the stair and two more down below." After a glance back at the still-open door, she twitched a shrug. "And he himself is out there walking the hall. Me and Besseta will be in the worst sort of trouble if ye try to run during our watch. Ye seem nice enough." Her gaze traveled over to Abby, then returned to Lyla. "And all upset 'bout being caught and such. Even Lady Katherine said so…so's me and Besseta volunteered to help with ye. But ye will behave for us, aye?"

Lyla blew out a disgruntled sigh and plopped back on the couch. How could she not *behave* just to keep these two out of trouble? "You have my word. We will behave." Besides, even though they needed to escape, she had no clue where they should go. The only place that came to mind was Edinburgh and Arthur's Seat. But what if they couldn't get back? What then? Better not think about it now. After all, she couldn't finish indulging in her nervous breakdown until they were alone.

CHAPTER FOUR

LYLA PERCHED ON the window ledge. It appeared to be the only safe place other than the dinner table while Eufamie and Besseta put the sitting room in order. Abby sat beside her, hugging her backpack.

With the efficiency of a relentless cleaning machine, the two maids removed the dust covers, wiped down the furniture, beat pillows and tapestries, mopped the floors, and lit the hearth to knock the chill from the room—or so Eufamie said. They spoke very little, but stole inquisitive glances so often, Lyla decided to use it to her advantage. If she made friends with the curious maids, perhaps she could convince them to let down their guard. With any luck, she might discover some useful information.

"Master Malcolm seemed very hesitant about this particular set of rooms," she said as Besseta toddled past with two buckets of steaming water. She hoped to trigger some sort of reaction, and it worked. Both maids halted, stared at her, then looked at each other as if silently hashing out what they should say. "My sister is worried about rats and spiders," she hurried to explain. "But so far, we have seen none."

"Ye willna see any rats here on the second floor," Eufamie reassured them, then returned to moving the candlesticks to a corner table for polishing.

So far, Besseta seemed the more talkative. Time to focus on her. Lyla aimed her questions at her. "Of course, we heard the chieftain's children confess about setting a mouse on Cook. Are those two always such mischief-makers?"

The maid smiled. "Always. A pair of feisty bairns, those two."

"But they can be dear sweet lambs, too," Eufamie hurried to interject as if afraid someone might accuse them of maligning their chieftain's offspring.

"The little girl—Fawna, I believe is her name—anyway, she told me her mother now lived in Heaven with the angels." Lyla held her breath, hoping one of them would comment and give up more information.

"Aye," Besseta said, her tone clipped. "Himself's wife is no longer with us."

"Died in childbirth?" Lyla asked in a sympathetic tone.

"We are nay allowed to speak of it," Eufamie announced, heading for one of the two doors leading to the private bedchambers. "Come, Besseta. Help me air them. We've much to do and little time in which to do it."

Besseta scurried after her, completely foiling Lyla's plan.

"That went well," Abby observed, still hugging the backpack.

"Just shut it. I don't see you doing anything to improve our situation." Lyla snatched up the other bag, retrieved the bottle of aspirin, and downed a couple of pills with a refreshing cup of water from the bounty provided by their captors.

After loading down the room's largest table with breads, cheeses, fruits, and preserves, the maids had fetched two pitchers of fresh water, a pitcher of ale, and a decanter of wine. At least their keepers didn't intend to starve them out.

She unzipped the main compartment of the pack and pulled out the last two bottles of homemade wine and added them to the small buffet. "Surely, it wasn't the wine that brought us here. I've had it before, and the worst it ever did was trigger a migraine."

"I fear we will never know what brought us here." Abby set the backpack on the window ledge and stared at it. Her despondent expression revealed the depths of her worries. She pulled up her knees, propped her arms on top of them, and buried her face.

Turtle-in-the-shell mode. Again. Lyla shook her head and stared at the fire. Burying one's head solved nothing.

"Is she unwell?" Besseta asked as she and Eufamie emerged from the bedchambers.

"She'll be all right," Lyla said, more to convince herself than the maid. "It has been a very long day."

"We're done with the cleaning and fresh linens, but we shall be back soon. Lady Katherine ordered proper clothes found for the two of ye." Eufamie fished the key out of her apron pocket and waited for Besseta to join her at the door. "Himself wishes ye brought down to the feast at the proper time."

That sounded as if he intended to serve them as the main course. Lyla rubbed her eyes, forcing herself to tighten her hold on what little of her sanity remained. After a grueling day of waking up in a different century, juggling lies, and riding a horse for the first time, she was exhausted. More jousting with words and making everyone believe she was from this time seemed a monumental task. With a stifled yawn, she massaged her still throbbing temples, wishing the aspirin would hurry and take effect. "We are prisoners here. He made that quite clear. Are you telling me he allows his captives at his dinner parties?"

"Himself is the chief. He can allow whatever he wishes." Euphemia herded Besseta out first, then closed the door behind them and locked it.

"Such blind acceptance," came Abby's muffled response, her head still buried in her arms. "Amazing."

"Not only amazing but problematic." Lyla went to the table, pinched off a bite of cheese, and popped it into her mouth. "I have never done blind acceptance. I'm not so sure I can."

Someone knocked on the door again.

"Knock all you want," Lyla called out as she refilled her cup of water. "We don't have the key and can't let you in."

Metal rattled in the latch, and the door swung open. Grant stood framed in the doorway, glowering as he tapped the key against his palm.

Her heart quickened to a pace that rendered her breathless. She had realized he was a hulking, well-muscled man, but the door frame nearly brushed the top of his blonde head and rubbed against his broad shoulders, which drove the point home. The back of her neck tingled, sending the short hairs standing on end again. Lyla rubbed at the sensation, determined to ignore her misfiring sixth sense about the enigmatic man holding her prisoner.

"Are ye injured?" His glower changed to an inquisitive scowl as he slipped the key into the pocket of his waistcoat and strode forward with a powerful, swaggering gait.

"No. Why?"

"Ye keep rubbing yer neck. Ye did it several times on the way back from Edinburgh." He stole uneasy glances all round, his eyes narrowing as if he expected an enemy to jump from the shadows at any moment.

"The maids did a fine job if that's what you're here to check." She waved at the table laden with food and beverages. "Would you like something?"

"No." He edged deeper into the room, his jaw tightening as he squinted at the second bedchamber door.

"No," she repeated. Not *no thank you*. Just a terse no. This one didn't beat around the bush or play games of mindless chatter. She rather liked that. She studied him closer. So why had he come here? With an internal shrug, she forged ahead. Best course of action was always to face demons head-on. She could be just as brash and straight to the point as he could. "What do you want?"

He started as though he had forgotten she was there. "What?"

"Why are you here?" she asked, stressing each word. "Just checking to make sure they really locked us up like you told them to?"

He looked so insulted she laughed, which made his expression even stormier.

"I know my people do as they are told. Without question." He noticed Abby balled up on the window ledge, then he turned back to her. "Again?"

Lyla nodded, blew out a heavy sigh, then shrugged outwardly this time. "Her nature."

"And what is yer nature Mistress Lyla?"

"To remind people to call me plain Lyla," she quipped.

"Fine." He forced a smile, clasping his hands to the small of his back as he resumed his uneasy pacing. The belted length of his great kilt swung behind him like a dragon's tail. "Would ye care to tell me the truth now, *Lyla?*"

"About what?"

"About why ye and yer sister were on the ridge above Edinburgh."

"I already told you. We were watching the stars last night and fell asleep."

"Ye traveled all the way from London to watch stars in the Scottish sky?" It did sound pretty unbelievable when he put it like that.

"Not specifically, but that's why we were on that peak above Edinburgh last night. The view is pure dead brilliant." Actually, in a long, convoluted sort of way, they had traveled from London for a better perspective on life. Abby had come because she and Mother feared Lyla wasn't handling either the miscarriage or divorce as they saw fit. And she had moved to Edinburgh after finalizing the split with her ex and never wishing to run into him *or* her mother ever again.

"I canna give ye free rein of the keep until ye tell me the truth, m'lady."

"I am not one of your children or your pet." She fixed him with the glare that always made the dogs she walked sit and obey.

He scratched at the blonde stubble dusting the squareness of his jaw. "And what is that supposed to mean?"

"It means you can't bribe me using freedom as a treat. I have told you everything. You are the one unable to believe it." She dismissed him with a flip of her hand. "Abby and I are exhausted. Go away."

"Go away?" Disbelief filled his tone, making his already deep voice rumble like thunder. "Might I remind ye whose keep this is?"

Her neck tingling increased to a zipping burn that stung like the dickens. Without thinking, she glared upward and blurted, "What the bloody hell? Stop it!"

He retreated a step. "Who do ye speak to?"

Still rubbing the back of her neck, she tried to shoo away his worries with her other hand. "Sorry. Don't mind me. I often talk to myself when I am overtired." She wasn't about to tell him about her instincts, intuition, or whatever the word of the day would be for the subtle sixth sense that told her what she should do—in the vaguest and most infuriating ways possible. They would think her a nutter for certain. Unfortunately, he didn't believe her flimsy excuse. She could tell by the look on his face. "Really. It's nothing. Just a quirk."

"She does it all the time," Abby said. "Always has."

Grant stared at Abby briefly, then riveted his steely focus back on Lyla. "Who do the two of ye work for?"

With a weary groan, Lyla dropped into the high-backed chair beside the hearth. Time to make up a tale to satisfy Chieftain Reddoch since he found the rather iffy truth so unbelievable. "We work for ourselves."

"Yerselves?"

She nodded, hoping Abby would listen close so she could help her keep the lie straight for future retellings. "After our father was murdered, and we made our oath, we sold everything so we could afford to track down his killer and have our revenge."

Grant lowered himself into the chair opposite her, leaned forward, and propped his forearms on his knees. "Ye are lying, m'lady."

"I am not. Do you not recall me telling you of our oath?" She smacked the thigh of her favorite jeans. "Of how we swore to dress this way until we avenged him?"

"Yer eyes have gone green again. Greener than a Highland glen in springtime."

His smugness infuriated her, but she refused to allow it to rattle her. "My eyes go green when I feel strongly about something. Emotions change eye color. Yours do the same. All stormy and gray one minute, then icy as a frozen loch the next."

"She is right, you know. Blood flow and sometimes even hormones can change the shade of your eyes." Abby slid off the window ledge and came to stand at Lyla's side. She rested a hand on her shoulder, as if proud of finding the emotional strength to contribute to the conversation.

His smug expression turned to one of bafflement. The furrow in his brow deepened as he eyed Abby. "What is a hormone?"

Bloody hell, now they needed to be experts on when a word was first used so they didn't use potentially dangerous terminology. "Abby is a healer. She's always using words I don't understand either." Lyla didn't know any other way to cover her sister's explanation. And it was the truth. Abby had a medical degree. She reached up and patted her twin's hand. "She is the best."

"Is she now?" Grant's eyes narrowed again. The man teetered between disbelief and outright denial. Lyla could smell his doubt quickly approaching its breaking point.

"Anyway," she continued before he had time to recover. "We sold everything and have been tracking the vile murderer of our father for the past year." She gave a dramatic shake of her head. "Slippery devil." A book she had read came to her rescue. "A cruel highwayman. Dick Turpin is his name. Known to torture and kill his victims. Usually works the roads close to London, but we tracked him to Edinburgh."

"And how exactly did ye follow the man, since neither of ye possess a horse? Or even sat one before today. *If* that be the truth."

Good question. She scrambled for the answer, breathing easier when it came to mind. "Carriages. What better way to trap a highwayman than in a carriage?"

"Ye had no weapons when we found ye." He leaned back in the chair and folded his arms across his massive chest.

Well, damn and blast it all. He had her there. "A quick death is too good for that man." She jutted her chin upward, daring him to challenge her. "Lashing him to a tree was our plan." She bared her teeth for effect. "Starvation for him. Or eaten by wild dogs." Surely, there were wild dogs in this era. She couldn't remember when the poor wolves had been hunted to extinction.

"Ye expect me to believe that two unarmed lasses as slight as yerselves could carry out such a task?" He arched a brow that was a shade darker than his thick, blonde hair pulled back in a ponytail.

"Revenge is a powerful thing." She left it at that, knowing that to a chieftain of what appeared to be a successful Scottish clan, revenge should not be an unknown concept.

He stared at them, working his mouth as though chewing on all she had told him. Without a word, he pushed up from the chair and strode to the door. His hand on the latch, he glanced back at her, pulled in a deep breath, then barely shook his head.

"Since you obviously don't believe me, I assume my sister and I will not be joining you for dinner." She sincerely hoped not. All she wanted was a nap and time to plan an escape, along with a place to go once they were free. "We totally understand." As soon as the words left her mouth, she knew she should not have said them.

"Yer maids will escort ye to the hall once they make ye presentable." He yanked open the door. Before he stormed out and slammed it shut behind him, Lyla caught sight of Malcolm hovering in the corridor.

"What if we are unwell?" she called through the closed door as he rattled the key in the lock.

"Ye willna be excused unless ye are dead," he roared, then hit the door so hard she jumped.

"You were so close," Abby said.

"I know." Lyla returned to the window and studied the outer wall. "I have never known when to shut it."

"Do you think he believed at least part of your story?"

"Even I don't believe it. Why should he?" Her inability to tell a convincing lie had always caused problems. "But we have to play the part. Maybe once we're costumed like everyone else, it'll be easier to convince him we are harmless and need to be let go."

"Let go *where*?"

She blew out a heavy sigh and shook her head. "I have no idea."

A loud thump from the nearest bedroom startled them both.

"Rats," Abby said in a hissing whisper. "I knew there would be rats."

Lyla grabbed the fire iron and eased across the room toward the bedchamber.

Her twin scurried back to the windowsill, pulled up her feet, and hugged her knees.

With the sturdy fireplace poker in her left hand, Lyla grasped the door handle with her right. Leaning in close, she held her breath and listened. Soft muffled thumps accompanied by whispering. Someone was in there, but how? With the iron lifted and ready to strike, she threw open the door and roared like a crazed beast.

Grant's children split the air with high-pitched squeals.

"What are you two doing in here?" She tossed the fire iron back out the door. That's all she needed was for the sneaky little scamps to say she had threatened to club them. "Better yet—how did you get in here?"

The pair remained silent, standing shoulder to shoulder, and giving each other side-eyed glances.

Abby appeared in the doorway. "I can't believe no one came running. Malcolm must be at the other end of the hall." She smiled at the children and gave them a happy nod. "At least it's not rats."

"You and rats." Lyla scrubbed a hand across her eyes and squatted down to the children's level. "How did you two get in here? I won't tell on you or get you in trouble. I just want to know how you snuck in with no one seeing you."

"Promise ye willna betray us?" Fawna wheedled, looking exactly like her leery father.

Lyla drew an *x* on her chest. "Cross my heart and hope to die."

Young Rory appeared suitably impressed. He pointed at the wall on the other side of the tall, four-poster bed. "Tunnels."

Lyla cast a meaningful look back at Abby, straightened to her full height, and went to where the child showed. All she found was white wood with a few scuff marks down close to the floor. Must be a secret door. "Show me how you open it."

"Watch." Fawna pushed past her and kicked the spot on the panel bearing all the black scuff marks. Nothing happened. "Sometimes the feckin' thing sticks."

"Ye're not 'posed to say *feckin'*," Rory scolded.

"Ye just said it whilst telling me not to say it." Fawna barreled forward as if about to chest-bump her brother.

"Stop fighting." Lyla pulled them apart and kicked the wall herself. This time, a waist-high section of the wall slid inward, revealing a dark tunnel.

"See?" Fawna pointed at the candle lantern sputtering on the floor. "That be our light. Nanny Greer thinks we be napping."

Rory giggled. "She be the one who needs a nap. Not us." He held up four fingers and a thumb. "We be almost five now. Next month."

"Someone's coming!" Still at the bedchamber door, Abby waved both hands. "Hide!"

"You better go." Lyla stepped around them and joined Abby. "Will the wall close or do we need to make it shut?"

"We can close it from inside," Fawna said. She grinned and

waved before shoving her brother into the passage. "Remember—dinna tell."

Lyla crossed her heart again, then closed the door and rushed back to the couch. Grant's children had provided the perfect escape route. Bless the little mischief makers and their nosiness. She owed them big.

Malcolm opened the door, gave a nervous glance inside, then stepped back out into the hall. Eufamie and Besseta entered, their arms piled high with colorful materials. Wool. Linen. Lacy-edged things. Ribbons and long thin strings. Heeled leather shoes hung in their apron pockets. Eufamie headed to the farthest bedchamber door, and Besseta waited in front of the one they had just vacated.

"I'll be helping ye dress, Mistress Lyla," Besseta said, her tone victorious as though she had won the coin toss.

Eufamie gave Abby a hesitant smile. "If ye are feeling better, Mistress Abby, there's water for washing in the stand beside the chamber pot, and then we can get ye dressed proper for supper."

Abby didn't answer. Just fixed Lyla with a glassy-eyed stare—her silent plea for help.

Lyla lifted both hands and gave her sister a sympathetic nod. There was no way out of this. Or at least none that she could figure. She waved Abby onward as she followed Besseta into the other room. A casual glance toward the secret panel reassured her that the beasties had escaped without issue. She hoped they would visit again so she could find out just how extensive the tunnel system was and all the places it might lead them.

"Lady Katherine herself sent some of these things." Besseta unloaded the things onto the bed, smiling down at the finds with pride. With a cheery clap of her hands, she hurried to the washstand and filled the basin with water. From the short bureau beside the stand, she selected a square of linen and a small brown crock filled with a white gelatinous substance. "If ye need to avail yerself of the chamber pot, 'tis behind that screen in a fine cabinet seat Himself had brought all the way from France."

At least that would stall the inevitable, and she did need a visit to the toilet. Lyla headed behind the tall, three-paneled screen of cloth decorated with the most elaborate embroidery she had ever seen. Flowers, squirrels, and rabbits. All frolicking within an impressive border of red flowers among trailing ivy. She eyed the chamber pot cabinet. Not quite sure how it worked. After some investigating, she discovered a hinged lid and lifted it. There, inset in its own frame, awaited a white ceramic pot, maybe even porcelain. She was not an expert on crockery.

"Be ye all right, mistress?"

"Yes. Uhm…I'll just be a bit."

"If ye be suffering from belly pain or yer courses, I can fetch herbs and extra rags."

Courses? Oh, bloody hell. What would she do when her period came and not a decent feminine hygiene product to be found? "Not necessary, but thank you, Besseta."

She sat on the cabinet, cringing at the loud pinging of urine hitting the vessel. Apparently, modesty had yet to be invented. Since toilet paper didn't exist either, she sorted through the drawers of the attached cabinet for something just as functional. Leaves and fluffs of wool filled one of the drawers; but were they to be used for what she hoped?

"Besseta?" The maid would surely think her odd, but perhaps she could blame it on being English.

"Aye?"

"The leaves and wool in this drawer."

"For wiping yer arse, mistress." A long pause followed. "What do the English use?"

What did the English use? She couldn't very well rattle off the brand name of toilet tissue from the corner shop. "Rags usually."

"I wouldna wish to be a laundress in England," Besseta muttered loud enough for Lyla to overhear.

Relieved and dry, Lyla came out from behind the screen, still not entirely certain how she would explain such modern things as jean zippers, her bra, or the stretchy lace on the waistline of her knickers.

"What's that in the crock?" she asked, stalling as long as possible.

"Mrs. Fintrie's best soap." The maid brought it to her nose and inhaled a long sniff. "She scents it with rose petals. Crushes and steeps them in oil." She held it out. "Have a smell, mistress."

While it had a pleasant floral fragrance, the main *essence* Lyla picked up on was old tallow barely a heartbeat away from turning rancid. "Very nice," she lied, hoping a tube of her body lotion was still in her backpack. It wouldn't substitute for deodorant or body spray, but it would be better than nothing. She didn't relish the thought of acquiring the natural earthiness of seventeenth-century hygiene.

Besseta smiled, obviously waiting.

Lyla sat on the bench at the foot of the bed, untied her hiking boots, and kicked them off. Socks came next. Then she sat there, wiggling her toes in the scratchy fibers of the woven rug covering most of the floor. Besseta patiently stood beside the washstand, her obedient smile glued in place.

Unable to stall any longer, Lyla stood, unzipped her jeans, and shucked them. Tossed her lightweight jacket on the bed and peeled off her favorite cotton tee that had been washed so many times, it was several shades lighter than when she bought it. Maybe if she didn't make eye contact with the maid, the girl wouldn't ask questions.

"Forgive me for asking, mistress, but what in the world are ye wearing?"

So much for not making eye contact to avoid questions. On to Plan B—clueless nonchalance "Whatever do you mean?" She stepped up to the washbasin, wet her face in the frigid water, then snatched the linen square out of Besseta's hand and dried it.

"Those." Eyes wide and her reddish brows rising, the girl tipped her head toward the pale pink lacy bra and matching panties.

"My...uhm...corset or uh...bodice." She patted the tiny ribbon between the bra's padded cups, then touched the waistband of her panties. "And these are my matching knickers."

"I have never seen the like." Besseta stared, obviously awestruck.

"Well, I am from London." Lyla hoped that would settle it.

"If ye say so, mistress." The maid scooped up another cloth, soused it in the water, then lathered it with the oily paste from the crock. "Take off the lot so we might wash ye. If ye entrust them to me, I shall see them laundered proper and returned to ye."

Lyla snatched the cloth from the maid. "I can wash myself, thank you." She started scrubbing before Besseta could argue.

"As ye wish, mistress. I shall set everything ready whilst ye do that." The maid wilted as if Lyla's announcement hurt her feelings.

Still rubbing the same spot on her forearm, Lyla watched Besseta sort out the multitude of garments with the sadness of a scolded puppy.

"Oh, bloody hell." She threw the cloth back into the bowl, unhooked her bra, and shed her panties. "I wash my lady bits," she said. "You wash everything else. Deal?"

Besseta blossomed like a flower opening to the sun. She rushed forward, took up the cloth, and started scrubbing Lyla's back. "Aye, m'lady."

After washing, then convincing Besseta to stoke the fire while she sparingly applied her favorite scented lotion and then stuffed it back in her backpack, Lyla eyed her underclothes, tempted to put them back on. After all, who knew if they would survive the keep's laundress? Before she could retrieve them, Besseta piled all her things beside the door and descended upon her with *proper* clothing.

A clean linen shift, then an underskirt with a stiff beige bodice sewn to the top of it. When Besseta tightened the laces of the bodice to where she couldn't breathe, Lyla's smallish breasts swelled above the neckline.

Self-conscious and needing air, Lyla pressed a hand over them. "Are you sure this is right? I can't draw a deep breath."

"Shallow, ladylike breaths, mistress, and aye, 'tis quite right. The kerchief will grant ye a bit of modesty."

In her opinion, the thin bit of laciness placed around her neck and tucked in front did little to hide her anything. And what if the delicate cloth slipped out? After every strained exhale, she checked to ensure it hadn't become dislodged.

"Leave it now," Besseta scolded. "Has it been that long since ye dressed like a lass?"

"It's been a while," Lyla hazarded to say.

"And now for the rest." The maid helped her step into what she called an outer petticoat of deep red and a lightweight waistcoat dyed the same color. Before bringing the front of the top together, she shoved a triangular panel of stiffened white linen in the front and pinned it in place. "Is the embroidery on the stomacher not truly fine?"

"Indeed." The delicate flowers glimmered as if stitched with threads of metal.

"No knickers?" Even though multiple layers covered her, Lyla felt strangely exposed with no panties.

Besseta shook her head. "Stockings, shoes, then I'll comb out yer hair and dress it for ye."

Lyla cast a longing look over at her favorite jeans and shirt. She had always pictured the past to be a simpler time, but if getting dressed was any sign, she had been sorely mistaken.

CHAPTER FIVE

GRANT SHIFTED IN his chair, his focus locked on the arch leading to the southern stairwell. The women should have been down long ago. What kept them? "If I find out they have refused this rare offer of hospitality extended to a prisoner—"

"Mind yer temper and settle yerself," his mother warned, hiding her quiet advice behind her pewter goblet. "Eufamie and Besseta willna fail to bring them. Those two can be more worrisome than a cloud of midges. The women will gladly join us to escape them."

"Can they sit wif me and Rory on this side?" Fawna asked from farther down the head table. "I like them."

"Me, too," Rory said. "They be nice ladies."

"The both of ye like them?" Grant eyed his precious bairns who rarely agreed on anything. His two wee ones appeared overly angelic this evening. A sure sign that once again, they had been up to something they shouldn't. "What have ye done now?"

Both children smiled up at him with the wide-eyed innocence of a pair of experienced criminals. "Nothing," they replied in unison.

"We be happy we get to sit at the chief's table 'stead of in the kitchen wif the rest of the bairns." Fawna sat taller and twisted a silvery curl around her tiny finger as if she were a woman grown.

"Aye," Rory said. "And we dinna have Nanny Greer making sure we eat what suits her 'stead of what suits us."

"Ye shall eat what suits me," Grant warned, knowing the two preferred honey cakes and buttery sweet tablet over anything else.

Lady Katherine cleared her throat. "Yer guests have arrived, my son."

Grant shifted his focus from his children to the other end of the great hall and went still. While Lyla had shocked him in her masculine attire, her more appropriate dress rattled him even more. He found it impossible to take his eyes off her. The rosiness of her cheeks and parted lips made the deep scarlet of her dress pale in comparison. He wondered if perhaps she felt unwell. Her tempting breasts rose and fell at a rapid pace, and the lacy edges of the kerchief covering them trembled uncontrollably with every breath she took. That aside, he found her lovely to the point of distraction. Narrow waist. Braided hair catching the light with the warm richness of dark honey. English or not, the woman was a beauty, and it did not escape his notice that he was not the only one who thought so. A sudden possessiveness pushed him to his feet. He rounded the head table, strode down the center aisle, and met the pair of lovely prisoners halfway.

He offered an arm to each of them. "Ladies."

Lyla sidled a nervous glance at her sister, who immediately shot one back. After darting the tip of her tongue across her lips, she took his arm. "Thank you, Chieftain Reddoch." She held tight, as if afraid she might fall.

"Yes. Thank you," Abby echoed, looking almost as lovely in a dress of dark blue.

Much to Grant's surprise, Malcolm stepped from the shadows and offered his arm to Abby. "M-my l-lady?"

Abby appeared relieved and didn't waste a moment. She took Malcolm's arm and fell in step beside him.

Good enough. Grant eased Lyla forward. Now he could

concentrate on her. "Ye look quite lovely this evening, m'lady."

"Thank you." She hitched in a shallow breath and almost whistled it out through clenched teeth. "I thought you promised no torture?"

Her words alarmed him, making him halt between the rows of crowded tables closest to the chieftain's dais. "How have ye been harmed?"

She twisted slightly and arched her back. "I cannot breathe," she said in a low voice meant for him alone. "Do these laces not have any give to them at all?"

He blinked, not quite sure he had heard her correctly. "Laces?"

"She pulled this bodice tighter than a sausage casing."

"That explains the redness of yer throat and cheeks." He turned and caught sight of the maids assigned to tend the English women. Both hovered close to the archway, watching their charges like nervous hens minding their first clutch of chicks. "Which one tended ye?"

"Besseta," she said, digging her nails into his arm. "But don't say anything. You'll embarrass her, and I don't want her to feel bad." She managed a deeper inhale. "I should not have complained. It is very important to her you be pleased, so do not get involved. Promise?"

"Ye place her well-being over yer own comfort?"

She rolled her eyes. "This time I do. As I said, I should not have complained. I get ratty when I'm overtired. Ignore me."

"I dinna believe I could ever ignore ye, m'lady." And he meant it. A fluttering at the table drew his attention to his children. Both sat with expectant smiles, waving for him to come to them. "It appears ye have made quite an impression on my bairns," he said. "Would ye care to explain how?"

"Children and dogs always know good people when they meet them." She shot a quick wink at Fawna, who struggled to wink back.

"And why are the two of ye winking?"

With feigned surprise, she squinted and blinked really hard as they rounded the end of the table. "That wasn't a wink. I had something in my eye."

"Ye do have something in yer eye," he said softly as he pulled out her chair. "I believe it is called a lie."

She graced him with an infuriating smile that tempted him to kiss it from her mouth. Once she was seated, he scooted her closer to the table, questioning his wisdom in keeping her so close. Perhaps he should have left her in her chambers. Her presence made it difficult to think. But how else could he discover the truth if not by keeping her near?

And Mother's immediate acceptance of the two strangely dressed women only made matters worse. Why hadn't she been the least bit leery of them? While he knew she had always believed in the old ways. The legends. The magic. Never did he think that would make her so accepting of such odd strangers.

He prided himself on control and knowing even the smallest detail of what went on in his keep. But with Lyla—God help him. He felt that control slipping. He sat beside her and motioned for her glass to be filled.

"Thank you." She leaned forward and looked past him. "Thank you for sending up such lovely clothes, Lady Katherine."

"Ye are most welcome, child." His mother preened like a proud peacock. "The red suits ye well. I knew it would. As I knew the blue would complement yer sister's coloring."

Grant stared straight ahead, irritated as hell and not really knowing why. The infernal woman brought out the worst in him, but the best in everyone else. "She says she canna breathe in them."

Lyla made a noise that sounded like a cross between an angry huff and a soft growl. "And I asked you to keep quiet about it, didn't I?" She leaned forward again and cast an imploring bow of her head toward his mother. "Please don't pay him any mind." She patted her chest. "I'm not accustomed to this style." Then her tongue tangled worse than Malcolm's in a room full of lasses.

"I...I m-mean. Well...you know—"

"After wearing those male things for a while, I am sure stays take getting used to all over again." Mother offered her an understanding smile, then fixed him with a look he remembered from when he was a bairn about to get his arse smacked.

"Exactly." Lyla graced him with a smug glare. "See? Your mother understands."

"Aye. Always." He drained his glass and held it up for a refill. What was it about this woman that pricked him like an itch he couldn't reach?

Servants filed in with overflowing platters. Roasted venison, birds, and hares. Boiled vegetables. Breads, cheeses, fruit of the season, and a steaming platter of greens dripping with butter.

"I dinna like greens," Rory said, eyeing the platter as if it held poison. "Daren't ye put any of that green stuff on my plate."

Fawna covered her platter with both hands to prevent the servant from spooning any in her direction. "I dinna like them either. Go on with ye."

Before Grant could comment, Lyla offered her plate to the maid with the greens and leaned toward the children. "You know, I never liked greens either, but I eat them because I don't want my ears to get long and pointy like a wood elf." She wrinkled her nose and shook her head. "Nasty little creatures that wild boars love to hunt so they can crunch on their bony ears. You don't want to be mistaken for one of them."

Both children stared at her for a long moment, then each of them felt their ears.

"How much greens does it take to keep the pointy ears away?" Fawna asked with a dubious look.

"Not many." Lyla pointed at the small mound of dark greens on her plate. "See? A few greens a day keep the pointiness away."

Fawna held up her plate. "Just a few," she instructed the maid, who was struggling not to smile.

"Aye, miss." The girl doled out a small amount on Fawna's plate, then placed the same amount on Rory's.

"And if you eat them with a chunk of stewed apple, they won't be bitter at all." Lyla popped the combination in her mouth, closing her eyes as if the delicacy was the best she had ever experienced. "Yum!" She turned to Grant, examined his plate, then shook her head. "You're going to have pointy ears if you don't eat any greens."

Fawna and Rory giggled.

Grant offered his plate to the maid. "A chief's share, if ye please."

The girl smiled and dipped her head, then spooned out a large portion onto his platter. "Aye, my chieftain."

"Happy now?" he asked Lyla, finding it impossible not to smile.

She grinned and pointed her spoon at him. "I would hate to see a wild boar munching on your ears."

"Indeed."

The longer the meal went on, the more Grant enjoyed the feast in the great hall. Since his wife's death, he had hated gatherings. But tonight, the covert glances of his people, some accusing and some filled with pity, didn't burrow beneath his skin as usual. His children's laughter, Lyla's fantastical tales of wood elves, wild boars, and other creatures made his keep feel like the home it had not been in a very long while. He didn't realize the lateness of the hour until Greer showed up to gather the children.

"But Da," Fawna whined. "We have been better than usual. Can we not stay?"

"Ye have been good, my wee one, but 'tis time for bed now." He scooted back from the table and opened his arms wide. "Give me yer hugs to keep me safe and warm 'til I see ye again come morning."

With pouty huffs and groans, the twins came to him as if walking to the gallows. They offered grudging hugs, which he gladly accepted, squeezing them both tightly, then kissing their cheeks. "I love ye both," he said with another hug, hoping they would always remember how much he loved them.

"I love ye, Da," Fawna said after kissing his cheek. With the sweetest smile, she adopted her craftiest look of innocence. "Can we break our fast with Mistress Lyla and Mistress Abby? Since we been so good tonight?"

"We shall see," he stalled, mildly jealous that his own children wished to start their day with the women rather than him. "There is still the matter of Cook and the mouse."

"'Twas Fawna's fault," Rory repeated with a solemn nod. "Always is."

"Then when will ye learn to think for yerself rather than follow wherever yer sister leads?" Grant struggled not to smile as his son wrinkled his nose and rolled his small shoulders. A sure sign the lad was deep in thought and searching for a suitable answer. "Think on it tonight. Ye can tell me in the morning, aye?"

"Aye, Da." With a dejected huff, the boy took hold of Greer's other hand, relinquishing victory to the adults.

"They are wonderful." Lyla smiled, watching the little ones as they left the great hall and disappeared up the stairs. "You are very blessed."

"That I am." He accepted the compliment with a gallant nod, frowning as the musicians in the alcove off to the side struck up a lively tune that threatened to shake the keep from its foundation. One played the pipe and tabor. One the fiddle. The lead man stood tall and proud with the bagpipes. The final player in the quartet plucked a clàrsach. Grant hated that harp. It had softly played during the entombing of his wife because she loved it so.

Lyla leaned toward him and motioned him closer still, so she might be heard over the Scottish reel and clapping and stomping.

God help him. At this angle, he couldn't help but appreciate the swell of her breasts above her neckline even more. He forced himself to tear his gaze from her cleavage and focus on her face. "Aye?" he encouraged loudly.

"Would it be all right if Abby and I retired?" She cringed as the pipes wailed even louder. "Dinner was lovely. Thanks ever so, but we are so weary. I am sure you understand."

"I would talk with ye first," he shouted while pointing to a nearby door. "Would ye walk with me in the garden?"

Her forced smiled said no, but much to his relief, she nodded yes.

Good. He didn't care much for the music either. It reminded him of times he preferred to forget. "I shall instruct Malcolm to see to yer sister, aye?"

She nodded again after a worried glance in Abby's direction.

He rose and offered his hand.

Before she took it, she moved to touch the back of her neck, then jerked her hand back down as if reminding herself to control the urge. Her neck had to be injured. Why else would she repeatedly rub it? As they walked to the door leading to the garden, he motioned for Malcolm to join them.

"Aye, my chieftain?" The war chief covered his ear on the side of the musicians and leaned the other closer.

"See to Mistress Abby," Grant bellowed, feeling somewhat sheepish as the final note of the first song played. "If she wishes to stay, then stay here with her. If she wishes to retire, escort her to her room."

Malcolm nodded, then dipped a polite bow at Lyla before returning to his seat.

Grant ushered her into the quietness of the short hall leading to the outer door. "Hurry, m'lady. Before the next song."

"I thought a chieftain always enjoyed the revelry of a feast. Especially one celebrating your return." She ran a finger behind her stomacher, grimaced, and yanked. "Oh, bloody hell. I made it worse."

"What exactly are ye trying to do, m'lady?" He had an idea, but far be it from him to hazard a guess with this lass.

"I am trying to breathe," she said. "You don't mind walking in the garden with a loose-bodiced woman, do you?"

"I would consider it an honor." He opened the outer door and pointed at the nearest torch stand. "Go to the light so ye can see to unpin yer stomacher and loosen yer laces. I shall stand watch to protect yer privacy."

"I will be eternally grateful." She untucked her lacy kerchief and whipped it from around her neck. "Here. Hold this."

He complied, then glanced back toward the door to make it look as though he stood watch. Of course, no one would interrupt him. At least, not if they valued their hide. This was his private garden, and everyone understood the chief was never to be disturbed unless it was dire. But he wasn't about to tell her that.

She unpinned the corners of her stomacher and held the tiny fasteners clamped between her lips like an experienced tailor. Unable to speak, she nodded for him to take the stiff embroidered panel as well. After failing to fish the laces out from the top of the bodice, she took the pins out of her mouth. "Would you mind if I pinned these into your sash? I can't tuck my chin down enough to see with them in my mouth."

"'Tis my kilt. Not a sash, m'lady." He held out his hand for the pins.

"Sorry." She tipped her head. "It is very nice. Much grander than—" She stopped and bit her lip.

"Grander than?"

"Grander than trousers." Her mouth trembled at the corners, revealing her nervousness. Had she caught herself before revealing another lie? Without a word, she spun around and stepped closer to the torch, muttering under her breath. Then she stomped her foot. "Oh bollocks!"

"What is it?"

"I have knotted the bloody laces. I am doomed to suffocate in this feckin' gown."

Before he could catch it, he laughed. Nay, he roared. Never had he met a woman like Lyla.

She turned and glared at him. "It is not funny," she said through clenched teeth.

"Aye, it is." He placed the stomacher, kerchief, and pins on the wooden bench beside the torch stand, then unsheathed his dirk. "Allow me to help, m'lady."

"If you cut the laces, Besseta will know and get embarrassed. Or ratty that I've ruined the borrowed clothes." She frowned at the dagger and shook her head while trying to pry the tight bodice outward. "I must not damage them. Your mother was kind enough to find us such nice things."

"Which do ye want more? Intact laces or breathing?" By the heightened redness to her cheeks even visible in the flickering torchlight, he knew the answer.

She stepped closer and presented her chest and the offensive knot. "Breathing. I'll think of something to explain the laces. Just don't cut the cloth, all right?"

He swallowed hard and nodded, not trusting himself to speak with her décolletage presented so nicely. With an artful flick of his blade, the lacing immediately relaxed, and the bodice eased open.

"You are pure dead brilliant." She pulled in a deep breath and blew it out. "I never realized air alone could give me such a rush."

"A rush?" He sheathed the dirk, quietly mourning the loss of her fine breasts mounded above her neckline.

"A giddiness." She twirled in place with her arms lifted. "I love breathing."

"Most do." He offered his arm. "Would ye care to walk a bit now that ye have sufficient air to do so?"

"I would love to." She granted him a teasing curtsy, then hooked her arm through his. Gazing upward, she pointed at the stars. "Look! There's Draco and Ursa Minor."

He stared up at the night sky. "What?"

She traced out the stars. "That string is called Draco. It's kind of shaped like a wingless dragon. See? There's the head, the body, and tail. It represents Ladon, the dragon that guarded the garden of Hesperides in Greek mythology. Then right beneath it, the one shaped like a ladle with the handle curved downward is Ursa Minor—Little Bear. More commonly known as the Little Dipper. See the shape?" She traced it out again. "The handle is Little

Bear's tail, and the cup is the bear's flank."

"No wonder my bairns like ye so. Yer storytelling is verra imaginative." And even though he knew he shouldn't, he liked this mysterious woman, too. "How do ye think up such tales?"

The excitement in her eyes dimmed, and her gaze fell from the stars to the ground. "I used to read a lot," she said quietly.

"What did I say to offend ye?" He missed the sudden loss of the childlike brightness that shone from her when she talked about the stars.

"Nothing." She gave his arm a friendly pat. "Don't mind me. I'm just tired." After a companionably silent stroll around the garden, she tipped her head toward her things on the bench. "If it's all right by you, might I go up now? As I said before, it has been a very long day."

He understood completely. "Aye, m'lady. I shall escort ye via my private stair. 'Twill be quieter than passing through the hall." He rested his hand on hers, tracing his thumb along the silkiness of her inner wrist. He didn't want her to go to her room. This was the first night he remembered enjoying at Eadar in a very long while. "I thank ye for indulging me, and I hope yer stay here is nay too uncomfortable."

She stared up into his eyes but didn't say a word, just twitched her shoulders as if something pained her—or she had an itch she couldn't scratch.

"Be it yer neck again?"

Her brows rose, and her eyes went wide. She blinked hard and fast as if waking from a dream. "What?"

He took hold of her shoulders and angled her back toward the light. "Allow me to see."

She tried to twist away, but he held her fast and studied her nape, shadowed by her braid. He gently moved it to better see. "Be still now. I willna hurt ye." With the lightest touch, he traced a fingertip along the base of her neck, then across the tiny hairs shimmering like gold in the flickering light.

She shivered, making him smile as the wee hairs stood on

end. "I have raised yer hackles, m'lady."

"You have no idea," she whispered, then erupted into a fit of coughing as though choking.

"God's beard." He lifted her arms, then thumped her between her shoulder blades. "Shall I fetch some water?"

Violently shaking her head, she banged on her chest with her fist. "No. I'll be…I'm…I'm fine. I must have sucked in a bug or something." She flipped a hand and forced an evasive smile. "You know, what with my deep breathing and all. Serves me right for letting you cut those laces."

Though he doubted the truthfulness of her excuse, this time, he would refrain from calling her a liar. It just didn't seem appropriate, since she had almost choked to death.

She rubbed her neck again, then yanked her hand back down and stomped her foot. "Oh, bloody hell! I cannot stop doing that."

"Are ye in pain? That is my only concern." He shoved her things to the far end of the bench, sat, and pulled her down beside him. "I dinna wish ye to suffer. We have a wise woman in a nearby village who might be of help with whatever ails ye."

Her delicate nostrils flared as her expression became more pained. The loveliness of her chest heaved up and down even faster. Tears shone in her eyes, and the wispy curls framing her cheeks trembled with a subtle shaking. She sniffed, then pressed the back of her hand against the tip of her nose.

"I will not cry," she said, her jaw tight and hard.

He decided she spoke to herself and not him. "Speak yer pain, m'lady. Let me help ye." Perhaps, she wasn't a spy. Maybe she and her sister sought sanctuary in the Highlands. What if they had fled England to save their own lives?

She covered her face with both hands and screeched a frustrated cry. "Bollocks! Bollocks! Bollocks! Damned if I am not as bad as Abby!" She shuddered in a deep breath and sobbed again. "And she is the logical one, not the intuitive twit that I am." She crumpled against him. "Maybe she has the right of it after all. We're both just going to suffer and die here. This is nothing but a jumbled mess. I don't care what my sixth sense keeps telling me with all that stupid zapping across my neck."

"Stupid sixth sense zapping?" He understood most of what she said, but not all, and he considered himself an educated man. And as God was his witness, a tearful woman terrified him more than the hangman's noose or an enemy's well-honed blade. "What is sixth sense zapping? A deadly malady?" He curled an arm around her and offered his shoulder to lay her head. He rather enjoyed her warm softness, but it would be so much better if she wasn't howling like a lost bairn.

"It's—intuitiveness." Her words came out muffled as she burrowed her face against him. "Knowing things without knowing how I know them. Feeling things no one else feels."

She must be one of the gifted. "Second sight, ye mean?"

"Yes!" She lifted her head so fast she banged his chin. Hard. "Oh no. Please forgive me." As she sorrowfully patted his jaw, her face crumpled with another wailing keen. "I am so sorry. I would never hurt you. Never in a million years. Not when my sixth sense keeps trying to tell me about you."

His mouth sagged open, and he stared at her, unsure what to say. For the first time since finding her, he had no doubt she finally told him the truth. "What is yer—*sixth sense* saying? About me?"

With her fingertips still nervously stroking his cheek, her tears welled again. "I don't know for sure. That's the crux of it all. It's just a feeling I get and snippets of things I'm not really certain about." She sniffed again, looking as heartbroken as if she was newly widowed. "I am not crazy. I promise." She twitched an unhappy shrug. "It just truly seems I am supposed to be here. With you. For whatever reason. But I do not know why."

His gaze slipped from her woeful eyes to her mouth. Lips so full. So close. So tempting.

She ran the tip of her tongue across the bottom one, then caught it between her teeth. The softness of her palm pressed tighter against his cheek while the side of her thumb rubbed the stubble along his jaw.

"I could really use a kiss right now," she whispered. "If that would be all right with you."

"That would indeed be verra all right." He tipped her head back and covered her mouth with his. She tasted of wine, mystery, and excitement. She tasted of everything he needed at this very moment. He deepened the kiss, pulling her harder against him with a hungry groan.

She responded in kind, welcoming him in and teasing his tongue with hers. Her fingers tangled in his hair and curled tight, locking her hold as if he would ever be foolish enough to try to escape her.

"Bless me, you are a brilliant kisser," she whispered across his mouth before taking it again.

He pulled her over into his lap, but a ripping sound made her stiffen and pull away.

"Oh no. We've torn something." She slid back to the bench and bent to free the lacy hem of her shift from a splintered knot on the bench's leg. "Bloody hell, I've torn off half the lace. Besseta will have my bum on a platter."

Words escaped him. All he could do was stare at this woman who had bespelled him as artfully as she bespelled everyone she encountered. God help him, he wanted her, but could he really trust her? If he took her to his bed, would he wake with a dagger in his heart?

He yearned to believe everything she said. Wanted more than anything to trust her. But could he? Thankfully, her hem ripping had prevented him from making a dire mistake. After he escorted her back to her room, he would go to the chapel and light a candle of thanks to whomever or whatever had protected him from himself. And he would think about things. Many things.

He stood and held out his hand. "Come. I shall take ye to yer room now, m'lady."

She didn't take his hand, just frowned up at him, chewing on her bottom lip as though flustered. Finally, she nodded, gathered her things, and rose. "Yes. I think that would be wise. I am full-on knackered, after all."

He had no idea what knackered was—unless it meant she was confused, frustrated, and didn't know what to do about the two of them. In that case, they made a good pair because he was full-on knackered, too.

CHAPTER SIX

"HE KISSED YOU?"

"Well, I did ask him to, so I suppose, technically, I kissed him." Lyla sat cross-legged on the floor, doing her best to repair the torn hem of her chemise. Grant had bought her some time by sending Besseta to fetch a warm herbal drink to settle her feigned upset stomach. "And from his reaction—well, and mine, too, really, I'm still not sure if it was a good thing or bad."

"Maybe it means he trusts you now. That would be good." Abby smoothed out the linen and held the lace in place as Lyla sewed. "At least it would make our stay here easier until we figure out a solid escape plan and a place to go."

Rather than respond, Lyla bent her head and intensified her focus on running the needle and thread through the cloth without stabbing herself too many times. Her twin would come unhinged if she confessed that the more she interacted with the people of Eadar, the more she realized she might be meant to be here. Call it fate, kismet, or destiny. Even before the kiss, her intuitiveness buzzed louder and longer here than an alarm with no snooze button. Could it be Grant was her other half, and the seventeenth century the timeline where she belonged?

She didn't love him. Not yet. But every zapping flash of *this feels right* said she might, eventually. This sensation had been sorely absent with her first marriage. In fact, she'd had misgivings from the start, but everyone told her to pass them off as cold feet. That farce had not ended well.

"Out with it." Abby nudged her knee. "What are you not saying to avoid a lecture?"

"What on earth are you talking about?" She hazarded a glance at her twin. Big mistake.

Abby arched a dark brow and paired it with an accusing glare.

Perhaps, it was time to ease Abby into her very strong gut instincts about this minor dilemma. "What if we get back to Edinburgh and find we're stuck here? Then what?" Lyla stared her down, determined to make her see sense. Logic always worked best with her twin. Abby had never been one to believe in psychics, mediums, or mumbo jumbo karma—as she always so sensitively put it. "We still don't know what triggered our little tumble back through time." She returned to stitching the hem, trying to sew faster without making a worse mess of it than she already had. Besseta could show up at any moment. She glanced up and fixed her twin with a no-nonsense stare. "If we can't get back, are you going to set up a psychiatric practice in Edinburgh and hope no one accuses you of heresy?"

"What are you really trying to say?" Abby slowly let go of the lace and folded her arms across her chest.

"There you go." Lyla nodded at her. "Your body language says you just shut me off. You're not willing to listen to anything that doesn't agree with what you already believe."

"You believe in more rubbish than anyone I have ever met." Abby yanked her skirts out of the way, rose from the floor, and flounced over to the open window. "I still hear music. I wonder how late their revelry lasts."

Lyla knotted the thread and bit it off. Not exactly good as new, but at least the hem was no longer in two sad pieces. Taking care not to undo her crude handiwork, she rose and tucked the needle and thread back in the portable sewing kit she kept in her backpack. She gave her sister a smug look. "Did Malcolm not tell you during your stroll around the courtyard? I saw you two coming from that direction."

"At least I didn't kiss him." Arms still hugged tight across her chest, she glared out the window. "We cannot stay here, Lyla. We can't."

"We may have no choice." Lyla settled on the couch and propped her feet on the long squatting table in front of it. "As a doctor of the mind, don't you think you should consider all possibilities so you can manage whatever happens?"

"Don't think I haven't," Abby said. "I merely prefer to think about the ones that make me feel more at ease." She shifted on the windowsill and cast a teary-eyed glance Lyla's way. "We have to at least try to get back, don't we?"

Lyla clicked the toes of her borrowed shoes together. They weren't ruby-colored slippers, but reddish-brown. The action reminded her of a very old movie, and how the little girl in it finally got back home from a strange place. But then the girl realized she missed a lot of the people she loved in that place so far from home. "If we have a safe haven here at Eadar, how can we risk it by trying to see if we can get back home? Then we'll have no protection at all in this time."

Abby pointed at the sitting-room door. "Have you forgotten we are locked in here? Held prisoner? Who knows what they might eventually decide to do with us?"

"I don't get that *feeling* from these people."

"You and your bloody feelings! I am so sick of them!" Abby hugged her knees to her chest and bared her teeth, resembling a cornered animal. "It is all a load of rubbish. A crutch. You blame everything that's gone wrong in your life on not listening to your sixth sense. Hokum, I say. Pure, unadulterated hokum. Your life is the way it is because of your choices. You have no one to blame for the shambles you've made of yourself but you."

"I see."

Abby clapped a hand over her mouth. "Lyla—I am so sorry. I

should not have said any of those things. It's just I am so stressed."

"Stressed? I would think a person in your profession could handle that." Lyla gritted her teeth to keep from adding anything more hurtful. Her sister had always possessed an off-putting bluntness. Tough love, she called it. Yet another reason Lyla always wondered if they shared the same DNA. Of course, Mother had been the same. Apparently, Abby's lack of compassion came from her. "Perhaps you should tell the guard to fetch Eufamie to help you get ready for bed. I'm retiring and won't be able to help you."

"Lyla—"

She held up a hand, unwilling to hear any more apologies. "No. You said what you meant. Leave it."

"I am sorry. Really, I am."

Lyla didn't bother to answer. Instead, she rose from the couch, crossed to her bedchamber, and closed the door. She leaned back against it, not knowing whether to laugh or cry. The shambles she had made of her life. What a lovely way her sister had put it.

Thankful for the layers of clothing to remove, she took her time. It would keep her mind occupied. Besseta had tied the ribbons holding her stockings so tight, it left an itchy red ring around her legs above the knees. She rubbed some of her precious body lotion on the marks until the itching stopped.

With slow, purposeful movements that kept her from falling apart, she folded everything and either placed it in a pile on the bureau or hung it on the hook beside the door. Down to nothing but her shift, she went to the window seat, pushed open the pane, and settled down, hoping the cool night air and her precious constellations would ease her heart. She wished there was a way to send Abby back to the twenty-first century. Surely over three hundred years apart would be enough distance to make her family leave her alone.

Someone pecked on the door.

"Go away."

"But I have yer tisane, mistress."

Lyla rubbed the corners of her eyes, gritty and burning from weariness and tears waiting to be shed. "Fine. Bring it in."

Besseta eased open the door, then closed it with a bump of her hip. She carried a tray with a steaming cup of something. "If ye wish to sip it in bed, I can fix yer pillows to support ye better. Shall I do that, mistress?"

"Don't go to such trouble." Lyla reached for the cup and sniffed the steam. She detected the clean, astringency of mint. Of course, mint would be what they brewed. Even in the twenty-first century, many practitioners of homeopathic options knew mint helped settle the stomach. She hazarded a sip and was pleased to discover it wasn't too bad. "Thank you, Besseta."

The maid stood there, nervously running the edge of the round tray through her fingers, turning it round and round.

After the third spin of the platter, Lyla couldn't stand it anymore. She snatched hold of the tray and halted it. "What?"

"Ye got ready for bed without my help." The young woman quivered a pitiful shrug, her gaze downcast. "Himself willna think ye need me, and Lady Katherine will send me back to either the laundress or the kitchens."

Lyla scooted over on the window seat and patted a spot beside her. "Sit."

Besseta's eyes flared wide. "Nay, mistress. It would nay be proper."

"Please?" She patted the cushion again. "I promise I won't tell a soul."

The maid perched on the edge of the cushion, sitting ramrod straight.

Lyla rubbed her eyes again, determined to come to an understanding with Besseta without revealing anything she shouldn't. She also needed more information about Grant before she could relax enough to sleep tonight. She needed details to sort through whatever her intuitiveness was trying to tell her. "I got ready for bed with no help because I've been doing that for myself ever since I figured out how to work buttons." She held out the tray. "But that doesn't mean I don't need you to help take care of me here. Especially since I'm not always sure about what I'm supposed to wear, or say, or do."

"Why is that, mistress? Is London all that different from Scotland?"

"Where I'm from it is." There. That was definitely not a lie.

"So, ye willna be sending me back to the laundress or the kitchens?"

"Absolutely not."

Besseta glowed with a relieved smile. She started to rise from her seat, but Lyla stopped her.

"But I would like some information before you go."

Besseta's smile disappeared. "Oh, dear."

"No matter what you tell me, I promise I will repeat it to no one." Lyla drew an *x* on her chest as she'd done with the children. "Cross my heart and hope to die."

The girl stared at her as if she'd threatened to call forth a horde of demons.

"It means I will keep my word and not betray you." The children had understood that. Why didn't Besseta?

"Aye, mistress." The maid eyed her and started turning the serving tray in her hands again.

Lyla did her best to ignore it. If it kept Besseta in place and possibly talking, she could bear it. Time to start with the basics and see how much she could find out. "When did the chieftain's wife die?"

Besseta's mouth closed, clamping tighter while her eyes opened wider. She shook her head. "I canna say."

"Why?"

"Himself and Lady Katherine forbid it."

She couldn't say, but she could nod or shake her head. Lyla shrugged. It was worth a try. "Did she die when she had his children?"

The maid clamped her mouth closed again and stared at the floor.

"You don't have to say it out loud. Just give me a nod or some sort of signal. That wouldn't be speaking of it, and you would still be obeying your orders." A twinge of guilt pricked her conscience, but she managed to silence it. She needed to know the keep's secrets to know which life path to take or avoid. "Did she die in childbirth?"

Besseta shifted in place and made a barely discernible shake of her head.

"So, she didn't die when the twins were born." Lyla frowned. That meant the woman had died at some point in time during the last five years since the twins hit that age next month. How could she narrow it down without turning her informational charades game into a game of twenty questions? "The twins turn five next month."

"Aye." The maid had no issue with sharing that, although she had started edging toward the door.

"Three years ago, then? Did their mother die when the children were two years old?"

Besseta shook her head while chewing the corner of her lip so hard it started to bleed.

Alarm filled Lyla. "Maybe you better go. I don't want to upset you so much that you bite through your lip."

The girl pulled a square of linen from her sleeve and pressed it to her mouth. As she did so, she crept forward while looking around, as if afraid someone might overhear. "'Twas just a little over a year ago," she whispered. "But the poor lady hadna been right since she brought her bairns into the world."

"What do you mean she wasn't right?"

Besseta frowned, as though regretting she had spoken. Either that, or she was having trouble finding the words. It turned out to be the latter. "She wanted nothing to do with the bairns. Wouldna even nurse them." She shook her head. "Poor thing cried all the time and just stared out the window. She was so sad."

"Why?"

With a disheartened shrug, the maid continued. "No one knew. She would never say. All we knew was that whenever Himself brought the children to her, she would cry all the harder and scream for him to leave her be." She stole a look back at the door. "Himself moved her to these rooms and kept the children from her. It seemed to make her better for a while. She even smiled now and then." Her pained look returned, and her knuckles went white with her grip on the tray. "Then we found her. Jumped out the window to hang herself." She crossed herself three times, then leaned closer. "Some say demons made her do it. Others say 'twas Himself's fault because she never wanted the arranged marriage. Just done it to obey her father and then Himself made it worse by leaving her be after he got her with child."

"And what do you think?" Lyla needed to know what Besseta believed about the poor woman's untreated depression that had driven her to suicide.

"I think she was just so sad she couldna bear it any longer." The maid's eyes glistened with unshed tears. "She was a kind woman before she had the bairns. Never happy, but content enough it seemed. I think Himself stayed away because that was what she wanted." She sniffed and dabbed at the corners of her eyes. "I pray for her soul every night. Just as I pray for Himself. Our poor chieftain is tormented by her death and by those who blame him for it."

"I shall pray for them, too." Lyla squeezed Besseta's arm. "Thank you for telling me, and I promise I won't tell a soul. Not even my sister." Even though Abby would know all the clinical details of what the woman suffered, she didn't need to hear about it.

Lyla found out long ago that her sister was too cold and detached about such things. She never understood why Abby possessed absolutely no compassion. How could she be so detached and still help patients? Abby said it was how she survived everything her patients told her. If she wasn't detached, she would succumb to their suffering just as they had.

"Can I go now, mistress?"

"Yes. Thank you, Besseta."

"When ye wake, have the guards let me know, aye? I'll help ye dress and bring ye food to break yer fast." She stood with her hand on the door and smiled. "I hope ye sleep well."

Lyla smiled back at the kind girl. "I hope you sleep well, too. I will see you in the morning."

"ARE WE FINALLY good now?"

"As long as you keep your opinions to yourself, we are good. At least, for now." Lyla took the lead, adjusting the herb basket on her arm. It had been almost a week since their argument, and the only reason she spoke to Abby now was because it was such a royal pain to punish her with the silent treatment while locked in the same suite of rooms. Thankfully, their daily releases from captivity into the wilds of the keep had grown longer each day, providing some relief from each other's company.

"Mistress Lyla!" Fawna and Rory charged toward them, leading a gaggle of children, a dog, and a goose that acted more like a canine than a fowl. It followed the children everywhere, and when they weren't available, it was the constant companion of the stable keeper's gigantic black dog named Dougal.

"What ye be doin' today?" Rory asked, tiptoeing to inspect the empty baskets. "Be ye going to pick berries?"

"Cook asked us to fetch her some herbs from the garden," Abby said, turning to cast a nervous glance back at the keep. "In fact, we best be on our way. You children run along now."

Lyla ignored her and barely refrained from rolling her eyes. She would much rather spend the day with the children than Abby. "I have seen no berry bushes here inside the wall." She looked wistfully at the iron-banded door beside the partially lowered portcullis. In the conspiratorial tone of a fellow mischief-maker, she bent closer and added, "You know we're not allowed outside the wall without guards to make sure we don't escape."

Fawna and Rory exchanged wily grins. "Us'll guard ye."

"Aye!" the rest of the children chimed in. "Ye canna escape all of us."

"Or Dougal," said the tallest lad as he ruffled the dog's floppy ears. "He could track ye anywhere."

The goose honked and flapped its wings as though promising to stand guard, too.

"See? Even Goosie'll watch ye!" Fawna tugged on Lyla's arm while waving Abby onward. "Mistress Abby can fetch Cook the herbs. We know where lots of raspberries and bilberries be waiting, ready to eat."

That plan suited Lyla fine. She itched to explore beyond the keep's walls. It would get her away from Abby, and she adored eating berries straight off the bush.

Abby shook her head. "You shouldn't, Lyla. What if they get angry? What might they do to you?"

"How can anyone get angry when I am well guarded by these fierce warriors and warrioresses, whom I could never escape?"

"Warrioresses is not a word." Abby gave her a stern, sisterly scowl.

"'Tis so a word." Fawna took hold of Lyla's hand. "Mistress Lyla's smart as my Da, and her just said it, so it's so."

Abby opened her mouth, but Lyla silenced her with a threatening look. "Not another word. Go fetch the herbs." She would not tolerate her sister correcting the children or lecturing her on the does and don'ts of being a compliant prisoner.

With a disgusted huff, Abby flounced off.

"Are ye sure her is yer *real* sister?" Rory asked.

"No. I am not." Lyla patted her basket. "But I am certain I won't let her ruin our day. Do you think one basket is enough?"

"We gots our aprons," offered a little girl with gorgeous blue eyes.

"I can use me cap," said a lad as he whipped it off his head.

"I'll fetch a couple of buckets from the stable." The tall lad took off at a fast lope with the dog and the goose hurrying to catch him.

"I hope Liam doesna get the ones his da uses to scoop shite from the stalls." Rory wrinkled his nose. "We best smell'm when he gets back."

"Good plan." Lyla took a step toward the portcullis, then stopped. "Is there a different way out? The guards might stop me if we go that way."

Fawna grinned and waved for her to follow. "Aye. There's another way. Come on."

"Shouldn't we wait for Liam?" Lyla didn't wish for any of the children to feel left out. She remembered that feeling all too well.

"I'm a comin'!" Liam pounded toward them, wooden buckets swinging from his hands. The dog also toted one, the bail of it in its mouth. The goose brought up the rear, scuttling along behind them with its wings outspread.

"Them's not the shite buckets, are they?" Fawna shouted at the boy.

Lyla wondered if she should correct the child, then decided against it. Perhaps when they were closer allies, she might guide the little girl on avoiding words that might make her look bad.

"Course they're not the shite buckets, ye wee eedjit." Liam gave her an insulted scowl, then stuck out his tongue.

Time to get involved. Lyla caught hold of Fawna and Rory just as they dove toward the boy. "No fighting. All that does is waste time when I'm trying to sneak out and pick loads of berries. You don't want me to get caught before we even get outside the wall, do you?"

"Naw," the two grumbled still glaring at their friend.

"What about it, Liam? Pax?" She had to get all of them on board. A quick count of heads revealed she was sorely outnumbered at seven to one.

"Pax?" the lad repeated. "What does *pax* mean?"

"Peace. Cease-fire. End of hostilities." Lyla held up her crossed fingers. "When you hold your fingers like this and say, 'pax' that means everyone stops fighting."

"That sounds like giving up or surrendering," said one of the shorter boys, siding with Liam.

Lyla shook her head. "No. It means everyone stops fighting so everybody wins. Like getting to pick berries and eat as many as we want."

"I do like me some berries." Liam bobbed his head and grinned.

"Then let's go." Lyla released Fawna and Rory. "Lead on my fine guards."

The children surrounded her. Fawna, Rory, the dog, and the goose took the lead. With as much nonchalance as their eclectic group could manage, they sauntered around to the back of the keep and squeezed into the space between a short-thatched building and the skirting wall. It was the same dwelling Lyla had seen from above and contemplated using to escape. The small cottage was where the dinner fowls were plucked and the feathers saved for pillows and bedding. The goose hissed and popped its beak as they strolled past the open door.

"Ye willna ever go there, Goosie," Fawna reassured. "Da promised. Neither yerself nor yer kin will ever be roasted at Eadar."

"Aye," Rory agreed. "Only chickens and wild birdies eaten here. No gooses."

"Geese," Liam corrected.

"Pax, Liam," Lyla gently reminded.

The lad held up crossed fingers and nodded. "Aye. Pax."

"Here 'tis, right here." Fawna bent and shoved aside a bushy clump of grass to reveal a hole in the base of the skirting wall.

Lyla squatted and peered into it. One block wide, one block tall, the passage would be a snug fit, barely wide enough for her shoulders. "Why on earth is there a hole here?"

"Grandmam says the first mason that started building the keep didna ken what he was doing." Rory added a solemn nod. "She said Grandda had him dragged behind a horse all the way back to Edinburgh where he found him."

"The next one did better," Fawna said.

"I imagine so." Lyla bent lower and squinted into it, not too keen on crawling through the cramped space. The wall looked to be a good three meters thick. Not a terribly long way to crawl, but long enough—especially while swaddled in layers of linen and wool rather than the much more crawl-friendly denim of her favorite jeans.

"Go ahead," Liam encouraged. "We'll stand watch for ye."

How could she refuse? Hiking her skirts out of the way of her knees, she crawled in and pushed her basket in front of her. At least, that would clear the way of any oversized bugs or vermin. "Eyes on the prize," she muttered aloud, trying to ignore the scratching rub of the stones on either side of her as the wall snagged her sleeves. "I can do this. I can do this. Daylight up ahead." She shoved through the other side and pulled in a deep breath. "Bless me, I'm glad that's over."

"I should think so," commented a familiar voice above her.

She contemplated not looking up in the hopes that Grant would somehow disappear, then a shove from behind left her no choice. "Oh no! You've caught me," she called out to whichever of the children had followed, hoping they would know the warning for what it was.

Fawna giggled, dashing that plan.

A large, powerful hand appeared right in front of her nose. "Allow me to help ye to yer feet, m'lady."

"Why thank you, Chieftain Reddoch," she said extra loud as she stood. Maybe the mites would skitter back out the other way and escape.

Grant dropped to one knee and glared into the tunnel. "Daren't ye run. Out here now. All of ye."

One by one, all seven children crawled through. The only

two escapees were the dog and the goose. Lyla could only assume that Liam had shooed the creatures to safety before crawling through to stand before his chieftain.

"This is not their fault," she began, then stopped at his frosty glower.

"Fawna. Rory." He rose to his feet, settled his arms in a stern fold across his chest, and tilted his head to a disapproving, parental angle. "Ye ken well enough that neither Mistress Lyla nor her sister are allowed outside the wall." His narrow-eyed look settled on his daughter. "Who showed her the hole and why?"

Lyla held up her basket. "I asked them to show me the way to some berries. They didn't want to because they didn't want to go against your word, but I talked them into it."

"Dinna teach my children to lie to their father," he growled under his breath.

Fair point. She shouldn't be such a poor example. But as the adult, it was her fault. Not theirs. "Please don't blame them. I should not have led them astray. I took advantage of them."

"Nay, Da. She didna take 'vantage of us." Rory strode forward with his tiny chest stuck out. "We wanted to go berry picking, and we promised to guard her. We nattered on and on for her to come wif us. On and on and on, we went, 'til she finally agreed just to get some peace."

"Aye, Da," Fawna chimed in. "Just like ye do when Grandmam asks ye the same thing over and over 'til ye finally do it just to get her to hush herself."

Lyla clamped her mouth shut and bit her lip. If she laughed now, it would be the dungeons for the lot of them.

"What say the rest of ye? Liam? Sawny? Jenna?" Grant ran his scowl across each child as he called them by name. "Fiona? Thomas?"

They each stepped forward and stood on either side of Fawna and Rory. "'Tis like Rory said." Liam nodded, as did the others. "Nattered and nattered."

"On and on," added Fiona, the smallest of the group.

"Then ye leave me no choice."

Lyla looked up, prepared to take her punishment with the rest of them.

With a deep breath that swelled his chest to an even more impressive size, Grant pointed to a large cluster of shrubs off in the distance. "If ye dinna pick enough berries to make cream crowdie for everyone, ye will all go to yer beds with no supper." He leveled his piercing gaze on her. "That includes yerself, Mistress Lyla."

She attempted a curtsy, but the rough ground caused her to stumble.

He caught her and swept her upright before she went down. In a low rumbling whisper, he added, "We shall discuss yer leading the children astray in private. For now, ye best pick berries like ye have never picked berries before, ye ken?"

"Yes, my chieftain," she said, struggling not to grin. Without thinking, she rubbed her tingling neck. "Will you be picking berries with us?"

"No, m'lady." He returned to his mount and settled back into the saddle. "I shall stand guard while the rest of ye take care of this evening's dessert." He nodded at her skirts. "Yer maid willna be pleased when she sees those skirts and yer sleeves."

"Oh, bloody hell." She had thought to avoid grass stains by hiking them up to her knees but sorely failed. Both elbows were stained as well. She examined the shoulders, relieved that the rough stones hadn't torn the material. "I thought you were out on a hunt or something." She picked her way across the rough grassiness, tromping in what she felt sure would be considered a very unladylike fashion.

"I was hunting." He kept his mount at a slow walk beside her while watching the children up ahead. "Malcolm fetched me."

"That damned Abby! She ratted me out, didn't she?"

"If ye are asking if yer sister betrayed ye? Then, aye. She did." He chuckled. "'Tis my understanding the two of ye have nay been speaking for several days. Ye dinna get on well with yer sister. Do ye?"

"No. I do not." Several juicy red raspberries on the nearest bush caught her eye. She showed them to him, then popped them in her mouth. "Quality control, you understand?"

"What?"

After swallowing the sweet juiciness, she offered him the next handful. "I had to try a few to make sure they were sweet enough."

He eyed the berries she held up to him, then scooped them out of her hand and ate them. As he chewed, he nodded. "Verra good. But I meant what I said. If ye dinna gather enough for Cook's use, ye will have no supper."

"If I am full of berries, I won't want any supper." She winked, then relented and placed the rest of the berries into her basket. "How are the other berry pickers doing? Can you see them?"

"I am sure they are doing well. They dinna like missing their supper."

She glanced up at the thoughtfulness in his tone. Now that they were alone, it was her chance to plead the children's case. "Please don't punish them because of me."

He resettled himself in the saddle and gave a heavy sigh. "They must learn that every decision they make has consequences. Someday, their verra lives will depend on the choices they make."

How could she argue with that? Especially at this point in Scotland's history. "I am sorry I got them into trouble." She picked faster, flinching as thorns raked across her hand. "Bollocks!" She licked away the blood, then sucked on the wound.

"How badly are ye hurt?" He swung down from the saddle and strode to her side.

"It's nothing." Droplets of blood bubbled up from the long, ragged scratch. "Serves me right for getting the babies in trouble."

"Where is yer square of linen?" He took her hand and frowned down at the minor injury.

"Oh. In my uhm." She patted the front of her bodice, then

arched a brow. "Close your eyes while I fish it out. I kind of shoved it pretty far down there because I really didn't think I would need it."

He stood there, her hand in his, staring.

"Are you going to close your eyes or not?"

He flashed a brilliant smile that revealed a dimple in his left cheek she had never noticed before. It and the devilishness of his expression set the back of her neck and other parts much lower on fire. "Well?"

"Nay. I believe I will keep them open."

"Never dare me." Eyes locked with his, she shoved her free hand down her front and retrieved the neat square of hemmed linen that Besseta had instructed she needed to carry at all times. She waved it in his face. "There. See?"

"Indeed." He snatched it from her, wrapped it around her bleeding hand, then tucked the ends in against her palm. Rather than release her hand, he stood there and held it, his gaze reaching into her and grabbing hold of her soul.

"What?" she whispered.

He leaned closer. So near, she drowned in the iciness of his eyes that suddenly didn't seem so cold after all. "Ye bewitch me, Mistress Lyla. I dinna ken what to do with ye."

She had a few suggestions but chose not to share them for fear of his thinking her a professional—or maybe even an amateur—whore. Instead, she softly breathed the words, "I think I am meant to be here. For us. In fact, I know it. I can't explain how, but you have to believe and know it, too."

"Da! Da! Is this enough?" Rory's hopeful cries broke the bewitchment Grant claimed so powerful.

Lyla stifled a groan as he released her hand and turned to the children galloping their way.

"Let me see," he said after clearing his throat.

As she ducked her head, Lyla allowed herself a smile. At least he felt it, too.

CHAPTER SEVEN

"I HAVE YET to satisfy Lady Napier's request." Grant walked along the alure behind the battlements of the skirting wall. "I canna rest until I fulfill the oath I gave my cousin. Especially since my last words with my uncle were not the best." He squinted against the brilliance of the cloudless sky and allowed his gaze to sweep across his beloved lands.

"We can set out at dawn if that is yer wish. Mounts and supplies can be ready with little enough trouble." Malcolm strolled along beside him. "All is quiet enough here at the keep. Quiet as it was the last time we set out for Edinburgh."

"Aye, but we have our English prisoners to consider now." Prisoners. What a laughable description for their *guests*. The two women had the run of the keep and had endeared themselves to everyone, from the lowliest scullery maid to his mother. Or at least Lyla had.

Not an unkind word or criticism ever came to his ear about her. A few commented on her sister Abby's nervous, standoffish temperament, but only good things were ever said about Lyla. And considering the effect she had on him, he understood why. He wanted the woman more than he wanted his next breath. Especially after that kiss. But he could not weaken to her charms.

At least—not yet.

"Grant? Chieftain? What say ye?"

He scrubbed a hand across his mouth, cursing himself for his inability to keep his mind where it should be rather than on the lass who had taken control of his thoughts. He even dreamed about her, and that had become maddening torture. "Forgive me, Malcolm. What did ye say?"

The war chief grinned and tucked his head. "I understand. Mistress Abby has the same effect on me."

Grant wheeled about and stared at his friend. "What has happened to us?" He leaned closer and thumped the man in the chest. "Have they bewitched us?"

Malcolm chuckled. "I remember Da saying how it was when he first met Mother." He grinned. "Said he went down like a felled stag shot through the heart." With a slow shake of his head, he stared off into the distance. "Died within days of each other after a lifetime of loving. They never could bear to be apart."

"Together in death and life." A twinge of jealousy ripped through Grant. He couldn't imagine such a precious bond with another. Especially after the disaster of his first marriage. He shook off the feeling and rested his hands atop the reassuring solidness of the waist-high stone battlement. "Now—what did ye say while I was trapped in my thoughts?"

"I said I think it is safe enough for us to be away for a few days. The more time I spend with Mistress Abby, the less I think her able to be a spy. We have men aplenty to watch them and guard the keep while we are gone. Shall we plan for tomorrow?"

"I canna do so in good conscience. Not yet." A flash of color close to the berry bushes to the south caught his attention. He strolled farther down the wall to observe Lyla and the herd of children that always followed her. "There is still something about those two that unnerves me. Have ye not noticed the way they sometimes cut off their speaking as if they fear their own words?"

"Aye, but I canna verra well judge a person for the way they speak. Not with my fickle tongue the way it is." Malcolm rolled his shoulders as if shaking off the embarrassment of his affliction. His bushy brows knotted as he studied the scene below. "What are they doing?"

The summer's breeze carried peals of laughter to the top of the skirting wall. Grant shook his head as Lyla covered her eyes, and the bairns scattered and hid, while the dog and that ridiculous goose remained on either side of her. "Another of her games she has taught them. Fawna and Rory love her. As does every wee one in the keep."

"Perhaps she would be a good mother to them." Malcolm cleared his throat and bumped him with a not-so-subtle nudge.

"An English woman to wife?"

Malcolm tipped his head, then blew out a grand huff. "Aye, well—ye could always say ye were trying to save her soul by making her a Scot."

"She is a sly one." Grant smiled as Lyla crouched and appeared to have a conversation with the dog and the goose. Then the trio charged off, rousting the children from their hiding places one by one and chasing them amid loud laughter, barking, honking, and squeals. "Did ye see that? Cheats at her own game. Used the dog and goose to find where the bairns hid." He shot Malcolm a knowing look. "And ye wonder why I still dinna trust them?"

The war chief made a face and flipped a hand toward the play. "'Tis naught but a game."

"Where is her sister?" Time to change the subject.

"Helping the weaver with new dyes." He frowned. "I believe that's what she said. Sometimes I dinna ken some of the words she uses."

"Aye. I know the problem." Grant leaned against the wall. He needed to keep his word and finish the task in Edinburgh, but couldn't bring himself to leave. Not with so many unanswered questions about the women—more importantly, about Lyla.

"If ye dinna wish to leave them here, why not take them with us?" Malcolm propped against the wall beside him, nodding down at the lovely dilemma as she continued the game. "Perhaps returning them to Edinburgh would be the test to see if we can trust them."

"Especially with rumblings about Cromwell heading north." Grant mulled over the prospect, studying it from every angle. If Lyla and her sister revealed themselves as spies, at least Eadar would be safe. Better to discover any potential dire news in Edinburgh rather than at his own hearth. He headed for the stair leading to the courtyard. "Come. Let us inform the ladies about their outing."

"WHY DO YOU think they asked us to come along? Malcolm said it was because they wanted to help us find our father's murderer. Do you really think that's what it is? They want to help us search for Dick Turpin? That man wasn't even born until the 1700s. Of course, I guess they can't know that, can they?"

Lyla continued brushing her hair, not bothering to wedge an answer into her sister's babbling. There wasn't any need. At least, not yet. Abby was like a wind-up toy. She spun around in circles, answering her own questions until she finally wound down, closed her mouth, and opened her ears.

"Are you still not talking to me? Why won't you answer?"

"Mainly because I can't get a word in edgewise." Lyla gathered her hair into a ponytail and pulled it forward, studying the tips for split ends. "Do they have scissors in this century?"

"Lyla." Abby's tone hit the level of distraught edginess that meant she might be ready to listen.

"I think they asked us to accompany them to Edinburgh because they still don't trust us. They don't want to leave their people unguarded." She flipped the ponytail to her back and turned in the chair, resting an arm across the back of it. In a voice of doom, she clawed at the air and bared her teeth like a dreaded beast. "They fear we will eat their people." She dropped her hands and shrugged. "After all, we are English."

Abby rolled her eyes. "How can they not trust us yet? We've been here almost a month." In nothing but her shift, perched in the chair beside the hearth, she drew up her knees and hugged them. "At least, near as I can tell, we've been here almost a month. I've been tying knots in a strip of cloth I keep hidden under my mattress." She gently swayed back and forth, rocking like she always did when upset. "I wonder if we can figure a way to get them to take us back to Arthur's Seat?"

"I don't want to go back." There. She had said it aloud. Her heart skipped a beat with the confession.

Abby stared at her, a worried frown puckering her brow. "I don't understand. Why not?" Before Lyla could answer, she continued, "I realize I've always been a complete cow about your life choices, but you seemed happy enough in *modern* Edinburgh. Were you not?"

Lyla pondered the question. It wasn't as simple as it might seem. "Not that I was unhappy." How could she explain it so her sister could understand? "I was restless. Empty and needing to be filled. Missing…something." She flitted a hand to encompass their surroundings. "But it's not like that here. After the initial shock of our landing in the seventeenth century wore off, I think I am as close to contended as I have ever been."

"Because of him?" The pucker in Abby's forehead deepened. "One kiss swayed you that much?"

"No, not just him." She rose and walked to the open window, stretching out her arms to let the breeze ripple her shift across her body. Deodorant and body spray had worn off long ago, but surprisingly enough, her natural *aroma* wasn't that bad thanks to daily washing with Besseta's crock of almost rancid rose oil soap. And for the first time in her life, she didn't wake up with her head plugged and her sinuses screaming for relief. Perhaps there was something to be said for the lack of air fresheners and perfumed toiletries full of chemicals she couldn't pronounce. Pollution-free air had its perks. "For the first time in my life, I belong. Or at least, seem to."

Abby scooted farther back into the chair and curled into a tighter ball. "I see," she said quietly.

"You probably don't, but that's all right." Lyla sat on the windowsill. "Besides, it would be easier to get you up to Arthur's Seat without me."

Her twin's frown returned, but instead of worried, she looked almost tearful. "Without you? I would never see you again."

"Abby. Come on." Lyla gave her a chiding look. "We might be twins, but we have never been close."

"Maybe not, but you are still my sister." Abby folded her hands on top of her knees and stared at them. "I do love you, Lyla. And care about you." She huffed a jerking shrug. "Whether you feel the same about me or not."

"You know I love you." She retrieved the hairbrush, went to Abby, and started brushing out the long dark curls she had always envied. "I just don't always like you very much. We look at things differently."

Abby didn't answer, just sniffed.

Lyla staunched a sigh and kept brushing. "What is the first thing you'll do when you get back? Take a hot shower? Brush your teeth with your electric toothbrush? Brew a delicious pot of black tea? Oh, I have it! You'll wrap yourself in toilet paper—right?"

"No. The first thing I'll do is cry for my lost sister." Abby rose and moved out of reach. "I guess we should go to bed now. They said we need to be ready to leave at dawn."

Guilt the size of a boulder weighed heavy on Lyla's soul. She had hurt Abby with the honesty she should have realized her sister couldn't handle. That had not been her intent. Well, perhaps a little hurt had been her intent, but she shouldn't have done it. A loving lie was always better than a hurtful truth. "I'm sorry, Abby. I shouldn't have said the things I did. You know I love you."

"I know," Abby sniffed. "I guess I'm just going to have to work harder at getting you to like me." She closed the bedchamber door behind her, ending the conversation.

"Well, bollocks." Lyla tossed the brush to the couch. "I handled that well."

A light knock on the sitting room door interrupted her fuming. She crossed to it and stood close so as not to disturb her sister. "I'm still up, but Abby's not," she said in a low tone. "Tell me who you are before I tell you where they hide the key."

"It is me, m'lady," replied the voice that made her steady herself by leaning against the wall.

"Well then, I guess you already know where the key is. Give me a minute to get a wrap or something. All I'm wearing is my shift." She dashed to her room, grabbed a light shawl, and threw it around her shoulders. This would have to do since she wasn't sure if robes or dressing gowns even existed. She returned to the door. "I'm ready."

It creaked open, and Grant stood framed in the opening as he had been on that very first day. "I wanted to check and make sure ye were well."

"Really?" His excuse made little sense. They had just seen each other at the last meal of the day. "And why is that?"

His fair brows drew together. "Why?"

"Did I seem unwell at supper?" She couldn't remember complaining about anything.

"No." He tipped his head toward the room. "Might I come in or do ye intend to keep me standing in the hall?"

"Proper ratty tonight, are we?" She stepped back and waved him in, directing him toward the couch.

Instead of seating himself, he paced back and forth in front of the hearth like a great, disgruntled dragon with his kilt swinging behind him. Fist to palm, he rubbed his hands together, scowling at the floor.

"Have you changed your mind about us coming with you?" That had to be it. What else could it be?

"No."

"No," she repeated. So much for that. "Are you going to tell me why you are really here?"

He halted and scowled at her. "Because I needed to see ye, damn ye."

She held her breath so as not to laugh in his face.

His nostrils flared like the great blonde beast that he was. Hands clenched, he resettled his feet as though preparing to charge. "I command ye to remove this spell."

She stared at him, not entirely sure how to proceed. Such a conversation in this era was dangerous. She should not handle it lightly. Her life depended on it. With the same serious calmness she used to settle wars between the children, she primly folded her hands. "I do not know how to cast spells because I am not a witch."

"Nay, but ye are a woman," he said. "And ye haunt my thoughts night and day."

That sounded promising. Perhaps if she attacked this from another angle. "It is not just women who possess that power. You are always in my thoughts, too."

He backed up a step. "What say ye?"

"I said I think about you all the time, too." She eased toward him, wondering if she should swerve to the right so she wasn't blocking the door. She didn't want him to feel trapped. "I have never had anyone kiss me like you did."

"Truly?"

She nodded and almost crossed her heart, then decided against it. "Truly."

"Well, then." He appeared to relax, pulled in a deep breath, then charged back across the room to the door. After he opened it, he glanced back and gave a perfunctory nod. "I shall see ye anon. Bright and early, aye?"

"Right. Dawn, I believe."

"Good, then." He stepped out into the hall, but before closing the door behind him, called out, "Sleep well." Then clicked it shut.

"You cheeky devil." Who would have thought such an alpha warrior type would have so much trouble wooing a lady? She assumed he was trying to woo her. Or at least, she hoped so.

HER WARM SOFTNESS both pleased and tormented him. Grant was thankful Lyla had spent her hours playing with the children rather than learning how to ride or else this closeness would no longer be necessary. Back in the saddle in front of him, her legs curved in front of his, and her fine round arse tucked tight between his thighs was Heaven as well as Hell. His poor cock throbbed until it ached. But if this trip proved fruitful in showing she could be trusted, he fully intended to grant his man parts the relief they needed and share more than a kiss to celebrate the discovery. Her sister rode with Malcolm. He felt sure those two would celebrate in a like manner.

"You never really said the reason for your trip to Edinburgh." She cast a smile back at him.

"No. I did not."

"I see. I assume you are not going to, either." She huffed a silent laugh and shook her head. "Besseta asked why we had been invited. I had to tell her I didn't know."

"Aye, m'lady. That was a truthful answer to yer maid." He smiled to himself, finding her artlessness at discovering more about him amusing. Yet more proof she was unlikely to be a spy.

"Do you think Malcolm could take Abby to the peak where you found us?"

Her question gave him pause. Perhaps she wasn't so artless after all. "Why?"

"She's the sentimental sort. That was a special place for her and Father."

He wished he could see her eyes to know if she was lying.

Her tone suggested it. "I see no harm in going there. In fact, studying Edinburgh from above before we enter might be wise."

"Oh, I don't want to go." She twisted around and looked him full in the face. Panic and something indescribable flashed in her eyes. "Abby wants to revisit it. Not me."

Damned if he could tell what she played at. "'Tis safer if we dinna separate."

She didn't argue, but she didn't agree. He could see it in her face.

"Malcolm!" He threw up a hand and waved the man over.

"Aye?"

"Let our first stop in Edinburgh be *Àrd-na-Said*, ye ken? Where we found the ladies?" He noted that Mistress Abby clutched a fist to her chest as soon as the words left his mouth. "I think it would be good to look down upon the city before entering. Do ye not agree?"

With a curt nod, Malcolm veered his mount in that direction.

The closer they drew to the vantage point overlooking the city, the more Lyla stiffened. It both worried and intrigued him. He didn't wish to prove her a spy or the enemy. She needed to be fleeing trouble or avenging her father's murder, as unbelievable as that tale sounded. He didn't wish to lose her to the truth. When they reached the top, he nodded for Malcolm to help Abby down, before dismounting and reaching for Lyla.

Staring down at him as though terrified, she clutched her fists against her middle and shook her head. "I'm fine, thanks. I'll wait until we get into town to stretch my legs."

He studied her. Rapid breathing. High color to her cheeks. Subtle trembling. Fear threatened to overcome her, but so did the determination not to tell him why. Naught to do but force her. He moved closer, took hold of her by the waist, and pulled her down.

"Don't!" She leapt into his arms and wrapped herself around him. Arms around his neck, one of her legs curled around his hip while the other dug at him as though trying to climb higher.

"Please don't."

"Lyla," he crooned softly, hugging her close. He hitched her up and supported her with an arm under her rump. "I will keep ye safe. I swear it."

"Then don't let me down," she pleaded. Her heart hammered against him.

"Why?" he gently prodded.

Abby rounded the horse. "It's all right, Lyla. The body is long gone. We won. He's not here, and no one is the wiser."

Lyla twisted to look at her sister but didn't speak.

Malcolm moved to Abby's side, frowning first at her, then at Lyla. "Come," he said, taking hold of Abby's arm and gently pulling. "Let us look upon the c-city from over there."

Grant silently thanked his friend for granting him the privacy to sort this through with Lyla. Loath to set her to the ground and lose her panicked embrace, he ambled closer to the edge of the cliff and turned her so she might see and hopefully explain. "Who, lass? Who is gone?"

"The man." Her gaze darted to just beyond the edge. "We pushed him over." She chewed on her bottom lip for a long moment. "Broke his neck in the fall. Made it look like an accident."

She hitched a shuddering breath.

"We lured him up here the night before you found us," she whispered. "Found him and avenged our father's death." She nodded first at him, then across the way where Malcolm and Abby stood looking down at the city. "When the two of you showed up, we were afraid you had found us out and meant to turn us in for the murder."

Grant thought back to the morning they found them. Their bottles of wine. The empty bottles and the blanket. Mistress Abby so distraught. Lyla full of lies. For the first time, what she said made sense. The only thing that didn't seem real was her fear now. He eased her down but kept hold, gently steadying her. "Ye were the strong one when we found ye. Now it is yer sister with the courage. Why?"

Her bottom lip quivered as she stared at him. "When you found us, I had nothing to lose. But now…I do."

He swallowed hard, her words hitting him like a hard shove to the chest. But he had to be certain. "What do ye have to lose now, m'lady?"

"You," she whispered. "At least, I hope so."

He gathered her back into his arms and clutched her as tightly as she had hugged him. "Aye," he rasped. "I fear ye do at that." And she had no idea just how afraid he was. Unable to move past his distrust, he gently set her aside. "Yer sister wished to come here, yet you did not. Why is that?"

"Closure, I guess." Lyla shrugged. "She mentioned needing to stand on this spot and see for herself that the die had been cast." She turned and gazed at her sister. "Abby finds it easier to trust than I do. At least she does once she sees proof." A fondness softened her features. "Logic to a fault, my Abby. I wish I could be more like her." Her gaze dropped, and she released a faint sigh. "I wish I could trust like she does, too."

He turned her back to face him and lifted her face to his. "Trusting can be the most difficult thing in the world." He wanted to say so much more, but this was neither the time nor the place. "We will take our time, you and I. We will learn to trust again. Together, aye?"

"Aye." She blinked her unshed tears away.

He leaned closer and allowed himself a grin. "Ye need to work on yer accent, m'lady."

Her smile brightened, lighting up her eyes. "I will do my best, my chieftain."

"A p-pub be in order, me thinks," Malcolm called out while offering his arm to Abby.

She smiled up at him as she took it. "I agree."

Grant held out a hand to Lyla. "Come, m'lady. I think Malcolm's idea a fine one."

She slid her hand into his. "Most definitely."

The galloping thud of horsemen approaching made him push

her behind him and draw his sword. Four riders crested the hill and came to a halt. The man furthest to the right seemed vaguely familiar, but Grant couldn't quite place him. Nor could he identify the riders by their colors, since their drab dress comprised dark trews, simple white tunics, and black, unadorned waistcoats.

"Be ye kin to the Montrose?" asked the man Grant had struggled to remember. It was then he recognized him. These four served the Earl of Argyll. They had taken hold of his uncle, James Graham, First Marquess of Montrose, at Ardvreck Castle when the Baron of Assynt betrayed him. They brought him to a false trial in Edinburgh, then ensured him executed as the traitor he had never been. All four unsheathed their swords. "Ye shall be hanged, drawn, and quartered just as he was."

Before he could answer, Abby moved to stand in front of Malcolm and motioned for Lyla to join her. Which, much to his shock, she did. Both had removed their kerchiefs and bared the mounds of their breasts swelling above their bodices.

"How dare you," Abby growled in the haughty tone that several back at the keep had brought to his attention. She pointed at her sister. "Do you have any idea who you are addressing?"

"I ken well enough ye speak like an English." The man didn't back down.

"His Royal Highness shall hear of this."

Three of the horsemen cast nervous glances between them, but the speaker jutted his chin to a more defiant angle. "And what exactly shall the king hear?"

"How his favorite mistresses and their protectors were insulted and delayed whilst they attempted to enjoy Edinburgh." Lyla strode forward with her head held high. "Does your master wish to fall from His Majesty's favor?"

"You expect us to believe that the king's favorite companions would be made to travel through Scotland on the back of a horse?"

"What better way to enjoy the beauty of this country?"

An answer for everything as always. Lyla stood her ground, but Grant itched to end this foolishness with his blade. He strode forward, offered her a gentlemanly bow, then stepped in front of her. "Be on yer way and no one shall hear of this." He caught the sunlight with his sword and flashed it in the man's eyes. "Or fight."

"Four to two?" The leader laughed. "Fine odds by me."

Grant twitched an uncaring shrug. "Some of ye will die before I do. Maybe not all. But some. Which of ye are ready to face the Creator with me?"

Malcolm appeared at his side, a wide grin splitting his reddish beard as he resettled his dagger in one hand and his sword in the other. "Aye—'tis as fine a day as any to die."

"Three to two!" Lyla shouted from behind him. Something lobbed through the air. Then the Argyll leader grabbed his head, fell from his horse, and went still.

"Two to two," she shouted again. Grant spotted the rock this time as it struck the second man right between the eyes. He hit the ground.

The remaining pair turned their mounts and fled, galloping down the hillside.

Grant wheeled about. "Woman! What the hell are ye doing?"

With a rock in each hand, she stared at him with an expression of confused surprise. "I was helping."

"She always has been the best rock thrower." Abby smiled proudly at her sister. "I knew if given half a chance, she would get them. All the boys in our neighborhood took care not to get on her bad side."

"This one's dead," Malcolm called out, nudging the leader with the toe of his boot.

"Bloody hell, I didn't mean to kill him." Lyla rushed to the man and touched his neck. She closed her eyes and blew out a relieved sigh. "He is not dead." She straightened and frowned down at him. "At least, not yet. He's not breathing quite right, is he?"

"We shall speak of this later." They had to leave. Now. There would be no visiting any public places. "To the horses. Now."

CHAPTER EIGHT

"**I** SAID I was sorry." Lyla waited for his response, willing him to be sensible. Men pouted so much more than women. She glared at his handsome profile, partially hidden in the shadows of the corner table. "Grant?"

He ignored her. Instead, he continuously scanned the dingy dining area of the questionable tavern owned by someone he supposedly trusted. Old Bill McCullough. Or at least, she thought that was the name he had said. Unfortunately, they now waited for the trustworthy Mr. McCullough to rise from his drunken stupor. None of the barmaids would let them a room without his say so.

Malcolm acted as though his tankard demanded his full attention while stealing glances to the left and the right. Abby sat with her hands in her lap, looking like her neighbor's cat after it ate Mrs. Bulgari's parakeet.

Lyla's stomach growled. Loudly. She huffed out a frustrated sigh and hugged her middle, trying not to notice the mouthwatering aroma of stewed meat and some sort of greasy deliciousness coming from the doorway behind the bar.

The weariest looking of the trio of barmaids slogged over with a pitcher in one hand and a tray of steaming bowls balanced on her hip. Without a word, she refilled their tankards, then turned to Grant and waited.

"Here." He tossed a few coins onto her tray. "Leave the food and bring bread as well, ye ken?"

She slid the bowls of boiled meat and vegetables onto the table, tucked the money into her apron pocket, and wandered off—still sullen and silent. Within minutes, she returned with a plate piled high with layers of flat, somewhat circular bread and plopped it in their midst.

"Thank you," Lyla said, more to Grant than the barmaid. She considered giving him a friendly pat on the arm just to irritate him but decided not to waste her time. Instead, she dug into the bowl of chunky boiled meat, carrots, and turnips with a flat of stale bread.

"Never again will ye do what ye did today," he said without looking up from his bowl. "Either of ye. Understand?"

Caught chewing a particularly tough piece of meat, she cut her eyes over at Abby, who took the coward's way out and responded with an obedient nod. Lyla forced down the bite, then took a deep breath, knowing she was about to poke the proverbial bear. "Which part exactly?"

He looked up from his food and pinned her with a steely glare. "Which part?" he repeated slowly.

Malcolm choked on his ale and turned aside, coughing and beating his chest.

She picked at her bread, dunking a corner of it in the watery gravy. "Yes. Which part? Acting like Charles II's mistresses or throwing the rocks?"

Even in the shadows, she could see the muscles twitching in his clenched jaw. In for a penny, in for a pound. After all, he was already angry. "Abby and I could not stand there like a couple of helpless numpties. Those men meant no good. They might have killed you."

Head slowly tilting as if finding her comment unbelievable, his infuriated scowl hit a fearsome level. "Malcolm and I had the situation well in hand."

"They outnumbered you." She couldn't let this go even though a little voice in her head kept shouting, *shut it!* Highland women sometimes fought, she silently reasoned. Or at least, she thought they did. It had been a long time since she studied any history. "If I can help keep you safe, why shouldn't I?"

Malcolm jumped up and held out a hand to Abby. "Come help me ch-check on the horses, aye?"

Abby nodded, tossed down her bread, and took his hand. Both hurried from the room.

Not a good sign at all. Like rats abandoning a sinking ship. Perhaps she should attempt to patch the damage she had already done. "I didn't mean to sound as if I thought you couldn't handle yourself. I just meant—"

"I protect my own," he interrupted, his tone cold and accusing. "Ye shamed me today."

"That was not my intent," she said. "I was afraid for you, and I've never been the sort to step back and let others handle things when I think I can make a difference. But I will try to do better. Can you try to forgive me? Please?"

"Will ye trust me to protect ye as I see fit?"

That wasn't anger in his eyes. It was injured pride. Heaven help her. She had never been one to rely overmuch on others, but apparently, he needed to be needed. "I will do my best to never bring shame upon you ever again."

He accepted her apology with a curt nod and went back to eating. Still silent. Still pouting.

She refrained from saying anything else for fear of making matters worse. Instead, she concentrated on finding the more edible parts of the greasy stew. It had smelled wonderful earlier. Now that she'd staved off the worst of her hunger, its appeal had lessened.

"Reddoch!" The shout vibrated through the low-ceilinged room, making heads turn. The loud, booming voice belonged to a barrel-chested man with unusually long, burly arms. She fully expected his knuckles to drag the floor as he lumbered toward them. He reminded her of the gorillas she had seen at the London Zoo. "Reddoch! Be that you?"

Grant jumped to his feet and met the man in front of their table. He caught the tavern keeper's forearm, grabbed his shoulder, and gave it a jerk. "Hush it, man. I dinna need my presence announced to all of Edinburgh."

McCullough grunted while waggling a gray, unruly brow. "Well, I be damned," he shouted with a theatrical look around the dining room. "Ye be the spitting image of Reddoch from north a here! Beg pardon, sir. Name's Bill McCullough. Me wenches said ye need a room. Got coin? I dinna let that room to just anybody."

With a nod toward their table, Grant clapped the man on the back again. "Coin, I have. Sit and I'll buy ye a drink, sir."

McCullough pulled out a chair and dropped into it. One of his eyes narrowed, focusing on her. The other remained fixed and wide open, his shaggy head tilting like a bewildered dog as he stared. "Ye are nay one of my wenches."

"This is Lady Lyla Smythe," Grant said with a hard look that she understood to mean he wished her to keep quiet. "She and her sister, Lady Abby Cornwalt, are traveling with Malcolm and myself."

McCullough made a face as though impressed. He leaned closer to Grant and lowered his voice. "I dinna want no trouble here at Deacon's Tavern, ye ken? I'll let ye a room because I owe ye me life, but I willna tolerate no trouble."

"There will be no trouble." Grant flagged down the weary barmaid, who suddenly seemed more energized with her employer sitting at the table. "If all goes to plan, I only need the room for the night. No longer."

With a huge knobby hand deformed by arthritis, McCullough drained his cup and banged it on the table for more. "I dinna have but the one room, but it has two beds." He cast another one-eyed glance her way. "Should be big enough for the four of ye. But willna leave yer women much privacy."

Unable to stay quiet any longer, Lyla opened her mouth to speak, only to be stopped by Grant's hand on top of hers.

"The women will stay in the room," he said. "Malcolm and I have business this evening." He leveled a hard gaze on his old friend. "I am charging ye with their safety. No harm must come to them, ye ken?"

McCullough dipped his head once and kept it there so long, Lyla thought he had nodded off. He came to life and shoved himself up from the table. Wrapping an arm around the barmaid bringing yet another round of drinks, he shook a finger at them. "Give them the keys—once ye get the money." Then he swerved around and lumbered off without another word.

Grant pulled a small leather pouch from inside his waistcoat and shook it. The coins inside clinked together, making the sullen woman smile. She went to take the money, but he held it out of her reach. "The key?"

Never taking her eyes from the money, she shoved her fingers down the front of her bodice and fished it out. With it clutched to her chest, she reached for the pouch of coins again. Grant let her take hold of it but didn't release it until she allowed him to take the key.

"'Tis even clean," she said before walking away.

"She can speak." Lyla folded her hands on the table. "So, what is this business you and Malcolm plan to do while Abby and I are enjoying the accommodations?"

"The less ye know, the better." He handed her the key. "There is not but the one room at the top of the stair. It isna much, but ye'll be safe there. I trust McCullough."

Abby exploded into the tavern, eyes wild, bits of straw in her hair, her sleeve and the hem of her skirt torn. Few patrons even bothered to notice as she ran to them. "Malcolm is hurt! Please hurry!"

"Where?" Grant grabbed her by the shoulders.

As soon as she choked out *the stable*, he set her aside and lunged a long stride in that direction, then stopped and pointed his sword at Lyla. "Hie to the room and stay there, ye ken?"

With an arm already around Abby, she nodded and turned them both toward the stairs. "Be safe!" she called out.

But he was already gone. "What happened?" she asked in a hushed tone as they climbed the narrow stairs.

Her sister didn't answer, just gave a jerking shake of her head.

Lyla didn't press her. Maybe once they reached the room, she could speak about it. At the top of the stairs, she steadied her against the wall, unlocked the door, and pushed it open. Enough light filtered in through the dingy window to lead her to one of the narrow beds. "Here. Sit a minute while I find a lantern or a candle." If forced, she would fetch the lantern from the hall and anyone climbing the stairs could just do so in the dark.

"The table by the window. Looks like a flint box beside the chamberstick," Abby said as though in a daze. "Not much of a candle left in it, though."

Her twin was right. The short, waxy stump wouldn't grant them light for long. She patted Abby's hand. The chill of it worried her. "I'll be right back. Lock the door behind me." She hurried out, eyed the lantern at the top of the stairs, and decided she could do better.

Down below, candles burned on either side of the tavern's main door, lighting the way to the bar. More tapers had to be somewhere close. She crept down the steps and kept to the shadows. A dingy wooden box, its edges caked in mud as though it had been used to scrape someone's shoes, sat in the corner beside the door. Maybe it held candles. She lifted the hinged lid and peered inside. Long wax tapers covered the bottom of the box. She grabbed a handful and vaulted back up the steps, unlocked the door, shot inside, then relocked it. If Grant caught her outside of the room, she would never hear the end of it.

"We'll have plenty of light now." She replaced the spent stub, lit a fresh candle, then perched on the edge of the rickety bed opposite Abby. "Now tell me what happened."

"I think it was one of those men. You know—from Arthur's Seat?" Abby hugged herself and chewed on the corner of her lip. "He jumped out of the shadows and hit Malcolm in the head with some kind of iron bar. And he had a knife, too. A long ugly one." She picked at her torn sleeve. "He stabbed at Malcolm before I hit him in the face with a shovel."

"Did you knock him out? Was he the only one? Two of them rode away from Arthur's Seat." Lyla eyed the door, wishing they had furniture heavy enough to use as a barricade. Neither of the beds or the rickety table between them would do much good. "What about Malcolm? Was he knocked out or—"

"You didn't let me finish."

"I'm sorry. You're right. I'll try to be quiet." She clenched her teeth, fighting to rein in her emotions. Abby's near-miss had her heart pounding.

"The shovel didn't knock him out. Just made him more crazed." Her twin paused and pulled in a deep, shuddering breath, then blew it out. "I kept away from him and got to the pitchfork before he did."

Lyla bit her lip to keep from interrupting.

Abby's face crumpled as tears spilled down her cheeks. "I think I killed him," she whispered. "How could I have killed another human being?"

"Self-defense." Lyla moved to sit beside her and gave her a hard hug. "I would rather him dead than you."

"I think he stabbed Malcolm before I got to him with the pitchfork." She shuddered with harder sobs. "There was so much blood. Malcolm can't be dead. He can't."

Lyla hugged her closer and gently rocked her. She knew Malcolm and Abby seemed more connected than her sister had ever connected with anyone. This confirmed it. "Grant will get him to safety," she assured, hoping it was true, and also hoping Abby wouldn't ask where safety was.

A thud hit the door, making them both jump and stare at it.

"Lyla!" The whispered growl made her heart leap.

"It's Grant." She ran to the door, cursing under her breath as she fumbled with the lock, then finally threw open the door.

Grant grunted and surged forward, half dragging, half carrying Malcolm. Shoved up under the wounded man's shoulder, he clutched him by the arm and hugged his waist to keep him from falling. Malcolm stumbled like a drunken bear, his head sagging forward, and a hand clutched to his bloody chest.

Lyla helped them maneuver to the nearest bed, cringing as Grant dropped Malcolm across it.

Abby rushed to him, dragging his feet up onto the bed and straightening his legs. She ripped open his tunic to check his chest wound. "It's a slash, not a puncture. Thank Heavens. I can deal with a slash."

"What about his head?" Lyla grabbed the poor excuse for a pillow from the other bed and helped Abby tuck it under the man's neck. "His color isn't good at all." The usually ruddy-cheeked warrior had gone a deathly pale. Eyes closed, his-reddish blonde lashes seemed so delicate as they rested on his colorless cheeks.

"Ye are a talented healer, then?" Grant asked Abby. "Ye must help him."

"Stay out of my way and I will."

Lyla stepped back, amazed. Abby had never exhibited such a take-charge attitude before. She took hold of Grant's arm. "Come, she'll help him best she can." She tugged him back beside the door.

Someone pecked on it. Grant drew his dagger before opening it a crack, then stepped back and allowed the bar wench in with a pitcher, basin, and several folds of linen hung across her arm. She set them on the small table between the beds. "McCullough said if this is nay enough, send for more." Then she left, closing the door behind her.

After locking the door again, Lyla tugged on his arm, making him stay beside her. "Let her work. She knows what she's doing. I promise."

He gave a grim smile, his focus locked on his friend. "Before he closed his eyes, he said yer braw sister saved him. Stabbed the bastard." He huffed a humorless laugh and shook his head. "Killed him with a pitchfork, no less."

"I think she cares about Malcolm," she said. "A lot."

His jaw flexed, then tightened as his gaze dropped to the floor. "He cares for her as well. It eases my heart to know she willna spurn him."

"Will your friend allow us to stay longer than tonight?" She leaned back against the door, hugging herself. With the room barely big enough for the pair of narrow beds and the table between them, she couldn't imagine staying there for days, but Malcolm couldn't possibly travel.

"'Tis not safe for us here. We leave tomorrow as planned." He leaned against the wall beside her, watching everything Abby did. "He's ridden in worse condition than this, and thankfully, 'tis not that long a trip, and the weather is fair."

"How can he possibly ride?"

"I will ride," came a weak growl from the bed.

Abby turned and glared at them. "Out into the hall if you insist on talking. He needs quiet and rest."

"Sorry." Lyla eyed Grant and tipped her head toward the hallway.

He nodded and motioned for her to lead the way.

"Do you think the other one came with him?" she asked once they closed the door behind them.

Grant leaned on the wall beside the door and stared at it. "If the other Argyll man had been there, I doubt yer sister wouldha been able to save herself or Malcolm."

Valid point. The thought of what could have happened gave her eerie chill bumps. She rubbed her arms, sent up a prayer of thanks, then rubbed the back of her neck.

"What does the sight tell ye?" He pushed away from the wall and stepped closer.

Without thinking, she reached for him, resting her hand on

his chest. "Coming to Edinburgh was a mistake. We have brought danger to you and Malcolm." She left unsaid that she would be heartsick if anything bad happened to him.

"Brought us danger?"

"You wouldn't have gone to Arthur's Seat if we hadn't been with you." She let her hand fall away.

"Arthur's Seat? I have always heard it called *Àrd-na-Said*. Height of arrows." He caught her hand back to his chest and held it there. "And who is to say we would not have come upon those heartless blackguards elsewhere in the city?"

"I want you safe," she said, tossing caution aside and voicing what she felt. "I cannot bear it if anything happens to you."

"There are no guarantees in this life, m'lady." But his deep voice resonated with a gentleness that softened the words.

"Death and taxes," she said, moving closer still. "And with any luck, a companion to help you fight whatever life throws at you."

With a hesitancy that made her soul ache, he traced his fingertips along her jaw, then cradled her cheek. "Is that yer second sight speaking?"

"No," she whispered. "My heart."

"Yer heart, ye say?" He nibbled a tender kiss across her lips, then deepened it as if claiming full possession.

Heart pounding, head spinning, she wished Deacon's Tavern had a second room available. She so needed to lose herself in his arms. Then a pained groan from beyond the door sent a wave of guilt through her. How could she think of her own wants and needs at a time like this?

"He sounds bad." She bowed her head and turned away, feeling her twin's pain.

Grant frowned at the door. "He is hurt, but he has known worse injury than this in the past and lived to tell the tale."

Somehow, she didn't find that very reassuring. All she knew for certain was that history's violence suddenly seemed all too real. It was no longer sterile words on a page or theatrical reenactments. This was life. And the permanency of death.

She forced herself to get hold of her emotions. Panicking helped nothing. She needed to get her mind on a positive solution. To plan some sort of helpful action. "What about the reason for this trip? You won't be able to do whatever that was now." Another dreadful worry came to her. "And if you return to Edinburgh later, won't more Argyll men be out to get you? Won't they spread the word and gather troops or something?"

"I canna delay my business here any longer. It would not bode well to do so." He wrinkled his nose and snorted as though clearing it of an unpleasant odor. "I will manage it alone. Tonight. Once I am certain yer sister has eased Malcolm as much as she can."

"You have no business roaming the streets of Edinburgh alone at night. Do you want to end up like Malcolm? Or worse?" She hated the worried quiver to her voice, but if it made him see sense, it was worth sounding like a helpless female.

He took hold of her shoulders and leaned in until the tip of his nose nearly touched hers. "I have to do this. I gave my word."

"Then let me help you." Whatever it was, she had to help. Somehow, even if it was something as simple as watching his horse. Anything to keep him from going out there alone and leaving her behind to worry. "My sixth sense can guide you. Protect you. But I can't connect unless I'm with you." A ridiculous lie, but she hoped the fear in her voice would make him believe it.

He stared at her, giving her a glimmer of hope. "My task is not a pleasant one."

"I promise you I can handle it." She couldn't tell him about her past. A past that happened far into the future. But if he would only allow it, she would prove she wasn't a coward. She rubbed the back of her neck for good measure, hoping to tip the scale in her favor.

After blowing out a deep sigh, he shook his head. "I feel sure I shall regret this, but yer second sight could verra well help me find the grave." Lips pursed, he studied her. "Have ye ever spoken to the dead?"

Unsure she heard him correctly, she blinked several times, then rubbed her neck that really tingled this time. "Uhm…no. I have never spoken to the dead." She wasn't about to admit she had once touted herself as an expert at the ouija board and held seances to pay the bills for a short time in London. Besides, didn't they accuse witches of consorting with the dead? Or was it just the devil? She shook herself free of her surprised stupor. "Did you say you are looking for a grave?"

"Aye." He went silent as a commotion at the bottom of the stairs interrupted him.

A pair of men. Half drunk. Shoving each other until they looked up and spied them. "Ho there! Wha's this?" one of them slurred.

She dove into Grant's arms and kissed him as though they were about to consummate the night right there in the hall.

"Ah, let him be," the other said between gulping belches. "He's just tryin' to get his money's worf."

Both drunks nodded, clapped each other on their backs, and stumbled toward the bar.

Lyla stepped back and smiled. "Sorry for the ambush. I wanted to look convincing."

He cleared his throat and adjusted his kilt where it tented in the front. "Ye convinced me." He hooked his hand around her neck, pulled her back, and kissed her again, groaning into her mouth. "Saints help me, woman. I could take ye right here against the wall."

"Don't tease me," she rasped, clutching him closer. Softness to hardness. Hungry need to starved yearning.

He groaned again, but this time pushed away, and stepped back, staring down at the floor. "I willna treat ye like some cheap whore bought in the pub." With a swipe of his hand across his mouth, he turned away, stared at the ceiling, and huffed noisy deep breaths in and out.

While she appreciated his chivalry, it left her aching and in dire need of relief. But she refused to complain or argue. He offered his respect, and she would take it. "This grave." She paused, cleared her throat, and took a few deep breaths of her own. "Who are we looking for?"

"My uncle. James Graham, the First Marquess of Montrose."

She knew that name, historically speaking, but couldn't remember all the details. Abby might know. She remembered names and dates so much better. "My condolences on the loss of your uncle. Are we finding his grave so you can pay your respects?"

Grant shook his head. "They excommunicated the Montrose before they hanged him, then buried him on unconsecrated land. The gallows ground on the Burgh Muir."

"I am so sorry." It sounded like either an unmarked or mass grave. A terrible thing for the man's family, denying them a last chance to mourn at their loved one's final resting place.

"Are you going to find the site and mark it?"

"Mark it?"

She nodded, slightly perplexed. Grant suddenly seemed more than a little uneasy. "With a headstone. Or a cross or something."

His jaw tightened as though he chewed on the words he was about to say. He shook his head. "I must find him so I can retrieve his heart and carry it to his niece. She means to have it embalmed and placed in a steel cask made from the blade of his sword. Then she will place the cask in a gold filigree box gifted to her family by a Doge of Venice."

"Excuse me?"

A sad smile cast his mouth to an unhappy angle. "I told ye this task would not be pleasant."

Now she remembered the name in full. James Graham, First Marquess of Montrose. Also known as the Great Montrose. One of Scotland's finest battlefield commanders. Betrayed. Hanged. Dismembered and beheaded. She also remembered a documentary that had shown the man's first grave before he was exhumed eleven years later, laid in state at Holyrood Palace, then entombed at St. Giles Cathedral. The effigy she had seen during a tour of St. Giles a few years ago had been stunning.

Grant would be so proud. Unfortunately, she could never tell him. She also couldn't tell him that the heart he wanted so badly to retrieve would eventually be lost for a while. However, his uncle would be so famous in death that two embalmed hearts that laboratories tested and assured were human would eventually be claimed to be the Great Montrose's. They would settle on one, but no one would really know for sure.

CHAPTER NINE

THE MOON SHONE full and bright, flooding the land with an eerie blue, white glow. Grant carried a torch to aid him once they arrived at the grave, but they did not need it to light their way. He kept close to Lyla as they scurried like common thieves through the streets of Edinburgh. She carried Malcolm's dagger. He kept his own at the ready.

"Are ye certain ye ken where the grave may be?" He prayed her second sight wouldn't fail them.

"You said they buried him on the gallows ground on Burgh Muir, right?"

"Aye, but 'tis a good-sized piece of land with several bodies laid to rest there." Her outlook amazed him. Fearless. Devoted. All that she was both thrilled and terrified him. God help him. Was this what love felt like? It damn sure wasn't as easy to manage as simple lust.

"There is Mercat Cross. And the gallows." She came to a halt. "I assume that field beyond is Burgh Muir?"

"Aye." Her question returned him to the grisly matter at hand, churning his guts harder. The sight of his uncle's head on a pike in front of the Tolbooth was still fresh in his thoughts. There was naught he could do about that indignity, but he could retrieve the courageous man's heart from the unconsecrated ground. He realized she stood there frowning at him. "What is it, lass? Did ye say something? Forgive me. I didna hear ye."

"I asked where we can find a shovel?"

"A shovel," he repeated, amazed at his own stupidity.

She scratched the tip of her nose as if trying not to say something she shouldn't. "Do you think there might be one by the gallows? Would they leave tools lying about?"

"Perhaps in the cart that carries the bodies away." He led the way, hoping no one would take notice of the torch. At this late hour, most had either passed out in the pubs or in their beds. He pointed at a small square object in the shadows under the gallows. "There is the cart."

"You go look." She cast a nervous glance all around. "I'll stand lookout."

He tried not to smile, pleased she finally seemed a wee bit squeamish. She should. 'Twas a gruesome duty that lay before them.

As he hoped, the gravediggers had left the tools of their trade propped against the cart. He grabbed both shovels, knowing the stubborn lass would probably be insulted if he didn't offer her one, too. Such a strange woman, she was. And he found her irresistible. Couldn't imagine life without her. A dangerous development, indeed.

"Where to, m'lady?" He offered her a shovel, and she took it, as he knew she would. Now to find the correct grave from among the several plots looking recently disturbed.

She eyed the gallows, then turned and looked back at the city. With a fearsome look of determination, she walked over to the bone-chilling structure, backed up to the southernmost post, then started walking, quietly counting off her steps. When she reached a freshly dug spot, she paused, studied the surrounding area, then gingerly stepped around it, and took off again. She halted at the next plot of broken ground, squatted beside it, and ever so reverently rested her hand on top of the mound. "This one," she quietly announced.

He strode across the grounds to join her, now and then casting a look around to ensure they were still alone. "Are ye certain?"

She nodded. "Look at the size. Didn't you say it was only his torso?"

"Aye." This plot couldn't hold a full-sized man, but it could hold a body bereft of its head, legs, and arms. He stuck the torch in the ground and started digging.

"What are you going to put it in?" she whispered even though there was no one about.

"I have a cloth sack, and dinna worry. We deliver it tonight. Even though Lady Napier fled Merchiston Castle because of my cousin supporting my uncle in his endeavors, she and the children found an ally here in the city to grant them safe haven."

"Lady Napier married your cousin?"

"Aye. Archibald Napier. He accompanied my uncle, the Montrose, when he left Scotland for Norway." He bent to the task, scooping up more earth. "Archibald is still abroad. 'Tis unsafe for him to return." His shovel thudded against wood. "They didna spare any effort to bury them deep, did they?"

"Disgraceful." Lyla crouched down, shoved her skirts out of the way, and used her spade to scrape the loose dirt away from the lid of the crude wooden box. "I hope he haunts every single person who treated him so poorly."

A chill washed across him as though the hand of his departed uncle rested on his shoulder. "I thought ye said ye knew no spells?"

"It's not a bloody spell," she said. "It's proper wishful thinking."

"Ye might wish to step back. This willna be pleasant." He waited for her to move away.

"They didn't embalm them?" She stared at him in horror.

He pulled a square of linen from inside his waistcoat, shook it out, and tied it over his mouth and nose. "Nay, they did not, and it's been over a month." He prayed the coolness of early summer had slowed the body's decay. "Shield yerself, m'lady."

She stepped farther back, covered her nose and mouth, then nodded.

With the tip of his spade, he pried open the lid and tried not to gag. Lyla's second sight had led them to the correct plot. Headless, limbless, stripped naked, the torso of his uncle lay before him. Curse every soul responsible for this reprehensible injustice. He readied the silken sack with the golden cord. Knowing the remains would quickly soak through the silk, he also readied two more bags of tightly woven cloth to hold the silk one. Breath held, eyes watering, he extracted the heart, placed it inside the silk, then slid it inside the other two sacks and cinched them shut. He held the bundle out to Lyla.

Nose covered with one hand and gagging repeatedly, she took the bag, then fled a few paces away and vomited. Grant understood completely as he replaced the lid and covered the coffin as quickly as he could. The stench would follow him all his days.

Still gagging, Lyla helped him rake the earth smooth, returning the grave as close to its previous state as possible.

"I will wash as soon as I can," he promised while wiping his dagger and hands on the grass.

"I understand." She kept her hand over her face and held out the bag. "Let's get it delivered, shall we? Then we'll find a pond or something and scrub ourselves and our clothes. If need be, we'll wash in the firth. I'll take seawater over that smell any day."

"Well said, m'lady." He tossed the shovels aside, took the heart from her, then motioned toward the west. "We'll leave the torch here. The moon will light our way well enough without calling any extra attention to our passing."

They traveled without speaking. He regretted scarring her with the terrible ordeal that would surely haunt her the rest of her days. "Forgive me, Lyla. I am so verra sorry."

"For what?" She kept her hand over her mouth as if afraid to vomit again.

"For involving ye in this. I should not have done so." He nodded toward the end of the lane. "There. Just up ahead. Not much longer."

"Is she expecting us?" She eyed the knotted cloth bag he carried.

"She will welcome us when we arrive. Stay close, aye? And keep that dagger ready." This area housed smugglers and those willing to do anything for God, king, and country. But that also included striking down any who might stand against them. He curled his free arm around her and pulled her closer. "I dinna wish ye hurt, m'love."

She stumbled and caught hold of him. "My love?"

"Aye." He didn't know whether or not to be insulted. Had he misread her? Surely not. "Any woman who would stay at my side and help with such a thing as this is most definitely *my love*."

"You are going to make me cry." Her face squinched up like a wee bairn about to wail for its supper.

"Dinna cry." He hugged her tighter. "I now know I love ye. That makes ye weep? Do ye despise me so? Is it such a bad thing?"

"Of course not! I would never despise you." She sniffed, coughed, then waved a hand in front of her face as if shooing away the tears. "Damn and blast it all! I love you, too. It's just taken you too bloody long to realize it and accept me the way I am."

"I feared ye, damn it! Ye are nay a usual woman."

She rubbed the back of her neck and smiled. "Thank you. I think."

"I will kiss ye later. When I dinna stink so and have relieved myself of this package." He doubted she would appreciate a passionate kiss while he held the heart.

"Thank you again."

He turned them down an alley leading to the back of the estate. "'Tis best we use the service entrance at this hour." They came to an iron gate, rusty and its posts unkempt. Ivy riddled with weeds and dried leaves that should've been cleared away back in the spring covered the walls. He pushed the gate open, flinching as its loud creaking groan interrupted the stillness of the night.

"Effective alarm system," Lyla whispered.

"That it is." He led the way across the courtyard, cluttered with broken barrels, spare wagon wheels, and several carts and wagons in varying states of disrepair.

She followed close on his heels. The winding path through the clutter was too narrow to walk side by side. "At least there's a light in the window," she whispered. "Will that be the kitchen, do you think?"

"Either that or where the servants dine." But he too took some comfort in the candle. At least they wouldn't have to rouse the entire household to get someone to open the door. He banged on one of the windowpanes in the tall window where the candle sat, then pounded on the door itself. He wanted this task finished.

The door opened the barest bit. "State yer business," a gruff voice growled. "The hour is late."

"Chieftain Reddoch for Lady Napier. Tell her I have fulfilled my oath."

The door clicked shut.

"Is that good or bad?" Lyla whispered.

"I am sure he has gone to fetch her." At least, he hoped so.

After an uncomfortably long amount of time passed, the door opened again, wide this time. There stood his cousin's wife, coif on her head, a shawl knotted around her shift. He didn't know the woman well, but what he knew of Lady Elizabeth Erskine Napier, he admired. After all, for her loyalty to the Montrose, she had once survived imprisonment in Edinburgh Castle.

"Dear cousin, ye have done as I begged ye?" Her voice trembled with such softness, it forced him to lean forward to hear her.

"Aye, m'lady." He held out the precious package. "Forgive me for taking so long."

She accepted the cloth bundle, cradling it in her hands as if it were a cherished gift. "I am sure the quest was fraught with danger and challenges. I am grateful ye remained steadfast." She turned and handed it off to someone behind her in the shadows. "Geoffrey, to the apothecary with it, aye? Take the greatest care and dinna be seen. Mr. Callender has the cask and the chest in which to seal it once he is finished with the embalming. Ye have the note and the money." Then she turned back and took Grant's hand with both of hers. "Thank ye, dear cousin. I shall deliver the Great Montrose's heart to the young Lord Montrose in exile in Flanders. We owe ye a great debt. As does Scotland." Her trembling smile turned sad. "Even though many are too foolish to realize it."

"What else might I do for ye, m'lady?" Even though he had done so much for this brave woman, he wished he could do more.

Her gaze flitted to Lyla, and her smile returned. "Ye can cherish yer lady love and never leave her side for anything as petty as war, ye ken?" She sniffed, pulled a handkerchief from her sleeve, and dabbed it to her nose. "I have decided that politics, countries, and land are not worth more than the love and contentment to be found in hearth and home." Her smile grew stronger as she clutched the cloth to her chest. "She is yer wife, aye? Who else would be at yer side during such a difficult yet noble duty?"

"Aye, she is. Forgive my manners." He turned, caught Lyla's hand, and gently pulled her forward. "Lyla, allow me to introduce ye to more of our family—Lady Elizabeth Napier." With a squeeze of her hand, pride surged through him as he turned back to his cousin. "My beloved wife, Lyla."

For the first time since he found her on that hillside, his precious lass appeared to be at a loss for words. After hesitating for a moment, she managed a polite nod. "It is an honor to meet you, Lady Napier. I would offer my hand, but I am too grubby." She fluttered her soiled hands, attempted a curtsy, then stumbled sideways.

Grant steadied her. Heaven help him. What would he do without this clumsy woman?

"English?" Lady Napier laughed. "It is a pleasure to meet ye, and I must say, 'tis surely a love that is true for a Scot to marry an English."

"It must be," Lyla murmured.

"We must go now. 'Tis late." Grant pulled a coin pouch from his inner pocket, placed it in his cousin's hand, and closed her fingers around it. "God be with ye, m'lady."

"He most surely is," she said, then offered Lyla a nod. "And may God bless ye and keep the both of ye safe in these troubled times." With the money clutched to her chest, she stepped back and gently closed the door.

"Come, m'lady." Grant offered his arm.

Lyla stood there, staring at the closed door as though entranced.

"Lyla?"

"Sorry." She jerked as though startled, then hurried to slide her arm through his.

"What is it?" He turned her to face him, but she avoided his gaze. She seemed thoughtful, yet ill at ease. "Is it because I told her ye are my wife? We will marry once we return to the keep. I promise it will be so. In fact, since I claimed ye as wife in front of two witnesses, we are actually married now by Scottish law."

She gave him a look that he didn't take as either kindly, accepting, or affectionate.

"Two witnesses?" she repeated in a tone that confirmed she was not pleased.

"Aye. Lady Napier and her servant, Geoffrey." Perhaps they should finish this discussion elsewhere. After leading her through the crowded courtyard and out the gate, he paused. "Why are ye angry?"

Her brows knotted into a confused furrow. "I am not angry. Exactly." She shook her head and turned aside. "I don't know what I am other than full-on knackered and in dire need of a wash before we pack in with Malcolm and Abby like two more sardines for the tin."

"Sardines for the tin?" And why had her eyes suddenly gone wide as though she feared herself in trouble? He tipped his head closer to hers. "Lyla? What does *sardines for a tin* mean? Explain yerself. For my sake. Please?"

She stared up at him, the corner of her lip caught between her teeth. Then her demeanor shifted. Her eyes went narrow, and she jerked with a nervous shrug. "When Abby and I were little, Mother would trap these tiny little fish, salt them down, and pack them tight in crocks. She called them *sardines* but Abby couldn't manage that word, so she called the fish *tin* and called their crocks that, too."

That had to be the worst lie she had told him yet. And how in the devil had they gone from planning their future to talking about fish? Did she not wish to marry? She hadn't refused, but nor had she accepted. Memories of his strained first marriage surfaced. The coldness. The detachment. He would not live like that again.

He tugged on her hand to hurry her. "Come. I know of a pond nearby. Secluded enough to grant us some privacy for a good scrubbing."

"Wonderful."

The relief in her voice stirred his misgivings even more. More proof that her story of fish and crocks was a lie. The more he thought about it, the angrier he became. He walked faster, pouring his frustrations into his stride.

She caught up her skirts and trotted along beside him. "You know, my legs are shorter than yours."

He didn't slow his pace. "Forgive me, m'lady. I thought ye wished to hurry."

She pulled her hand from his and came to a full stop. "Now you've gone all ratty. Why?"

"Because ye dinna wish to marry me!"

"Says who?"

"The way ye reacted. Yer lie about fish and crocks. No joy. No smile. Nothing. Ye didna even say yes."

"I didn't say yes, because you bloody well didn't ask me!" She surged toward him as if ready to do battle. "Even my first husband did a proper job with the proposing part, and he was a loser of the first sort."

"Ye have been married before?" The news pushed him back a step.

She stared at him, astonishment dropping her jaw. "*That* is all you got from what I just said?"

"Answer the question." The rest of what she said caught up with him, but he hesitated to admit his own error. He hadn't asked her to be his wife. That was true, and he should have rather than assuming she wished to marry. But that was not the matter at hand. "Where is yer husband, m'lady?"

"You *m'lady* me in that tone one more time, and I'm going to pop you in the nose." She shoved around him, heading for the grove of trees clustered at the base of an undulating hillside on the outskirts of town. "I assume your pond is down there?" she shouted back, without slowing her pace.

"Answer the question," he bellowed.

"Sod off!" She threw up some sort of hand sign he didn't understand, then disappeared into the trees.

"Sod off?" he repeated, storming after her. "What the feck is *sod off*?" He knew it to be an insult, just didn't know how offended he should be. And married? Not once had she ever mentioned a husband before. Was that what had brought her to Scotland? Running from her responsibilities? Just as he entered the trees, something hit his chest. And then another something narrowly missed his head. "Stop throwing whatever it is ye're throwing at me!"

"It's my shoes, you numpty. Lucky for you, I have found no rocks good enough for slinging!"

The small pool reflected the light of the full moon, but when she darted back beneath the trees, the shadows hid her. He had to keep her talking to pinpoint her exact location. "So, are ye running from me just like ye ran from yer husband? Is that it? Ye run from yer troubles rather than face them?"

"I never run," she growled from somewhere off to the right. "I solve my problems by ridding myself of all the arses who cause them. That includes you!"

That sounded like she had killed the man. He slipped toward a rustling in the bushes, silent as if on a hunt. "Are ye married or not?"

"Not!" she barked the word like a cornered dog. "And I don't plan on being again until I can find a man who doesn't act like a bloody fool."

The swish of branches and a movement in the shadows confirmed her whereabouts. He lunged through the bushes, caught hold of her arm, and yanked her out from behind a tangle of saplings. Barefooted, hair unbraided, and already stripped down to her shift, she roared like a banshee and swung at him.

He caught that arm, too, and held her in place. "Cease! Just answer my feckin' questions. Preferably with the truth this time!" The thought of her married to another man inflamed him with more jealous rage than he ever thought possible. Holding tight to both her wrists, he yanked her closer to the pond, into the light. He needed to see her face while she told her lies. "Or are ye even capable of the truth?"

"Are you even capable of opening your ears and actually listening to every word?" Chest heaving and teeth bared, she glared at him with more fury and hatred than any woman had ever offered him. 'Twas a wonder he didn't turn to ash and scatter to the winds. She tried to yank her arms free, but he held fast.

"Answer my questions, damn ye." He braced himself for the worst.

"I am not married," she said. "I was. But I'm not anymore. I divorced the bastard." She clenched her teeth, then tore her gaze aside. "Or he divorced me. Either way, neither of us wanted to be married to each other anymore, so we ended it." She snapped her focus back to him and sneered, "Next question, Chieftain Reddoch?"

While her answer eased him some, he feared it to be untrue. He needed to know more. "Why did ye divorce? The real reason? Not some made-up fantasy no fool would ever believe."

"Because I had a miscarriage and lost the baby he never wanted, anyway." She bared her teeth again, her cheeks shining with tears. "The rat bastard said he was glad. Said we were better off and thought I was crazy for not feeling the same." She yanked free of his relaxed grip. As she turned toward the water, a heart-wrenching sob escaped her. "She was so tiny. They let me hold her before they took her away. So peaceful. So brilliantly perfect. Her precious little toes. Velvety hair." Lyla's shoulders shook as she bowed her head. "And she had the daintiest fingers. I'm sure she's playing the harp with the angels right now." She hitched in a sniff and lifted her gaze to the moon. "I named her Avery. It means one who is a wise ruler because I knew she would have changed the world if she had lived."

His gut clenched with her suffering, squeezing the air from his lungs. "I am so verra sorry, Lyla. I swear I am." He almost choked on the words, so overcome with hurting for her. God help his dear lady love. She had known such pain. Not a doubt remained that she told the truth this time. He took a step toward her, but she held up a hand and stopped him.

"I am so sorry," he repeated. "I swear I didna mean to be so heartless and cause ye to relive yer pain."

"You are not heartless," she whispered. "None of my past is your fault."

"Can ye ever truly forgive me?" he asked softly. "And if ye find it in yer heart to do so, will ye grant me the joy and honor of becoming my wife?"

She wiped her cheeks and slowly turned to face him. Fresh sorrow written on her face made him fear what she was about to say.

"There is something else you need to know about me first," she said quietly.

Whatever it was, he didn't want to hear it. He could tell by her expression. But he had never been one to cower. "And what is that, m'love?"

Her gaze locked on the ground; she clasped her hands in front of her. "I almost died when I lost Avery. Physically as well as emotionally." She tucked her chin and shifted a pitiful shrug. "And she is the only child I will ever have. They told me I won't be able to have more children. Too much damage from the miscarriage."

He eased out the breath he hadn't realized he held. Her plight was terrible for certain, but he had feared it might be so much worse. "My Fawna and Rory need a mother. Do ye think ye could ever love them as yer own?" He opened his arms and waited. "I know they could love ye. They have told everyone at the keep how much they like ye."

She stared at him, her bottom lip quivering. "You really mean it?"

"If I didna mean it, lass, I wouldna say it." Arms still open wide, he watched her, praying she would believe him and accept. "I love ye, and my children will love ye. Will ye do us the blessing of making our family whole?"

Tears streaming down her face, she walked into his arms, rested her head on his chest, and hugged him tight. "Yes," she whispered. "And thank you for sharing your precious babies with me."

He closed his arms around her. "We will never let ye go, my dearest one. We all will be one."

She lifted her face and pulled him down for a kiss, opening to him, reigniting the burn she had set simmering within him with that first kiss days ago.

"In the water," she rasped against his lips.

He swept her up into his arms and waded in fully clothed.

Afloat with her arms around his neck, her eyes danced. "I guess you took me seriously when I said we should scrub clothes and all."

He grinned, submerged them both, then rose and laughed as she sputtered and spit. "I always take ye seriously, m'love."

She whipped her wet hair back from her face and shimmied her linen chemise off her shoulders and down to her waist. "Then go ashore, take off your clothes, and get back in here." She winked. "I'll toss you my shift once you set me down."

"As ye wish, m'love."

CHAPTER TEN

T HE MOONLIGHT TURNED the surface of the pool to quicksilver. As Grant entered the water, the muscular planes of his sculpted body gleamed like polished marble. He waded toward her slow and proud, offering a feast for her eyes. The man was magnificent. Bold, ripped, scarred by battle, and utterly irresistible.

He joined her in the deeper water, making the ripples lap against the base of her breasts. This early in the season, the water was colder than she had expected. She hoped it didn't cause that deliciously impressive length of his to shrink away and hide.

As soon as he came within reach, she ran her hands across the slippery hardness of his shoulders and wrapped her legs around him. "Rubbing on each other should help with the washing. Don't you think?"

He answered by crushing her to his chest and kissing her long and deep.

Without warning, he floundered backward, and they both went under.

Lyla surfaced first, coughing and spewing.

Grant splashed up from the depths, snorting curses. "Feckin' pond scum. Slippery as goose shite!"

Still coughing, she laughed, caught his hand, and tugged him back toward shore. "Shall we try out the leaves, then wash them off later?"

"A fine idea." With a sheepish dip of his head, he ran his other hand down his front and rubbed himself under the water. "The water's chill has nay done the devil's work yet, but it could."

As the water level lowered, so did Lyla's gaze. She smiled. Proud Grant worried for no reason. The sight rushed a flood of aching heat through her, and her nipples pearled into harder buttons. As they reached a mossy nest higher up the embankment, she dropped and pulled him down with her.

"You know, they say we should savor the first time slowly," she said, rolling to her back and reaching for him. "But I have never been a patient woman."

"Nor I a patient man." He settled over her and pushed in deep and hard as if welcoming himself back home. "God's beard," he groaned. He slid a hand down her side and grabbed the meat of her arse, settling into a tantalizing rhythm. He stoked the dance with another deep kiss, teasing his fingertips across the slipperiness where they joined. After another rumbling groan, he lifted his head and stared deep into her eyes. "Ye are mine now, ye ken? Forevermore."

She couldn't help but smile while touching his cheek. "That goes both ways." She arched into him and raked her nails down his back to get him moving again. Her not-so-subtle hint worked nicely.

He pounded harder and faster as if driving his intentions home. She matched him thrust for thrust, reveling in the way his muscles rippled beneath her hands.

Time and space exploded within her. A gritty moan wrenched free of her throat as wave after wave of indescribable ecstasy set fire to every nerve ending she possessed, and even some she didn't know existed. She was no stranger to orgasms but never had she enjoyed one like this. Clinging to him, she gave in to the blinding bliss and let it wash across her.

Grant's wonderful pounding took on renewed fervor, then he shoved in deep and halted as though every fiber in his body had locked. A low throated growl rumbled from him; a ground-shaking bellow followed. He spasmed and shuddered, then collapsed, moaning as he sagged across her.

"M'love," he gasped, nuzzling kisses along her throat.

"My love," she murmured, still floaty and light with the afterglow's effervescence.

He shifted to the side, curled her into his arm, and pillowed her head on his shoulder. Eyes closed, she tickled her fingertips through the hairs on his chest. She couldn't remember if they were light or dark but didn't bother looking. The shadows would hide them, anyway. And while in the pool, her focus had been elsewhere. She gave a contented sigh. Grant had done his century proud.

"And what kind of wedding do ye wish, my dear one?" He kissed the top of her head.

"Nothing fancy. A priest and a couple of witnesses will be fine." After all, it wasn't the ceremony that made a marriage last. She had learned that the hard way. But then she remembered Lady Napier's observation about a Scot marrying an English. "The people of Eadar Keep welcomed me as a prisoner. Are you sure they will accept me as your wife?"

"There will always be some ye canna please," he said. "But they will accept ye and treat ye with respect. I will tolerate nothing less." He flattened her hand on his chest and held it there, his strong, steady heartbeat tapping into her palm.

Satisfaction and weariness lulled her into a drowsy state that risked becoming complete slumber. While the pond seemed secluded enough now, she wasn't too sure about sleeping there and being discovered by a passing citizen of Edinburgh come morning. She grudgingly pushed herself up to a sitting position. "I hate to kill the mood, but shouldn't we rinse off and get back to Malcolm and Abby?"

After a heavy sigh, he sat up beside her. With a loving smile, he tenderly touched her cheek. "Now that we have chosen our path, I could stay here forever. Loving ye until I canna love ye anymore."

"Don't make me cry." She swallowed hard, struggling to believe that all that had happened wasn't some wild dream and that any minute she would wake up and be alone again. Back in Edinburgh. She touched the stubble on his cheek, loving the scratchiness against her palm. "I have never felt so…"

"Never felt so what?" His mouth slanted with a pleased with himself smile that revealed his dimple.

She stroked that devilish dimple with her thumb. "I have never felt so wonderfully alive."

"Good." He stood and offered his hand. "Come, m'lady. Time for a quick dip, then we shall try to dress."

"Try?"

He rested his fingers at the base of her throat and swept them all the way down in a suggestive caress past her belly button. "Aye," he rasped in a hungry whisper, leaning forward to nuzzle her neck. "We shall try to dress because I canna get my fill of ye."

"I cannot be the voice of reason here. Willpower is not my strong suit." She stepped closer and molded herself against the hard length of him.

He cupped a breast in each hand, teasing her nipples with his thumbs. "One more time afore we go," he whispered, bending to taste each of them.

Who was she to argue? She cradled his head in her arms as he suckled her breasts while lowering her back to the ground. This time was slower. More methodical as they fully explored and enjoyed each other's bodies. Touching. Tasting. Caressing. Pure pleasuring. Their cries soon filled the small woods again, startling birds from their evening roosts.

As she tried to catch her breath, she stared up through the canopy of branches. The moon had slipped lower in the sky, but the stars had disappeared. She studied the velvety darkness with the moon only showing itself now and then. Storm clouds gathered like a soft gray blanket unfolding across the night. "We are in for a drenching."

Grant glanced upward. "Aye, we are at that. Best hurry and dress." He rose and grabbed his clothes from a nearby bush, laughing as he snapped them in the air. "Mine are well dampened already."

"Well, mine are not." Correction. Her shift was, but the rest was dry. Pity the shift came first. She wrung as much water from it as she could, then shook it out. "Oh, bless it. I don't suppose you remember where my shoes landed when I threw them at you?"

"I will find them. Do ye ken what ye did with yer stockings?"

"Everything else should be in a pile. Over there where you found me." She caught her lip between her teeth and chewed on it, remembering all she had confessed. Thank Heaven, she had said nothing she shouldn't. Maybe someday she would share the truth of her century with him, but not for a very long while. Instinct told her he couldn't handle it. Grant's trust would be hard-won. She still had work to do in that area.

"I found one of yer shoes," he called out from the other side of the pond.

She envied how he had dressed in record time. Of course, males didn't have to fool with stays, bodices, laces, or so much clothing. She wore more layers than an onion. "How is it you stripped down and all your things stayed in one place?"

With a pompous grin, he returned to her side and held out both her shoes. "Because I didna throw my things at anyone."

"You deserved it." She plopped down, straightened her stockings, and retied the cloth ties above her knees. Shoes on, she tightened those laces as well. "By the way, how will your mother feel about us? She has been so kind. I'd hate for her to feel as if I betrayed her or something. Mothers and sons, you know?"

"She likes ye." He tossed a length of his kilt over his shoulder, tightened his belt, then went still. "And she shares a kinship with ye even though she doesna ken it yet. She, too, lost her daughters. Both my sisters died when they were naught but a few months old." He gave a sad shake of his head and stared at the ground. "I was but a wee lad, but I can still remember her wailing. She discovered them dead a few weeks apart. In their cradles. The first was barely a month old. The other only lived a little while longer."

Lyla covered her mouth with trembling fingers and closed her eyes against the burn of tears. She understood. Wholeheartedly. Even though she had miscarried Avery late in her last trimester, she had loved her daughter with all her heart. "I can't imagine her pain at losing two babies."

"It was a dark time at Eadar." He offered his arm. "Come. Let us see if we can find our way back to Deacon's Tavern without the moon to light our way."

Whether by Divine Providence or sheer luck, the full moon peeped through the clouds often enough to light their way back to the ramshackle public house. They eased inside, stepping around a few patrons who slept on the stairs. At the top of the staircase, they discovered old Bill McCullough, on the floor, propped against the wall, sound asleep beside their room. Arms folded across his barrel chest, he hugged a wicked-looking club, cuddling it like a child would hold a beloved teddy bear.

"Dinna startle him," Grant whispered.

"Don't worry. I'm sure he's pure dead brilliant with that weapon." She held out a hand. "Hand me the key, and I'll try to get us in there without waking him."

Grant shook his head. "Nay, m'love. He'll hear it and attack." He motioned toward the other side of the hall. "Stand over there while I let him know he can go to his bed."

She fought the temptation to argue. No. It was late. And Grant knew the man, whereas she didn't. She did as instructed and braced herself for whatever he was about to do.

After rubbing his hands together, Grant sidled closer and pounced faster than a cat. He grabbed the club, put McCullough in a headlock, and held on tight. "Wake yerself, man. Ye can go to yer bed now."

McCullough sputtered and kicked briefly, then relaxed, and thumped Grant's arm twice.

"Ye're fully awake now, aye?" Grant maintained his hold until McCullough smacked at his arm twice more. He leapt back, still holding the club, and offered the man a hand. "I thank ye for guarding my kinsman."

"Ye be me friend, and I've nay got that many." The old man huffed and groaned as Grant helped him clamber up from the floor. "Too old to sleep like that. Me bones dinna like it."

"Ye're still a fierce old bull." Grant thumped him on the back as he returned the club. "'Tis still a few hours afore dawn. Go to yer bed, old friend, and again, I thank ye."

The tavern keeper bobbed his head, huffed something unintelligible, then slowly lumbered down the steps, scratching his back with the end of the club.

Lyla hurried to unlock the door and eased it open, hoping to find both Malcolm and Abby sleeping peacefully. The lone candle on the table between the beds burned low, casting a soft glow across the stained linens piled in the basin beside it. She squinted to make out the shadowy shapes, frowning at the empty bed to the left. But the more her eyes adjusted to the dim light, the more her frown became a smile.

Malcolm lay partially propped up in the small bed with one arm hugged around Abby, and the other hand resting on his stomach. Still wearing his boots, his feet stuck out from under his kilt that worked well as a makeshift blanket.

Abby, still fully clothed, slept with her head nestled in the dip of his shoulder, an arm hugged just below his bandaged chest, and her leg protectively curled across his thighs. Both of them snored, Abby's louder than Malcolm's nasally whine.

"She always sounded like a bloody freight train," Lyla quietly observed. When Grant didn't comment, she realized what she said and almost panicked until a passable lie sprang to mind. "At least Mother always said she reminded her of the noisy carts that rumbled past our lodgings in London. Headed to the docks with goods at all hours. Mother called them freight trains because it seemed like there were always so many at once. Not just one or two, but several." She needed to stop babbling now, face him, and sell the lie, because he still hadn't said a word, just softly closed the door behind them. After easing in a trembling breath, she turned and offered her hand. "Do you want the side by the wall or the table?"

He stared at her hand with an expression she couldn't read, then took it and brushed a kiss across her fingers. "Ye sleep by the wall so I can protect ye should anyone break in, ye ken?"

Not trusting herself to speak, she nodded and clambered onto the bed. She had done so well lately about not saying anything that might betray her. It had to be the weariness, and maybe the lovemaking had caused her to become lax. Whatever it was, she had to regain control and better filter her words before they came out of her mouth.

As he reclined beside her, his continued silence fed her worries and kept her awake. He wasn't asleep either. She could tell by his breathing. "What is it?" she whispered, unable to stand it any longer.

"It hurts me when ye lie."

Her heart fell. She curled closer, resting her head on his shoulder, but he didn't move. No hug. Not the slightest caress. No pulling her tighter against him. His arm lay limp against her. How could she handle this without telling him things he was not prepared to hear?

"I'm sorry," she finally said. "I lie to keep myself safe—it's better that way. For now."

He still didn't react, just stared up into the darkness. His chest rose, then fell with a deep sigh. "I would never harm ye. Surely, ye know that?"

"To lose you now would harm me worse than if you ordered me flogged and tossed into your dungeons." How could she make him know that perhaps someday she could share everything? But not now. "I'm afraid if I tell you all about myself, you'll throw me away and never look back." She shuddered out the breath she had been holding. "And then I'll be alone all over again. But it'll be worse this time because I'll know what I could have had if you hadn't left me." She smoothed her hand across his chest, blinking hard and fast to fight back tears. "I have never loved like this before. The way I feel about you scares the bloody hell out of me."

"I love ye, Lyla," he whispered. "But yer lies trouble me. Make me worry I canna entrust ye with the safety of my home, my children, but most importantly with my heart."

"I understand." She rolled away and faced the wall, wishing she knew what to do. "You don't have to marry me. No one knows what happened between us tonight, and I doubt we'll run into your cousin any time soon. We can just act like nothing ever happened. Like nothing was ever said." She swallowed hard, determined not to cry. "Like I said before, I understand." She prayed he would argue but knew in her heart he wouldn't. No. She had muddled things again.

"Ye should sleep," he said with as much emotion as if she had just commented on the weather. The bed shook as he shifted positions and moved farther from her. "With any hope, Malcolm will be well enough to travel come daybreak."

The space he purposely placed between his back and hers pulsated like a pair of magnets turned the wrong way. She clenched her hands until her fingernails dug into her palms. Curse her stupid sixth sense, and bollocks to whatever force had shot her back to this damn century. At least being alone in her time had been easier with friends, dogs, and staying so busy she didn't have time to overthink her mistakes. At sunrise, she would talk to Abby about their trying to survive in Edinburgh on their own. Surely, after all he had just said, Grant would be more than glad to be rid of her.

"You look like proper shit this morning," Abby said quietly.

Lyla held up the bed linen as a makeshift screen to grant her sister some privacy with the chamber pot. She mulled over several responses, then settled on the safest one. "It was a long night." Muscles knotted and aching, eyes dry and itchy from too many tears. She resettled her stance after stealing a glance back at the sleeping men. "When you're finished, we're going for a walk."

Her twin stepped out from behind the sheet, took it, and gently piled it on the end of the bed. "Sounds ominous."

"Best not say anymore." Lyla tipped her head toward the door and waved her sister forward. Once out in the hallway, she cringed as the door groaned with a loud creak before it shut. She stood there and waited, listening.

Abby scowled at her with such a harsh glare it was visible in the early morning shadows. "What is wrong with you? I really don't like leaving Malcolm for very long. There's no fever, but who knows what sort of bacteria is in that wound?"

"You should've washed it with whisky." Lyla crept down the stairs. As she held open the tavern door, she hurried her sister out. "Isn't that what they do in all the movies?"

"We can talk medicine later. Now, tell me what is wrong. I haven't seen you this ratty since London." She lowered her voice. "Was it the grave robbing?" A shudder stole across her. "Malcolm told me. I'm sure it had to be bloody awful."

Lyla chose to ignore that. Burying the memory of digging up a corpse and cutting out its heart was not her highest priority at the moment. "I am going to tell Grant to go back to Eadar without us. I think we should stay here and make a go of it on our own."

Abby halted and backed up a step. "You cannot be serious?"

"I can, and I am." She stole a glance around the deserted

street, thankful they appeared to be the first ones to rise with the sun. "I feel sure he will agree."

Her sister's eyes narrowed. "What happened last night? The truth."

"I am so sick of that word I could vomit." Lyla rubbed the burning inner corners of her eyes. Abby had used all the water last night, so she'd not even had the benefit of a proper face wash this morning. "For once in your life, can you just support a decision I've made and leave it at that?"

Abby's scowl softened. "This is between you and him, isn't it?" She stepped closer. "What went wrong? You thought him the bee's knees yesterday. Today, you want nothing to do with him and act ready to strike out on your own and conquer the universe. Which would probably be a lot less hostile and easier to adapt to than seventeenth-century Edinburgh."

Lyla emitted a hiss dripping with sarcasm. "Yesterday, he wanted to marry me, but during the hours before dawn, he said he could never trust me with his family, his children, or his heart because I am a habitual liar." She halted her march down the lane and leaned back against the building, not giving two shits that she might appear to be a prostitute waiting for her next customer.

"I don't know what to say." Abby stood there wringing her hands. "I am so sorry." She pulled her into a hug and squeezed her tight. "No wonder you're gutted."

"Gutted or not, I do not feel inclined to go back to Eadar and act like nothing happened." With a feigned, half-hearted shrug, she extracted herself from Abby's hold. She could easily convince her twin she was just fine. "Besides, he will eventually remarry. Do you really think his next wife will tolerate him having a pair of English women for pets?"

"But I think I love Malcolm." Hesitance and worry filled Abby's voice. "And I'm fairly certain he loves me back."

Lyla swept a hand across her brow. So, she really would be all alone again. Well, she survived it before. She would bloody well survive it again. She managed a smile and tossed up both hands.

"Then forget I said anything. You go with Malcolm. With my blessing, I might add. I will stay here in Edinburgh. I'm more adaptable than you are, anyway."

Grant exploded out of the tavern, charged a few paces into the muddy street, then wildly looked from side to side. As soon as he set eyes on Lyla, he pointed a shaking finger at her. "Woman!"

"You better retreat and run back up to Malcolm. If Grant's up, I'm sure yours is awake, too." Lyla braced herself, flattening her back to the wall.

"Are you sure?" Abby took hold of her arm and squeezed. "If you want me here—I'm here."

She shook her head, gauging the few seconds it would take for Grant to close the distance between them. "Run. Now."

Abby dashed away, her skirts lifted to her knees.

Nostrils flaring, teeth bared, and both hands fisted, the mighty Scottish warlord had risen in a foul mood. "Have ye any notion the fright ye just put into me?"

She calmly folded her arms across her chest and forced a nonchalant air. "Why?"

"Why?" he repeated, bellowing the single word like a battle cry. "I wake, and ye're gone? Not in the hall. Not in the pub. But gone as if ye were never there?" He smacked the wall beside her. "And in a dangerous part of town. A woman alone is not safe here on the street."

Since he was already enraged, she might as well tell him her plan now and save him the trouble of getting all worked up all over again. "I plan to stay here in Edinburgh."

"Ye what?"

"Do you have to shout everything? I am not deaf." She resettled her stance and lifted her chin to a defensive level.

Jaw working as though barely holding back another roar, Grant stumbled a step back and turned aside.

"When a woman works in a pub, do they ever give her a place to stay?" She needed to know these things, and who better to ask than Grant?

He slowly turned and glowered at her with murder in his eyes.

A subtle sense of victory shivered through her. She had made him as miserable as he had made her. Good. "Or do you know of any boarding houses?" She paused, wondering if that's what they called them in this era.

So tense that the loose strands of blonde hair around his face trembled, Grant moved closer. "Why are ye asking these things? Why would ye say any of this?" He drew his dagger, flipped it in his hand, and offered her the handle. "Dinna continue this torture, m'love." He thumped his chest. "Cut out my heart and end my agony now."

She swallowed hard, determined not to show how much he had hurt her. By jings, she didn't have much, but she still had her pride. "You made it very clear that you wanted nothing to do with me because you couldn't trust me. Abby's going back to be with Malcolm, but it will be a cold day in Hell before I go back to Eadar just to be your pet—like some bloody English songbird you keep in a cage to show off whenever you have company. Besides, I'm sure whoever you choose as your next wife would not approve of my presence."

He sheathed his dagger, bowed his head, and took several long deep breaths. "I said it hurt me when ye told lies to hide the story of yer life. How can we ever be close as a man and wife should be if I canna believe a word ye say?" He lifted his head and leveled a sorrowful gaze with hers. "My first wife was a complete stranger who hated me and loved another. Yet she honored her clan's wishes and married me. Once she fulfilled her duty and carried my child, her doors remained locked to me, but open to other men just to spite me and her kin." His gaze shifted off to the side, staring back into his past. He frowned and slowly shook his head. "Then she changed. Right before the bairns were born. Apologized for all her sins. Begged my forgiveness. Gave me hope that we might have a genuine marriage after all. At least one where we didn't hate each other."

Lyla wished he would stop. She knew how this ended.

"But after Fawna and Rory came…" He turned away, scrubbed a hand across his face, then flipped it in the air. "I am sure yer maids already told ye how her life ended." He shook his head again. "Or how I killed her. When they told me how she was, I shouldha had her locked away and bars placed on her windows, for her own safety."

She couldn't stand to hear anymore. Pushing away from the wall, she gathered him into a hug. "It was not your fault. The sickness in her mind killed her. You couldn't have known." Severe depression was still a terrible beast raging strong in the twenty-first century. How could they hope to deal with it in this time? "You didn't end her," she said, holding him tight. "She ended herself because it was the only way she knew how to stop her pain."

He clutched her, gently swaying as he dug his fingers deep into her hair. "Do not leave me," he rasped. "I was weary last night and spoke poorly. I never wish ye to go. Never."

She closed her eyes, both thrilled and terrified with his admission. "I will never leave you," she promised, hoping it was the right thing to do. Her intuition hadn't nudged her a single time since the pond. Either she had finally done things right, or once again, done them horribly wrong.

CHAPTER ELEVEN

G RANT KEPT HIS pace to a slow stroll so Malcolm could keep up. The man still suffered from a fierce aching in his head that sometimes addled his balance. The chest wound nay troubled him. Lyla's sister had cleaned that well enough and sewn it nicely. But the blow to the head still troubled him. As soon as they entered the great hall, Grant decided the slowness of their ambling benefited them both. The barely controlled chaos filling the room brought to mind the clash of two clans on the battle-field.

"Saints' bones, have ye ever seen such doings?" He almost collided with a maid as she darted across his path.

"Beg pardon, my chief," she called back without slowing.

Malcolm squinted as though in pain, scanning the hall from the rafters down to the floor. "Did ye not tell me Mistress Lyla wished for nothing more than a simple ceremony?" He scratched his head. "Or did I dream it?"

"Ye nay dreamt it." Grant did a silent headcount of the maids and scullery lads swarming the place. He never realized they had this many servants. The powerful stench of lye water used to scrub the tables and floors stung his nostrils. The foul acidic smell was inescapable. He rubbed his nose, attempted to snort it away, and failed. "Her exact words were she wanted nothing fancy. Only a priest and two witnesses to make it binding."

"Did she change her mind?" Malcolm turned in a slow circle as they walked, tipping his head back and lifting his gaze to the lads beating the dust from the banners hung from the gallery railing encircling the second floor. "Abby willna speak of it. She smiles and tells me not to worry."

The double doors to the keep swung open. Mrs. Fintrie waved in a line of servants carrying the longest garland of braided ivy Grant had ever seen. He immediately knew the instigator of this chaos. "This is Mother's work. I would lay odds on it."

"Grant!"

"And at the sound of her name, the queen appears," he said, turning to greet her. "Mother."

Her arms were covered with what appeared to be several long swatches of laces and silks, she strode across the great hall, weaving around the servants with amazing speed and accuracy.

"Where is yer lady love?" She opened her arms, displaying the materials draped across them like winglike sleeves nearly dragging the floor. "The seamstress is beside herself. She canna finish the gown without another fitting and knowing which edgings Lyla prefers. The wedding is in two days. We must do this."

"Is this not a lovely garland, m'lady?" The housekeeper joined them, preening with the pride of a mother hen with new chicks. "Ye wish it hung above the head table, aye?"

Lady Katherine turned to inspect the handiwork and approved it with a nod and a smile. "Well done, Mrs. Fintrie. And above the head table will be perfect."

Grant contemplated escaping, but his mother caught him easing away.

"Oh no. Not until ye say where ye have hidden Lyla."

"I have nay hidden her." He lifted both hands in surrender. "In fact, I was about to search for her myself."

"And how are ye feeling, dear Malcolm?" Not giving him

time to answer, Lady Katherine revealed her true intentions. "Do ye ken where yer lady might be? Surely, she is with her sister. Or at least knows where Lyla might be."

"Uh…uh…" Malcolm coughed, then grabbed his head, flinching as though stricken with terrible pain.

"Hie to yer bed, man," Grant ordered. "Ye have been up overlong. Seek some rest."

Malcolm gave a grateful nod to them both and hurried away, stumbling and bumping off the tables and benches.

"Shame on ye, Mother." Grant fixed a rare look of sternness upon her. "He struggles to speak to ye on a good day, and yet ye attack the man when he's not even healed?"

Lady Katherine assumed a contrite demeanor he didn't believe for a moment. "Ye are right, my son. I should nay have done that. To atone, I shall instruct Cook to prepare Malcolm's favorite meat pies and send them to his chambers." She drew up, standing taller as if ready to resume the battle. "Now about Lyla—"

"Choose for her." He made a sweeping motion that took in all the trappings. "She has mentioned more than once how she appreciates the choices in clothing ye keep sending her. I am certain whatever ye select will please her."

"I dinna wish to be overbearing."

"Since when?"

"Grant!"

He closed his eyes and rubbed his mouth to keep from inciting a further scolding. After a roll of his shoulders, he granted her an apologetic smile. "She doesna think ye overbearing. In fact, she told me just yesterday how fortunate I am to have a mother such as yerself."

That melted her. Just as he had known it would.

"Poor lamb." She picked at the satiny ribbons on her arm, then lowered her voice. "Besseta told me about Lyla's mother and how the two of them were nay close at all."

"Did she now?" He didn't like Lyla's personal maid reporting back to his mother. He would speak to her before the day ended.

After a nod at the finery on his mother's arms, he turned to go. "As I said, make the choices for her, and when I find her, I will let her know the seamstress needs her for another fitting."

"Today," his mother stressed.

"Aye. Today."

"Verra well then." Lady Katherine swept away.

While he loved her, Grant felt certain she always left a trail of relief in her wake because of her sometimes overpowering nature. He had a fair idea where Lyla might be after overhearing Rory and Fawna whispering about the tunnels. The only problem was figuring out which run of secret passages they chose to explore today. The hidden trails honeycombed the walls of the keep.

He doubted they would be so foolish as to hide in the ones connected to Lyla's chambers. After all, that would be the first place Lady Katherine would instruct the maids to look. Perhaps the run is connected to the larder? That would afford them ways to sneak in food and remain concealed all the longer.

Almost certain of it, he headed to the kitchens at the back of the keep, and immediately regretted it. While the aromas of the meats roasting, breads baking, and whatever else bubbling and steaming smelled wondrous, Cook's domain rivaled the upheaval going on in the great hall. He sidled along as close to the walls as the hanging pots and bundles of dried herbs would allow, then slipped into the quiet confines of the larder.

With a hunter's stealth, he eased to the back wall and the section of shelving that always remained empty to assure they could swing it open with ease. A hidden hinge on the side closest to the corner connected it to the wall. He pulled it open and leaned down, tilting an ear toward the passage.

A faint giggling echoed through the darkness. A sense of victory made him smile. He knew that giggle. His lovely wee daughter was somewhere deeper in the passage. He selected a chamberstick from the several stored on the top shelf of the hinged cabinet, inserted a candle, and lit it with the tinderbox included in the supplies.

Forced to bend low to enter the short opening to the tunnel, he straightened to his full height once inside. Once he got closer to the wee imps and their wily leader, he'd douse his candle. He knew the tunnels as well as he knew his name and had walked them many times in the pitch blackness. As chieftain, he felt it his duty to lead his people to safety with or without light. Who knew if they could find time to make a flame in the middle of a siege?

After moving through several turns and inclines, he paused and listened again.

"Here, Rory. You can have the rest of my cheese. I am quite stuffed."

Grant smiled, envisioning Lyla sharing her food with his wee lad, who ate as much as a man full grown.

"Can I have the rest of yer apple?" Fawna asked, always vying to outdo her brother.

A crisp crunch echoed louder than the conversation. "Of course you can," Lyla said. "I just needed one more bite."

He pinched out his flame and continued on. As his eyes grew accustomed to the darkness, he detected a faint glow up ahead. While still well in the shadows, he eased to a stop. His heart warmed at the sight he found.

Lyla, Rory, and Fawna sat blocking the tunnel, their feast and the candle in the middle of them. Lyla's back was to him, but occasionally the glow of the light highlighted her profile. More often though, it silhouetted her, creating a halo around her. An angel right now, but also a devilish wee minx.

"When ye marry, Da, what will ye have us call ye?" Rory asked.

"Aye, what shall we?" Fawna added.

Lyla scooted to the side and leaned back against the wall, stretching her legs out in front of her and crossing them at the ankles. "What do you want to call me?" She folded her hands and rested them in her lap.

"We remember Mama, ye ken?" Fawna said in a small voice

that broke Grant's heart. "She didna want us around."

"Aye," Rory said. "She didna love us, but I dinna ken why. No one would ever tell us what we did wrong."

"First off," Lyla said. "Neither of you did anything wrong to make your mother not love you." She shook a finger at both of them. "I know you get into mischief, but that's because you're absolutely brilliant."

Hesitant smiles flickered across their faces, but then their forlorn looks returned. "Then why did she not love us?" Fawna asked.

As Lyla folded her hands back in her lap, her head tilted, and she stared off into the distance. "Have either of you ever been so sick you had to stay in your bed?"

"Me once," Rory said. "Hurt all over, and me skin felt on fire."

"When you were sick like that, did you want to get up and play with your friends, or pull tricks on Cook, or hide your sister's things?" Lyla kept her focus pinned on the boy.

Rory frowned. The tip of his tongue peeked out the corner of his mouth.

Grant ground his teeth together, knowing his son was thinking hard to come up with an answer. His heart ached. He wanted to scoop his children up into a hug and tell them how much he loved them. But he held back, curious to hear what Lyla had to say.

After puckering his mouth and narrowing his eyes, the lad shook his head. "Nah. I just wanted to curl up in me bed and feel better. I didna even wish to talk to anyone."

"Well, even though your mother loved you both with all her heart, the terrible sickness inside her head made it impossible for her to be a proper mother to you." Lyla slowly shook her head. "She couldn't help it. It was the sickness."

"But we're five now," Fawna argued. "And she didna die until we done turned three."

"And a half," Rory added.

"Some people stay sick for a very long time before the ailment makes them die." Lyla leaned forward and gave them each a pointed look. "But she loved you both and was very proud of you. Still is."

"How do ye know?" Rory dared.

Lyla took on a mysterious air. "Because I have the sight, and she told me."

"Ye lie," Fawna challenged.

"Do not." Lyla held up a finger and made an 'x' across her front. "Cross my heart and hope to die."

Grant covered his mouth and held his breath, yearning to make his presence known, but he wanted, nay, he needed to hear the rest.

"So, what do ye wish us to call ye?" Rory asked again. "After ye marry our Da."

"Whatever you want to call me." She paused for a moment, then added, "As long as it is respectful and kind, that is."

"We would never be unkind to ye," Fawna said. "We love ye."

"Aye! We do," Rory agreed.

"Aww." Lyla pulled them both into a hug. "I love you, too."

"And I love all of ye," Grant said, unable to keep quiet any longer.

Lyla and the children pierced the darkness with high-pitched shrieks. Then she jumped to her feet and shoved him. "What is wrong with you? Are you trying to give me a bloody heart attack?"

He laughed and pulled her into his arms. "'Tis a wise chieftain who always knows what goes on within his own walls."

"Ye scared us good, Da," Rory said.

"And I am nay done," Grant said with a growl. He curled his fingers like great claws and unleashed a bellowing roar. "Ye better run before the tunnel beastie gets ye!"

Both children screamed and ran.

"They don't have their candle," Lyla tried to hand it to him.

"They know all the tunnels in the dark." Pride that they weren't afraid of the dark made him grin. "They brought the candle for ye." He sidled a few steps farther and roared long and loud so it would travel deep into the passage. "This way joins with a tunnel to Fawna's room. We keep torches well-tended in both her tunnel and Rory's. Wait here. I'll be back soon as I herd the wee scamps into Nanny Greer's waiting arms."

Then he charged off into the darkness to the squealing delight of his children. Their cries worked better than a candle at alerting him to the turn that went to Fawna's room. He stomped and slapped his hands against the stone walls as he bellowed. "Here I come!"

Just as he entered the turn, both his wee bairns attacked, grabbing hold of his legs and yelling, "Ye canna best us, ye vile beast!"

"Oh, no! Ye have foiled my plan! Whatever shall I do?" He pretended to stumble and fall to his knees, grabbing them both into his arms and tickling them with squeaking kisses against their necks.

They giggled and squealed until the grating sound of stone rubbing against stone alerted them that the entrance to the tunnel was opening.

"Ye best be bringing yerselves out here," Nanny Greer called out. "Dinna make me come in there after ye."

"Dinna breathe," Rory whispered. "Her hears everything."

"Rory!" Nanny Greer's voice seemed louder, as if she had entered the tunnel.

"I told ye," he said.

"Shh!" Fawna shoved him.

"Ye best go to her," Grant said, somewhat disappointed that the game was already over.

"But Da," Fawna whined.

"No, my wee lass. A Reddoch doesna whine." He set them both on their feet and turned them in that direction. "Nanny Greer takes good care of ye. Now go, and dinna make her duties any more difficult than ye already do, ye ken?"

"If we must." After a sullen hug, Fawna patted him. "Ye will help Mistress Lyla find her way out, aye? She doesna ken the tunnels as we do."

"I promise I will help her." As they disappeared from view, Grant thanked God Almighty for those two precious demons. "I dinna ken what I would do without them," he said softly as he backtracked through the passage.

Again, he paused while still well beyond the reach of the candle's glow, enjoying the sight of Lyla placing the food scraps in a large square of linen and tying the corners.

"I heard you this time." She turned and shook a finger in his direction. "I know you are there."

"I shouldha crept softer." He took her hands, helped her rise from the floor, and pulled her into his arms. "Mother is looking for ye." He kissed the tip of her nose. "Something about the seamstress needing ye for more fittings?"

Her mouth went tight as though she struggled to hold back words she didn't want him to hear.

"I know how she is, m'love." He apologized with a kiss to her forehead and a suggestive squeeze of her arse. "'Tis only because she cares about ye. Ye know that, aye?"

"I know that, but she is driving me mad." She pressed tighter against him and added a suggestive wiggle. "Why do you think I'm hiding in these tunnels?"

"Do ye nay wish to marry in a lovely garment befitting a beauty such as yerself?" As he talked, he worked her skirts higher, trailing his fingers along her sides, then between her thighs and up into her warm wetness.

She did the same to his kilt, reaching between them to take hold and treat his cock to a loving squeeze. "I don't care if we are stark naked when we marry." She arched and rubbed the tip of him against the satin of her belly, then lower. "It would save time after the ceremony."

"That it would," he said. He walked her back to the wall,

lifted her up, and pinned her with a firm thrust into her heat.

"I love these tunnels." She hugged him with her legs while wrapping her arms around his neck. Her gasping squeaks and soft groans excited him as much as her wriggling. The passages echoed with them.

He pounded harder, clutching her buttocks with both hands. "I love these tunnels, too."

She clung to him, gripping his shoulders as hard shuddering overtook her. She erupted with a loud, joyous growl. Her spasming delight finished his control. He buried deep and stayed, emptying himself into her with a growl of his own.

Still holding her tight against the wall, he nuzzled kisses along her neck, then made his way to her mouth. She tasted of happiness and joy. Most of all, she tasted like she loved him. "I will never get enough of ye, my wee English fury."

With a tender half-smile, she framed his face in her hands. "Good. I hope you never do."

He pressed his forehead to hers and pulled in a deep breath.

"Don't say it." She caught hold of his ears and pulled him back. "I am never leaving these tunnels."

He released the sigh he had held. "That willna stop her. She knows every passage as well as I do."

"Well, bollocks!" She smacked his shoulder, but lightly. "Then I guess you had better let me down so I can sort myself and face my executioner."

A laughing snort escaped him. "I thought ye liked Mother?"

"I do like her when she's not acting like a bloody war commander preparing for battle."

"An apt description." Grudgingly, he stepped back and eased her feet to the floor, giving her arse one last squeeze before allowing her skirts to fall back in place. "Once the wedding is behind us, I'm sure she'll leave ye in peace."

"I'll aim her at Abby and Malcolm." She turned, facing her back toward the light. "How bad is the back of my dress? These walls are rather damp and slimy in spots."

He eyed the dark, greenish stain running from her shoulders to her waist, then striping her skirts wherever the folds had pressed against the wall. "Ye need to change afore ye visit the seamstress."

"That bad?" She cringed, eyeing him as though hoping for reassurance.

"Aye. 'Tis quite clear I took ye up against the wall." He wanted to laugh, but her expression warned him he best not. "We can take the tunnels to the left. They connect with the ones that lead to yer chambers."

"My sitting room is where the seamstress is. You don't think your mother is standing guard at the escape hatch beside the bed?" She brushed at her skirts, then wrinkled her nose as she looked down at her hands. "Why is that wall so wet? The one I leaned against for lunch was dry. I felt it."

He tapped on the wall in question. "The laundress and the well house are on the other side." He shrugged. "I guess the steam and water soak through the stones."

She pulled a fresh candle from the cloth bag tied to her belt and lit it from the old one. After pinching out the flame on the dwindling stub, she plucked it free of the chamberstick and settled the fresh candle in place. "Lead on, my chieftain. If your mother isn't in there, you can help hide this one so I can postpone Besseta's dirty looks."

"Dirty looks?" He took the chamberstick in one hand and her hand in the other, then started down the passage.

"She doesn't like it when I stain my clothes." Lyla shook her head. "She says nothing, but I can tell she's not happy. Of course, I suppose she has the right to be ratty, though. She's the one stuck helping the laundress get them clean."

"Ye would do well to mind what ye say in front of and to Besseta."

"Why?"

"Because she carries yer words back to Mother." He took the second tunnel to the left, then slowed to help her manage the flight of slippery stone steps leading to the next floor. "I dinna believe she does so to be malicious, mind ye. But ye need to be aware she's a gossipy wee hen. If ye wish, I can replace her."

"No. Don't replace her." She returned to walking at his side as the passage widened. "I like Besseta and besides, she was probably told to do it at the beginning. I'll have a word with her."

Her hand clasped in his, they continued on, the candle burning lower. These tunnels would be forever changed for him. He had never known such contentment. "Not much farther. One more flight of steps and then just a few paces 'til yer door."

"I really hope your mother isn't there. Does she know we…?" She gave a light cough. "Did you tell her about me? She knows I've been married before, right? And the fact I can't have any more children."

He halted and faced her. "What passes between us stays between us alone. I dinna run to my mother and tell her everything. 'Tis none of her affair."

Her pained look made him pull her closer while trying to keep from singeing her hair with the candle. "I don't want to be the source of problems between you and your mother," she said. "I do like her. Very much. And the children adore her—as they should. Grandmothers are supposed to spoil their grandchildren rotten with sweets and toys and letting them stay up late to watch their favorite cartoons." She stiffened in his arms. "Fish. In a bowl. Kept as pets. You feed them breadcrumbs. Mother got ours from a foreign lady. She called them cartoons."

The lies again. He clenched his teeth and rested his face against her hair. When would she trust him enough to tell him the truth? How could she still fear him? "We should go," he said softly. "Yer door is just up ahead."

"Yes. Right." She eased away, reminding him of a cowering animal that feared its master.

"Lyla." He caught hold of her arm. "Why do ye still fear me?"

"I don't fear you." Her gaze dropped, but she gently reached for his hand. "I fear losing you."

"Ye willna lose me." He brushed the softness of her cheek, then hooked a finger under her chin and lifted. "I swear it."

"In time," she whispered with a faint smile that struck him as almost sad. "I promise you will understand. In time."

He reminded himself to be patient. A task he had never mastered. But for her, he would find a way.

CHAPTER TWELVE

LYLA BACKED AWAY from Besseta, Lady Katherine, and the seamstress, Mrs. Taffrey, until she bumped into the wall. "You have to be joking. Another?" She already wore two underskirts.

"Fullness for the satin," Mrs. Taffrey explained in a tone that let Lyla know she had insulted the elderly woman yet again. "Ye dinna wish to go to yer chieftain with nothing 'neath yer finery but yer shift, do ye?"

Well, she did. But she probably shouldn't tell these three that. She had never been one for dressing up, and all the layers and pomp of the satin and lace wedding gown made her long for her favorite jeans. What if she spilled something on it? What if she stumbled and tore it? She contemplated skittering along the wall to the right and escaping.

Abby stepped in and blocked her way. "The more you fight us, the longer and more unpleasant this is going to be, and you were supposed to be down to the chapel several minutes ago."

"*Et tu, Brute?*" Lyla glared at her twin, who would thoroughly enjoy an opportunity to dress like a collectible doll. Abby always had been the fancier one. She pressed against the wall, knowing it futile to fight but unable to give in—yet. "How am I supposed to keep from overheating in all these layers?"

"Dinna fash yerself," Besseta said, creeping forward with the laciest and hopefully last of the three underskirts ready to toss over Lyla's head. "Ye give me the nod when ye feel yerself soaked through yer shift, and I'll help ye change it for a fresh one."

"Bollocks to that. Once I strip down naked, I will not reload."

All the women nudged each other and smiled.

"Enough cowering," Abby said. "We are already fashionably late, and you know how he is. Do you want him storming up here to see if you abandoned him?"

"Yer sister makes a fair point, lass." Lady Katherine cocked her head to a knowing angle.

"Fine." She couldn't fight them all. And Abby was right about Grant. She lifted her arms and bent forward. "Do what you will."

The third underskirt fell down in place, and the maid tied the waistband snug.

"Now the stays." Mrs. Tafferty held out a creamy beige satin bodice embroidered with dark blue flowers that matched the midnight hue of the gown. "Cinch it good and tight, now. Her bosoms need to round up nicely to make her groom's heartbeat faster."

"I also need to breathe," Lyla reminded after Besseta's first hard pull on the ties.

"Ye can breathe in yer marriage bed." The maid grunted and yanked again. "Hold on to the bedpost, so ye willna hop back every time I tighten them, aye?"

"It is tight enough." Lyla turned and showed her breasts about to spill out from the sadistic bustier. "See? My boobies are hitting my chin."

"The bodice needs to be tight as can be to smooth the lines of the gown." Besseta took her by the arm, led her to the bed, and planted her hands on the bedpost. She smiled and bobbed a respectful nod. "Hold fast, m'lady."

After another rib-crunching pull, the determined maid tied and tucked the ends of the laces down between her shoulder blades. "I canna pull them any tighter lest the edges overlap and make a ridge in the back."

"Praise God for that." Lyla released the bedpost and pulled in the deepest breath the torturous bodice allowed. Her nipples popped out over the edge. She turned and pointed. "See? I told you it was too tight."

"'Twill be fine. Tuck them back in." Entirely too proud of herself, Besseta waved the others forward. "And now the lovely last layer."

Lady Katherine circled like a vulture while the maid and seamstress hoisted the dark blue yardage of satin up and over Lyla's head. Abby fluffed out the abundant folds of the skirt over the mound of underskirts, helping the material flow into place. The snug, off-the-shoulder sleeves required some maneuvering to pull in place. Adorned at the wrist with delicate, cascading lace, Lyla envisioned dragging them through everything served at the banquet.

"Stand straight," Mrs. Tafferty ordered as she brought the front panels of the gown's jacket together and fastened it to the waistband with three pearl buttons. The creamy white bodice made a stunning wide *v* between the midnight blue panels of the jacket, secured the rest of the way with pins. The seamstress stepped back, surveyed the results, and smiled. "Himself will be verra pleased."

"Let me fetch the stool." Besseta scurried out of sight.

"The stool?" Lyla started to turn, then stopped. "Bless me, this weighs a bloody ton."

"But you are gorgeous," Abby said wistfully.

"She needs the stool to reach yer hair, child." Lady Katherine stepped forward with a long, narrow box in her hands. "I have a gift for ye."

Guilt about being so ratty about dressing shamed Lyla into bowing her head. "A gift?" She clasped her hands at her waist, thankful the tight sleeves allowed the motion. She didn't deserve a gift. Not after behaving like a full-on brat. "But you have already been so generous."

Lady Katherine didn't respond. Instead, she opened the box and slowly lifted a silver necklace from its depths. From the chain hung a breathtaking, dark blue sapphire. "Grant's father gave this to me on our wedding day. I think it verra appropriate that it now belong to ye."

Overwhelmed by the gesture, Lyla's eyes stung with the threat of tears. She pressed a hand to her chest, struggling to find the words to express how much this meant to her. "It is…I am…"

"Ye are quite welcome, my new daughter." Lady Katherine moved forward, fastened it around her neck, then patted her shoulder. "Ye have brought my son great joy," she said. "And in doing so, ye have blessed me with joy as well."

The weighty coolness of the stone nestled at the base of her throat, slowly warming to her flesh. Lyla touched it with trembling fingers, closed her eyes, and bowed her head, thanking whatever force had brought her to the seventeenth century. "Thank you so much," she whispered, lifting her head and hoping Lady Katherine would someday understand how much this meant to her. "Words fail me right now."

"Good." Lady Katherine clapped and hurried Besseta forward. "Hie wi' now. We shouldha been at the chapel an age ago."

"I'll go tell everyone not to worry," Abby said. She offered a teary-eyed smile. "You are so beautiful." Before Lyla could respond, she shot out the door.

With the footstool as close as Lyla's full skirts allowed, Besseta brushed out her hair and sectioned it off. "M'lady," she said, addressing Lady Katherine. "Her hair is so thick. The irons are ready for her curls, but I dinna believe there are enough in the coals to do her hair quickly."

Lady Katherine came closer, tapping her chin as she studied Lyla's mane.

Visions of red-hot rods sizzling her bald made Lyla forget her vow to cooperate. "No irons! Pull it back into a chignon or a bun. Please?" She offered an example by grabbing her hair and twisting it back. "We are already late, and I don't want to keep Grant waiting any longer than necessary." She gave what she hoped was a convincing shrug. "Besides, with this gorgeous gown, and this beautiful sapphire, a simple hairstyle will set them off better than an overdone thatch of curls. Don't you agree?"

Her dressers studied her, their heads tilting to the side in one synchronized move.

"Be she right, Lady Katherine?" Besseta asked in a reverent whisper.

Mrs. Tafferty twitched a rounded shoulder and nodded. "I believe she is. What say ye, Lady Katherine?"

Grant's mother clicked her tongue while making a slow circuit around Lyla. "Aye, she is. Especially about not making my son wait any longer. I feel sure the lateness of the hour has already given him a fit of the red arse."

Lyla breathed somewhat easier. She might have to succumb to the dangerous curling rods someday, but today was not that day. However, with that matter settled, her stomach churned with a fresh set of butterflies spreading their wings. Married. Again. As soon as Besseta finished with her hair.

Gaze locked straight ahead, Lyla idly chewed on her bottom lip. She had yet to share all her truths with Grant. Or any of his family, for that matter. Was it really fair to marry him without his knowing she came from the future?

"All done, m'lady, and ye look so verra lovely." Besseta stepped down from the stool and moved away, beaming like a freshly lit candle.

"Come, my daughter," Lady Katherine motioned toward the door. "It is time."

"It is time," Lyla repeated under her breath. She loved Grant but didn't really know him any more than he knew her. Of course, she had the upper hand on the time travel thing, but other than that, she knew nothing.

"It is only natural to feel a mite ill at ease." Lady Katherine took hold of Lyla's arm and gave a very conspiratorial wink. "I met Grant's father on our wedding day, but we shared many happy years together until a vile attack of apoplexy stole him from me." Her voice softened as she bowed her head. "I miss him still. So verra much."

Lyla sidled a glance at her future mother-in-law, then decided to share as much as she dared. "I fear that once he gets to know the *real* me, he will regret this day."

"Even in the best of marriages, ye both regret the wedding day at some time or another." Lady Katherine took the lead as they descended the stairs. "There will be days when ye would as soon kill him as to look at him." She tossed a smile back over her shoulder. "And he will wish to shake ye 'til yer teeth fly out." As they reached the first landing, she paused. "But neither of ye will do so. Ye will breathe, apologize for yer harsh words, and then ye will have a glorious bout in the bedchamber." She urged her to go first down the remaining steps.

As Lyla emerged from the archway, a gasp escaped her. A sea of smiling faces gave her the urge to run back up the steps. But the weight of her gown, along with Lady Katherine blocking the way, made escape impossible. Sly old woman. She wouldn't make the mistake of underestimating her mother-in-law ever again.

Clansmen and women, some she recognized, most she didn't, lined the way to the chapel, creating a wall of bodies on either side of her. She suddenly wished she hadn't passed on that whisky Besseta had offered. In fact, she should have indulged in several. Then up ahead, waiting outside the chapel, stood Grant.

It didn't matter that her bodice was too tight because the sight of him made her forget to breathe. Full Highland dress. Kilt belted and pinned to the shoulder of his freshly brushed black coat even though it was midsummer. She didn't know how it was possible, but his shoulders looked even broader than before. His blonde hair gleamed in the sunlight, slicked back, and tied in a proper braid at the back of his neck. He had shaved away the short stubble that usually dusted his face. His squared jaw was slick and strong, the muscles ticking in his cheek as he opened and closed his hands at his sides.

She tensed and held her breath as his gaze swept across her. When his eyes lit on the jewel at her neck, the faintest smile tugged at the corner of his mouth. The dimple in his cheek made a rare appearance.

Then he strode forward and offered his arm. "I thought ye had changed yer mind, m'lady."

"I almost did," she confessed after a hard swallow. If her stomach churned any worse, she'd chunder her breakfast all over his boots. Which looked to have been polished for the occasion. "Are you sure about this? We haven't known each other that long." Sixth sense or not, this marriage ceremony suddenly seemed all too real.

He came to a halt halfway up the aisle to the altar and turned her to face him. He touched her cheek, then grazed her lip with his thumb. "I canna imagine my life without ye. Ye have brought a brightness into my home and a flame of hope into my heart. I love ye, my dear one, and will only grow to love ye more as we make a life together."

Her neck tingled like it never tingled before. She rolled her shoulders, determined not to rub it like a dog scratching fleas. "I really feel as though I am meant to be here," she said. "And I love you, too." The tingling disappeared as though never there.

Grant fished a silver band from his waistcoat pocket, slid it onto her finger, then turned and bellowed, "Priest!"

The stern-faced man stormed down the altar steps and charged toward them. "Aye?"

"We have said our vows, and I have given her the ring." He offered her a tender smile, then turned and glowered at the holy man. "Finish the ceremony, ye ken?"

"My chieftain." The man resettled his footing as though about to wage battle. "'Tis customary for the couple to exchange their vows before God Almighty while standing at the altar."

"Are ye telling me God canna hear us from the middle of the kirk?"

Lyla clamped her lips tight, determined not to laugh or smile.

The priest didn't answer, just puckered his scowl tighter. With nostrils flared, he cleared his throat and then gave a disapproving growl. He flipped open his tattered black book, made the sign of the cross over them, then snapped it shut. "By the power granted to me by the Church of Scotland and God Almighty, I hereby pronounce ye man and wife. Let no man dare put asunder what God himself hath joined." He gave another loud hurrumph, then jerked a nod their way. "Ye may kiss yer bride, my chieftain."

As he bent his head, she expected the usual slow, chaste kiss of most marriage ceremonies. She was wrong. With one of his hands at the back of her neck and the other at the small of her back, he crushed her close, opening her mouth with his, then laid claim to her soul. She gladly returned the fervor, welcoming his taste of whisky and passion. Yes. This was so right. For the first time in her life, she felt in perfect sync with life and how she should live it. Then she thought she heard thunder. No. Not thunder. Applause and cheering. She nudged a last nibble of his lips, then gently pushed away and glanced around.

The small stone chapel had filled to bursting. Every pew. The side aisles along the walls. They had even packed into the center aisle on either side of them. Every man, woman, and child who could fit in the kirk had pushed in to see the sealing kiss between their chieftain and his new wife.

She spotted Fawna and Rory wiggling through the crowd and reached to help them. "Make way. Let my children through." It felt so good to say that. Her heart filled with such warmth, she couldn't breathe. She tried to bend to hug them, but the fullness of her gown and the tightness of the bodice forbade it. So, she squatted and pulled them into her arms.

"Dinna step on her dress!" Fawna warned her brother.

"I am nay on her dress, ye cow!" he shot back.

"Pax?" Lyla said, squeezing them tight. "At least for today. Yes?"

They both held up crossed fingers. "Aye, pax."

"What does *pax* mean?" Grant helped her stand.

"Cease-fire." She gave him a serious nod, knowing the children watched her. "Not surrender. Just standing down so everyone wins."

"A fine plan to enjoy this day." He leaned close, brushed a kiss on her cheek, then whispered in her ear, "As wise as ye are beautiful."

"Thank you." A rare blush warmed her chest, ran up her throat, and heated her cheeks. The crowd jammed into the close confines of the chapel seemed to press closer, renewing the dangerous churning in her middle. She needed space and some air or would soon be toes up and showing everyone how many underskirts she wore. "Might we go outside? It is very close in here."

"Lead the way, Fawna and Rory." He hooked her arm through his. "Ye are beautiful, m'love."

"It's because I am so very happy." Once they stepped outside, she pulled in as deep a breath as her garments allowed and pressed a hand to her stomach. "Much better. Thank you." She scanned the crowd for her sister. "Have you seen Abby? Or Malcolm?"

"The last I saw them, they were at the altar, speaking to the priest before ye finished dressing." His eyes narrowed into suspicious slits. "As our official witnesses who signed the contract, I thought little of it at the time. However, now I wonder if something else was afoot."

"You don't think…" She turned and stared back into the chapel but couldn't see anything because of the crowd following them out.

He shrugged. "I have never seen Malcolm so taken with a woman as he is with yer sister."

"If that cheeky little bird married him without telling me, I will shake her silly." She didn't know whether to feel slighted or happy that Abby had also found love in the seventeenth century.

Both of Grant's brows rose. "Cheeky little bird?"

"It's an English thing," she explained. Which wasn't a lie. It was just terminology used in the future. Teeth clenched behind her smile, she scolded herself. It seemed like the more she became relaxed about the current era, the more she slipped up and mentioned things in the future—or at least used twenty-first-century language. That had to stop. Especially since she wasn't quite ready to confess all to Grant. She needed to return his attention to the matter at hand. "Do you really think they married without telling anyone? Who would have witnessed it?"

"Many had already gathered inside. Malcolm could have pulled a pair of witnesses from the crowd." He patted her hand on his arm. "Enough of them. Today is ours, ye ken?"

"Ye should see all the food," Rory called back to them.

"Can we go on ahead and find Liam and them?" Fawna asked.

"Aye, go on wi' now." Grant hugged her arm tighter to his side. "Ye dinna mind, do ye?"

"Not at all. I am sure they would much rather sit with their chums than us." Him asking if she minded filled her with happiness. He had truly meant it when he said his children would become her children, too.

Cheers, stomping, and tankards banging welcomed them into the great hall. Lyla clutched his arm tighter. So many had gathered. Some must have traveled in from the nearest village and beyond. As he pulled out her chair at the head table, she motioned him in for a whisper. "Are all these people part of your clan?"

"*Our* clan, m'love." He tipped a subtle nod and helped her maneuver her skirts and sit.

"Bloody hell," she muttered, wrestling with the gown's fullness. If she hadn't sweated through her shift before, she had now. A relieved huff escaped her as she settled into her seat and shoved her skirts inside the armrests.

Grant watched with a lop-sided grin. "Are ye settled now?"

She silently counted to ten to make sure she said nothing she shouldn't. "Yes. Thank you." As he seated himself beside her, she added, "I have never owned a gown this regal before." True enough. "You married a poor commoner."

He lifted her hand for a kiss, his gaze inescapable as he brushed his lips across her knuckles. "And why, my precious minx, do I gather ye would rather wear simple garb than the many layers of plenty?"

He had read her well. She tipped her head closer to his and smiled. "Because these layers of plenty weigh as much as this table, take a village to get me into and out of, and are as uncomfortable as nettle rash." And she had yet to figure out how to hit the chamber pot without wetting through one or all of her underskirts and wasn't sure who she felt comfortable asking.

With a rumbling chuckle, Grant motioned for the maid to fill their goblets, then lifted his. "To many years blessed with comfort, aye?"

"Indeed." She clinked her glass to his, then took the barest sip. Since she didn't know how to take a successful pee, she best limit her intake of fluids. Although, she wouldn't mind a whisky. A nervousness had settled over her. It couldn't be about the wedding night. After all, they had already consummated their union. Several times, in fact. She had the nagging sense it had something to do with her continued need to hide her past.

Just as she was about to flag down a servant and ask for whisky, Abby and Malcolm entered. They paused just inside the large double doors that had been left open to bless the hall with air. As they walked hand in hand down the center aisle between the rows of tables and benches, several delayed Malcolm with pats on his back and by lifting their tankards.

"Yer sister's left hand," Grant said from behind his glass. "Is that a ring I see?"

"Oh, she married him, all right. Look at her eyes. Dead giveaway. She couldn't hide a guilty look if her life depended on it."

"Ye dinna like Malcolm?"

"I like Malcolm fine. She should have told me. I'm her sister."

Hurt feelings aside, she was happy for Abby. "I'll talk to her later. We'll get it cleared between us."

He nodded and set his drink on the table. But then he sat there, staring down at his goblet while thoughtfully rubbing a knuckle against his lip.

She rested a hand on his arm and leaned close. "What's wrong?"

His jaw tightened as he sat taller and rested his hands on the armrests of his chair. "I dinna wish there to be any untruths between us."

She released him, placed both hands in her lap, and clenched them into fists. This conversation was not a good omen.

With a pained look, he shifted in his seat and faced her. "I told Mother ye had been married before but were widowed, rather than telling her of yer divorce. I also told her ye had lost a child, but she doesna ken that ye are now barren."

Why had he chosen to share all this in the middle of their wedding feast? She didn't mind, but had he done it to keep her from going off her trolley and causing a scene? She glanced up and down the table. With the dull roar of so many conversations, the only person who might hear was the girl standing at the ready to refill their wine. "Why are you telling me this now?"

He dipped his chin and kept his gaze lowered. "I shouldha told ye before. Forgive me." Then he lifted his gaze, and she picked up on a decided glint in his eyes. "As a coward would think, I waited until after we married to tell ye I had betrayed yer confidence. I thought it more likely ye could find it in yer heart to forgive a husband. Before, I was just yer lover. And lovers are easily spurned." He took her hands in his and smiled. "Just as I shared, now ye can share the truths ye feared to tell me. Do ye not agree?"

So that was his game. Wily, but not wily enough. She squeezed his hands. "Not just yet." She cast a glance across the many gathered in the room. "And definitely not in front of an audience."

Enlightenment filled his face, then he huffed a soft laugh and shook his head. "I am a fool." Still holding tight to her left hand, he straightened in his chair. "Delicate matters require privacy. Forgive me, my own. I can only blame it on the fact that I hate for anything, any questions or fears, to remain between us."

She understood he was dying to know her secrets, but she wasn't ready just yet. Close. But not quite there. "I don't want anything between us either, but I need a little more time. Please?"

He kissed her hand again, but it had changed from a loving caress to a nervous peck. "Of course, m'love."

She hated for anything to overshadow their wedding day. "Tomorrow," she blurted. It came out before she realized she had even opened her mouth. "Tomorrow night, after we have enjoyed an entire day as a married couple, I will tell you everything."

"Aye, m'love. Tomorrow night it is." He leaned over and gifted her with a lingering kiss that made her wonder how much longer they really needed to stay in the hall. All she hungered for was him.

"Might we go upstairs now?" she whispered.

Without a word, he rose and offered his arm. "As ye wish, m'lady love. Always and whenever ye wish."

CHAPTER THIRTEEN

GRANT POURED THEM both a whisky while trying to recall if he had told her how her beauty had rendered him unable to move. The sight of her had almost taken him to his knees right there in front of the chapel. He smiled to himself. Even if he had already told her, it needed repeating. "When ye walked toward me today…" He couldn't finish. No words could describe how he had felt. Still felt, in fact.

She turned from gazing out the open window of his solar. With a nervous twiddling of her hands across the rounded top of the upholstered chair beside it, she arched both brows higher and turned her head as though straining to hear him. "When I walked toward you today?" she encouraged. "It isn't nice to leave a woman hanging with a sentence like that."

"I canna describe yer beauty, dear one." He offered her the drink as he joined her in front of the window. "And it was not the gown, nor my mother's sapphire around yer lovely throat that cast the spell upon me." A sip of the fiery liquid failed to sort his thoughts. After a self-deprecating laugh, he shook his head. "I canna describe it. It was as though the sun had filled ye with its golden glow and set a brilliant ring of light around ye. Ye looked descended from Heaven as the purest hope for happiness."

She went still with her glass partway to her mouth, staring at him as though about to burst into tears. Either that or laugh in his face. He wasn't certain which. "The dress is verra nice, too," he hurried to add. "But not as stunning as the woman wearing it."

"I fear I am going to fall." She took an impressive gulp of whisky, not flinching at the heat that surely had to be burning down her throat. Admirable, indeed.

"Fall?" He strode back to the long, mahogany cabinet filled with decanters and water pitchers and fetched the whisky bottle. "Fall from where?" he asked after returning to her side.

"That pedestal you've put me on." She held out her glass and tipped a nod toward the bottle. "Abby would say that is not healthy, because at some point I will disappoint you." Her lovely bare shoulders lifted in a shrug. "I am real, Grant, and trust me, very fallible."

"As am I." He filled her glass, then clicked his to it. "If one of us falls, we shall rise together, aye?"

"Well said." She turned back to staring into the night. "You have a better view than I do. I can see more stars from here."

He placed the bottle and glass on the small round table beside the chair. Something troubled her. Her uneasiness filled the air as surely as the sweet floral fragrance of her hair. The nervousness stiffened her neck and strained the slant of her shoulders. With a careful gentleness, as if she were a skittish colt, he slid his arms around her and rested his chin on her shoulder. "This is yer view now, too. Besseta will see that the rest of yer things are moved in here tomorrow."

She shivered with a soft, forced laugh. "I didn't know if we would be a couple who shared the same quarters or not. You know some never sleep in the same bed unless...well, you know."

"What troubles ye, m'love?" He turned her in his arms and made her look him in the eyes. "'Tis not as though we dinna ken how to enjoy each other, and yet ye're behaving like a shy virgin." He tried to read the shadows shifting in her eyes. "Or as if ye fear me." He squeezed her shoulders. "Tell me, Lyla. What distresses ye so?"

She touched his face, trailing her fingertips along his cheek. "I want to make you happy. More than anything." A lopsided smile tugged at the fullness of her mouth. She closed her hand into a fist and pressed it to her chest. "I know with all my being I was meant to be your wife. I am more content, happier, and aligned with life than I have ever been before."

He waited, sensing she hadn't finished. Perhaps she had decided to reveal her mysterious truths tonight rather than tomorrow.

After a deep breath and a sad shake of her head, she continued. "But it has been a standard in my life that whenever I am at my happiest, something always mucks it up. Either something I say or do, or some outside force that makes a mess of everything for me." Her voice softened to a hushed whisper full of emotion. "I don't want that to happen here. Not with you. I—"

He hushed her with a long, slow kiss, then pressed his forehead to hers. "Life is never without risk. All we can do is face whatever comes. Together."

Easing back a step, she rested her fingers on the brooch pinning his kilt to his shoulder. Her brow furrowed the slightest bit as she idly traced the outline of the mighty lion reared on its hind legs as if ready for battle. After giving the crest a hesitant pat, she smiled. "It is a warm night. Shall we get out of these clothes?"

"Allow me to help ye." He frowned down at her front. "How does this satin creation come off?"

She tapped the pearl buttons at her waist. "Unbutton these and then the pins should be easier to find. I don't know how many they used." With her chin tucked, she studied her chest, eying the embroidered edging of the gown's jacket. She grazed her fingertips along it. "Mrs. Tafferty and Besseta hid them well."

"I never realized a woman's dressing could be so complicated." He unbuttoned the waist, then found the first pin when it pricked his finger. "Shite!"

"Don't bleed on the bodice!" She caught hold of his wounded finger and stuck it into her mouth.

His cock roared with jealousy, making him groan.

Her smile took on a wicked tilt. "Sorry." She sucked it one more time, then pushed his hand away. "I'll remove the rest of the pins to protect you from injury. After that, you can help me peel the jacket off so I don't snag the lace on the sleeves."

He started to unpin his brooch, but she stopped him.

"No. I get to undress you tonight." Eyes sparkling, she teased him with a suggestive look. "After all, we should properly christen your solar before we christen the bed. Don't you agree?"

"Absolutely, m'love." He helped her peel off the fitted jacket and snug sleeves while keeping his gaze locked on the creamy white mounds of her breasts.

Much to his disappointment, she turned and directed him to her back. "And now to release me from my bonds."

He fished out the tucked ends of the ties, smiling when she flexed as his fingers brushed against her skin. "It looks verra tight."

"It is." She rested her hands on her hips and glanced back at him. "Besseta made me hold on to the bloody bedpost so she could yank them harder. I'm surprised she didn't plant her foot on my bum to get more leverage."

The process she described made him laugh. As he loosened the ties, the bodice sagged open. Lyla held it to her chest and faced him. With a devilish look, she lifted both arms, exposing herself in the sheer laciness of her wedding shift. "You can pull it off over my head if you like. That way you don't have to keep fiddling with the laces."

Without hesitation, he did as she wished, thankful that the ultimate reward of having her in his bed would arrive faster that way. When she teased him by tugging the neckline of her chemise higher to cover herself, he couldn't resist hooking a finger in the delicate edging and pulling it back down. "Never hide yerself from me, m'love. Allow me to drink ye in and relish ye like fine whisky."

She took hold of his wrists and guided his hands to her breasts. "Skin on skin feels so much better than rib-cracking satin and whalebone."

"I much prefer skin on skin as well." He took the pleasure of nibbling her collarbone as she removed his crest from his shoulder, then deftly unfastened his belt as well. His kilt slid off and piled onto the floor.

Sliding her hands under his léine, she treated him to a slow seductive massage with one hand while palming his bollocks in the other. "You know, we really should finish undressing before indulging in the good stuff," she said in a breathy whisper.

He shed his jacket and let it drop, then ran his fingers up under the buttons of his waistcoat, popping them open in record time. It joined the growing pile on the floor. Much to his dismay, she let go of his manparts and backed up a step. "Help me with all these skirts."

Their level of fluffiness gave him pause as he unbuttoned the waistband to the midnight blue outer skirt. "How many are there?"

"Counting this one?" She held up her fingers. "Four."

He lifted it off over her head and tossed it across the back of the chair. "Why so many?"

She rolled her eyes and kept her arms in the air for the next one. "I asked the same thing. Mrs. Tafferty mentioned something about floofiness."

"Floofiness," he repeated more to himself than her, uncertain he understood. He lifted off the next skirt, then considered pulling his dagger from his boot to cut the others away.

"I can get rid of the rest of them if you'd like to pull off your boots." She untied the waistbands and let the remaining under-skirts drop to the floor before he could respond.

As he sat to kick off his boots, he glanced up and went still. Lyla sat perched on the windowsill, untying the ribbons above her knees and rolling her silk stockings off.

"You better hurry and catch up." She grinned as she hopped off the ledge and stripped her shift over her head. Partially hidden by the high-backed chair, she stretched, reaching for the ceiling. "At last. The night air is wonderful."

He shed his léine, joined her at the window, and pulled her into his arms. "Yer flesh against mine is better than any breeze's touch."

"I would most definitely have to agree," she said, pressing her softness tighter against him.

"But as ye said, it is a verra warm night." He lifted her up, returned her to the wide ledge of the windowsill, and stepped between her knees. He slid his hands up her thighs, spreading her legs farther apart. "Hold tight, m'love." He knelt, then he tasted, reveling in her high-pitched, gasping squeaks.

One hand buried in his hair, she pulled him in, directing his tongue deeper as she leaned back. She looped her legs over his shoulders and hugged his head with her thighs. The squeaks turned into throaty groans that told him she was close to reaching her bliss. So, he slipped a finger inside and sucked hard as she had sucked on his finger.

She yanked his head closer still, both hands tangled in his hair. A shriek escaped her, followed by a series of shudders and clenching. Her pleasure nearly undid him. He ached to bury himself inside her and ride to his own relief. As her quaking subsided, he pulled her from the window. He sat in the nearby chair and settled her on his lap. "I need ye, woman," he groaned, running his hands down to her hips and squeezing.

"Not yet." She set a foot on the floor between his and knelt. "My turn." As she settled in place, she smoothed her hands along his sides, then took him in her mouth, sucking and pulling him in deeper.

He clutched the chair arms, fighting for control. Upholstery ripped and the wooden frame creaked as she sucked him harder. "God's beard," he groaned through clenched teeth. "I can bear no more!" He lifted her off him, rolled her to her back, and buried himself in the perfection of her wet heat. And he pounded, scraping his knees on the weave covering the floor and not giving a damn about the pain.

She arched and thrashed, slamming into him thrust for thrust. Then she screamed, and he joined his roaring with hers. As his seed left him, so did his strength. He sagged on top of her, propped on his elbows to keep from crushing his lady love. Still gasping for precious air, his mouth pressed to her ear. He wanted to make her know how much she had healed his life, filled his heart, and renewed his soul. But flowery words escaped him.

"I love ye, my own," he whispered, praying she would feel the words as their hearts pounded against each other as if trying to meld into one.

She rubbed her hands up and down his back, pressing her cheek to his. "I love you more."

They lay there for the longest time. Or it seemed like a long while before he noticed her occasional wriggling and barely audible grunts. He raised up and studied her.

"I am so sorry," she said, relief filling her face. "The scratchiness of this rug is eating me alive. Can we move to the couch or the bed?"

"Ye shouldha said something sooner." He pushed up to his knees, then flinched.

"You are bleeding." She cringed, staring at his knee.

He gifted her a sheepish grin as he stood and offered her a hand up. "Aye. A wee bit."

She ignored his hand. Instead, she rolled to her hands and knees, making him groan and go hard all over again.

"Does it hurt very badly?" she questioned, hopping to her feet without looking back. She headed toward the water pitcher. "Rug burns can be the worst. Go to the couch. I'll wet a cloth. That should ease it some."

"Rug burns," he repeated, staring down at his scraped knees. An apt description since the stinging pain resembled the feel of a burn. He strolled to the couch and sat, sprawling his arms across the back and his legs out in front of it. "'Twas worth it."

She returned with a cool, wet linen and dabbed it to each knee, blotting the blood away. Her kneeling in front of him reminded him of earlier, his cock throbbed for another treat of her wondrous mouth.

"I'm glad it was worth it," she said. "But I don't want you incapacitated after just one round." She grinned up at him. "After all, this is our wedding night. We need to make certain we are properly consummated. Yes?"

"Absolutely, wife." He pulled her up to straddle him. "Ye could always sit in my lap and distract me from my knees."

"I shall do my best." With her hands planted on his shoulders, she wiggled in place, burying him inside her while rubbing her breasts in his face. "I did say I wished to christen the couch. If you're ready, I am."

"More than ready," he rasped, squeezing her breasts while contemplating which nipple to enjoy first.

⸻⧓⸻

LYLA MANAGED A drowsy smile. Her nose itched, but she didn't have the strength to scratch it. She fully expected them to find her in this same position at daybreak. Head resting in the dip of Grant's shoulder, arm across his chest, and a leg thrown across his thighs. Dead from blissful exhaustion.

His heartbeat thumped a steady beat, tickling the underneath of her arm. She breathed in his warmth and smiled. His smell, his unique musk, filled her with a euphoric sense of being safe, being loved. The unmistakable aroma of their lovemaking marked the bedchamber, probably the sitting room, too. Anyone entering the rooms would know they had well consummated their union. Several times.

"Sleep," he rumbled slow and deep, his voice vibrating through her like a lazy caress.

She pressed a kiss to his salty, sweet skin. "I am enjoying the afterglow, dear husband."

"Afterglow?"

She almost laughed. The slowness of his speech revealed slumber wasn't far from claiming him. "A floaty feeling of being well-loved."

His arm curled tighter around her, then relaxed and slid into the curve of her side. "Aye, dear one. That ye are." His breathing settled into a slower rise and fall that said her fine Highlander had relinquished the battle. Sleep conquered him at last.

She wished sleep would claim her, too. While undeniably sated and too tired to move, her whirring thoughts and worries refused to grant her any peace that might allow slumber. Her promise to tell him the truth tomorrow nagged at her. Especially since tomorrow had become today. According to the diminished height of the night candle, the sun would peep above the horizon soon. She dreaded it more than she had ever dreaded anything in her life. Her gut warned her, and her heart agreed that once she told him everything, nothing would be the same. In fact, she feared the repercussions would be so much worse than she could bear. But she couldn't make up another cover story. Not after tonight. She had promised him the complete truth.

"I am not a witch," she whispered, testing the waters.

He didn't respond, and the rhythm of his breathing didn't change.

Maybe she should tell him now. While he slept. That way she didn't really risk him hearing her. It might be a bit dodgy and underhanded, but her life was at stake here. Tomorrow she would say she had already told him everything and act hurt when he didn't remember. It wouldn't be a lie. And with his pride, it might just work. The longer she pondered the plan, the more convinced she became. Renewed hope and determination filled her.

Everything she should say tumbled through her mind in a confusing avalanche of desperate babbling. She pulled in a deep breath and eased it out, regaining control. Stick to the basics. One thing at a time and don't embellish. If she talked too long or loudly, he might wake.

"I was born on July 13, 1989," she started, speaking in the softest whisper. "I know it's shocking, but Abby and I traveled back through time from the year 2019 while watching a meteor shower from Arthur's Seat in Edinburgh. You found us right after we arrived, remember?" She thought back over the short confession, inwardly cringing. That sounded like pure rubbish. Thank goodness he was asleep. Of course, he would remember where he found them and how daft they had been. How could he not?

"Say that again, lass."

The alert leeriness in his tone shot fear through her. He had heard. The bloody truth became a monster threatening to tear her and her happiness to pieces. His body tensed against her as if coiled to strike. She clenched her teeth and remained silent, praying he would think it all a dream.

"Lyla." Louder. Strong and awake. Not a doubt remained she had his full attention. "Repeat what ye just said to me?" He slid out from under her and pushed himself upright back against the headboard.

She pondered faking sleep. But even cloaked in the dim light from the night candle, she doubted that would work. The sheer terror in his face was unmistakable. He stared at her as if he had never seen her before.

Clutching the bedsheets to her throat, she scooted upward and leaned back against the headboard beside him. "What exactly did you hear?"

"Dates that canna be possible." His voice broke. "Repeat what ye said. All of it."

Her heart plummeted, then shot a knot of emotions up to choke her. True to form, she had just ruined the best thing in her life. She rubbed her forehead and looked aside, unable to face him. "The date of my birth is July 13, 1989. Manchester, England.

I was born a few minutes before Abby." She kept her gaze fixed on a spot on the floor beside the bed and waited.

"And the rest?"

"It was May something, 2019, when we found ourselves thrown back here. To this century." With her bottom lip caught between her teeth, she closed her eyes and bit until the coppery taste of blood filled her mouth. Did he really love her enough to believe her? "This is my truth," she whispered when he didn't speak. "The one I have tried to hide with all those stupid lies you always saw through." She stole a glance at him. "Because I knew you would react like this."

Her stomach churned with the same agony filling her heart. She gaged the distance between the screen hiding the chamber pot and the bed. Vomiting was inevitable. Bile burned at the back of her throat, warning she better get ready. The open window was closer. She hoped nobody was under it.

Without commenting, he stared up at the ceiling, seeming to watch the dancing shadows.

"I promise it is the truth." She swallowed hard, trying not to throw up. They needed to talk, and she couldn't very well manage a conversation while chundering the contents of her stomach out the window. "I swear it. Tell me what I can say to help you believe me." Her gut rumbled and clenched one final warning. She launched from the bed, hung her head out the window, and heaved harder than she had ever wretched before. Tears ran and dripped off her nose as she vomited. He thought her a witch. Or even worse, he thought her mad. Either way, she would soon die as she had lived. Alone. Her happiness had ended in record time.

The bedchamber door thudded, making her turn. The latch clicked and rattled, then went still.

Grant was gone. After a swipe of her hand across her mouth, she ran to the door, determined to chase after him. Convince him. Make him understand. She tried to yank it open, but it refused to give. The latch seemed frozen. Then it hit her. Grant was not only gone; he had locked her away.

"Grant!" She pounded on the door with both fists. "Grant! I promise I am not lying this time." She rammed into it with her shoulder, then kicked it for good measure. The solid oak didn't give. "You have to come back," she yelled against the crack of the doorway. "You have to listen!"

Silence answered. She turned and sagged against the door, then slid to the floor in a crumpled heap. Uncontrollable sobs wrenched free of her as she lay on her side and curled into the fetal position. "Grant," she shouted as loud as she could, hating herself for destroying their precious new bond. "Grant, please. Please come back."

Not a sound came to her through the darkness. Only her weeping filled the chamber.

CHAPTER FOURTEEN

"HOW CAN SHE be so addled and yet seem so sane at the same time?" Grant stared at his land, but the glorious view of lush forests, sparkling streams, and a gently rolling glen brought him no comfort this day. His heart, nay, not just his heart but his entire being suffered unbearable pain. How had everything gone wrong in the blink of an eye?

With his forearms propped atop the stone battlement, he shifted his gaze to Malcolm, praying the man would have some type of wisdom to explain Lyla's descent into madness. "Has her sister said anything of the year she was born or about coming from another time?"

Malcolm blew out a heavy sigh and slowly shook his head. "Nay, my friend. All she said is that yer wife is not mad." He pinched the bridge of his nose and rubbed the corners of his eyes. "But she fears ye will order her locked away as well. So, her words may be guarded."

"I ordered Lyla locked in a room with barred windows because I will not lose another wife to hanging." Even though he had not loved the mother of his children, her death had both saddened and shamed him. Lyla would be different. He could not bear the thought of her taking her own life and refused to allow it. He hoped to protect her from herself until her mind healed from whatever malady ailed it. If it would heal. God Almighty, he prayed it would heal. He cleared his throat and softened his tone. "I am protecting Lyla. Make certain yer wife understands that, ye ken? Surely, she doesna wish her sister to harm herself?"

"I have explained such to her. Several times, in fact." He sidled a worried glance his way that almost made Grant cringe. "Will ye visit her?"

"Aye. 'Tis my hope to guide her back to sanity." He flattened his hands on the rough stone blocks, hating himself for the dread he felt at the prospect. What if she was worse? Her shouts and cries as the guards took her away still tormented him.

"Might her sister visit?" Malcolm quietly asked. "'Twould ease my precious Abby's heart to see yer Lyla with her own eyes." He paused, the furrow in his brow growing deeper. "And she asked if she might take their old things to her. Both the odd bags they had with them when we found them. Abby feels it might help her sister's spirits."

"Absolutely not. I have ordered all that locked away, and I alone have the key." He shook his head. "I fear it could worsen her madness. Yer wife may visit Lyla anytime she wishes, but that is all. And the key to the tower room remains with the guard." He couldn't trust that Abby wouldn't try to help her sister escape the safety of her new chambers.

"There ye are!"

Grant closed his eyes and sent up a prayer of deliverance. That was the last thing he needed right now. "I am quite busy, Mother. We will speak later, aye?"

"We will not." She came to a halt beside him. "We will speak of this now and resolve it."

For the first time in his life, he didn't hold back. "Ye will remember yer place, woman. I am chieftain here. Not you." He pushed away from the wall and faced her, squaring his shoulders and settling his stance for battle. "This is not yer concern. Go back downstairs and tend to yer grandchildren, ye ken?"

She stared at him as if struck mute. After a tense moment, she bowed her head and retreated a step. "It is my beloved grandchildren's welfare that brings me here, my chieftain."

Jaw clenched so tight it ached, he scowled at her. "Are they unwell?"

She shook her head. "Nay. They wish to visit their mother."

"Their mother is dead."

After a slow, deep breath, she bowed her head again. "Forgive me for being unclear. They wish to see their stepmother." She leveled a knowing look at him. "But her chambers are empty as are yers."

He refused to lay bare the death of all his hopes and dreams. Not yet. "My wife is unwell. I had her moved to the tower."

"The tower?" The shock in her tone made the words sound like a dreaded curse. "Grant—my son, Lyla in the tower?"

"It is best for now. For her own protection." He turned his back on her, refusing to say more.

"I see," she whispered.

He ignored the weight of her compassionate touch on his shoulder. Nothing brought him comfort this dark day.

"I will pray for her." She stepped away, turning toward the steps leading down to the courtyard. "I will pray for ye as well, my son."

"Tell the children I will speak with them later. I have much to attend to this morning."

"I will tell them," she said, then hurried down the steps.

"What can I do?" Malcolm asked.

"If my beloved is no better in a sennight," he said. "Find me a battle. I canna remain idle while waiting for her madness to leave."

"With Cromwell headed to Edinburgh, I feel certain that willna be a problem."

"Good enough, then." Grant dismissed him with a nod. He needed to be alone with his suffering.

DRESSED IN NOTHING but her torn shift. Barefoot. Hair ratty and hanging in long, loose tangles. Lyla knew the guards considered her demon-possessed or cursed. Or a deranged animal. Or all three. She had fought, screamed, cried, and spit at them. Everything she could do to twist away and escape. Nothing worked. Gentle but firm, silent as stone, they had caught her up by the wrists and ankles and carried her to this bloody hellhole.

She hugged her knees tighter, perching in the wide window-sill overlooking the courtyard. Rusty iron bars, the spaces between them narrow and crosshatched with wire, prevented her from leaning out to see any better. From this height, only part of the cobblestoned yard was visible. She was too tired and hoarse to scream anymore. The barred window was large. If Grant planned to keep her here during the winter, she would surely freeze to death, since nothing but a rickety square of rotting planks covered the hole to keep out the wind and the rain. But maybe that's what he wanted. She closed her eyes. They still burned from the last tear-jag. She pressed her forehead to the coolness of the metal barrier. "I have to get calm and figure this out. I have to fix this."

A longer study of her new quarters didn't help. No furniture. No blankets. Not even a candle stub or a chamberstick. Her current assets were daylight, an enormous pile of straw, and a wooden bucket with no bale. She assumed the pail was for bodily functions since the circular room provided no other accommodations. Although stark, the space appeared clean enough. Even the straw seemed fresh from the field.

Boots thumped and metal clattered on the other side of the door, interrupting her gloomy assessment. A key rattled in the lock. She prayed it was Grant. Surely, he would come. A muted conversation between the guard and a female dashed that hope. At least it was Besseta. "I hope she's still my friend," she said under her breath.

Besseta's arrival meant water. She hoped so. A drink would help her raw throat. The thought of food only nauseated her. Hunger left her whenever her world went out of balance. As off-kilter as it was right now, she doubted she would ever eat again. She didn't rise from her seat on the window ledge as the door creaked open. Manners could just be damned.

"Ye call out if ye get afraid," the guard instructed as the door swung wider.

"Lady Lyla would never hurt anyone." Besseta strolled in with a pile of clothing draped over one arm and a large tray in her hands. She glanced back at whoever had warned her. "I will be fine, Geordie. Lock the door in case Master Malcolm or Himself comes. Ye dinna need any more trouble, ye ken?"

"I dinna like locking ye in," he argued.

"I won't hurt her," Lyla shouted, doubting it would reassure him and not really caring if it did or not. She started to add *cross my heart and hope to die,* but that made her think of the children. "Damn and blast it all!" She closed her eyes and turned away, trying not to cry.

"There. Ye see?" Besseta glared at him while impatiently tapping a toe.

Geordie huffed out a long-suffering groan and shook his shaggy head, before yanking the heavy door shut and locking it.

As Besseta turned, her self-assured attitude melted into one of caring worry. "Oh, m'lady. What happened?" She wrinkled her nose at the wooden bucket, then set the tray on top of it to make a table. After carefully folding the tray's linen covering aside, she picked up a small pitcher and filled a wooden cup with water. "Here. I feel sure ye need this."

"Thank you." Lyla sniffed it first, then offered an apologetic shrug at Besseta's wounded expression. "Sorry. It's not that I don't trust you, but it has been a rough morning. I'm not sure who I can trust anymore." The cool water both helped and hurt her throat, making her flinch and then cough. She held her throat and forced down another swallow. "I guess it serves me right for screaming at the guards."

"I shall bring some herbs to help with yer throat." Besseta frowned at the surroundings, the furrow in her brow growing deeper by the minute. "I canna believe they dragged ye up here in nothing but yer shift." Her gaze swept from the top of Lyla's head down to her toes. "Not even stockings or shoes. Shame on them all! Ye will surely catch yer death. 'Tis unbelievable. Especially with Himself saying ye needed to be here to protect ye from harming yerself."

"Protect me from harming myself?" Lyla scooted to the part of the windowsill still catching the direct sunlight. It might be summer, but castle stone became a cold hard seat in the shade.

Besseta stole a glance back at the door, then returned to the tray and uncovered a plate of bread. "Himself is afeared ye will do the same as his first wife. Remember how I told ye 'bout her hanging herself?" The girl sidled a glance at the metal grating across the window. "I grant ye that's why he ordered ye put up here."

Lyla pondered that news while sipping the water. The more she drank, the more her throat eased. At least he had labeled her as crazy and not a witch. That offered some comfort. But it didn't answer how long he planned to keep her locked up. She lifted her cup in a mock toast. "I promise I am not suicidal."

Head cocked like a dog listening to its master; Besseta offered the plate of bread. "Ye are not what?"

"I do not wish to end my life," Lyla said. And she didn't. She wished to repair it from the mucked-up mess she had made of it. With a gentle but firm shove, she pushed the bread away.

Besseta's scowl said she didn't approve, but she obeyed and returned the plate to the tray. "If ye dinna wish to end yer life, why does Himself fear ye mad?" Her mouth tightened as if she regretted saying that. "Leastwise that's what Mrs. Fintrie said. That Himself fears ye addled like his first wife and canna bear the possibility of yer dying."

So, he had confessed to the housekeeper? Lyla wondered how much he told her. Setting her cup on the ledge, she hugged her knees again and resumed looking out the window. "If I tell you, you will think me mad, too." She shrugged. "So, I would rather not." The only person who needed to believe her was Grant. She swallowed hard, determined not to cry anymore.

"But I can help." Besseta held up the garments. "I brought ye clothes and will fetch yer shoes, too. Why would they keep yer shoes? I mean, whatever for?" She glanced around the room again. "And even though it be summer, I'll see about having a brazier fetched to knock the chill from these stones."

"Bring me my bag. Or Abby's." Why hadn't she thought of it before? She could show Grant the labels. The trademarks. The aspirin bottle or the headlamps. Those things would have dates on them. Then he could see she was telling the truth. "And the clothes I wore the day I arrived. Can you do that? Bring me everything I had that day?"

The maid gave a sad shake of her head. "I am sorry, m'lady. But Himself had the trunk removed from yer chambers and locked away. I dinna ken where he had it taken. Mrs. Fintrie said it was cursed and probably what brought on yer madness. Only the chieftain has the key."

Lyla's heart fell, and her spirits sank even lower. "Please, just tell me everything Grant told you." She didn't care about anything Besseta might be able to bring if she couldn't get hold of the backpacks. All she cared about was Grant and making him understand.

"Himself said nothing to me. He told Mrs. Fintrie ye were nay well, and that ye needed to be here to keep ye safe. Her being housekeeper and all, she needed to know to tell the rest of us how to care for ye."

"Do I seem unwell?" Lyla glared at her.

The furrow in Besseta's brow deepened. "Ye dinna appear to be ailing, but ye dinna look well either." She shook out a dark blue kirtle and held it ready. "Yer poor eyes are red as fire from crying all night. Nose red, too. Willna eat and ye sit there shivering like a leaf in a windstorm." She stepped closer, lifting the dress like a net to throw over Lyla's head. "Ye didna reject him in the marriage bed, did ye? Is that the true reason he sent ye here? Ye ken how men can be."

"Well, of course not." Lyla shoved her arms into the lightweight wool dress, jerked it on over her head, and wriggled it the rest of the way down. "Last night's sex was the best I've ever had. That is not our problem."

Besseta's brows arched so high they nearly disappeared beneath the edge of her white linen coif. She retrieved a knitted shawl from the dwindling pile of clothing on the floor. "Well, that is a good thing." After tossing the wrap around Lyla's shoulders, she snatched up the stockings and held them out. "I didna mean to pry, m'lady, but something dire mustha happened for him to send ye to the tower."

"That's where this is?" In her fight to get the guards to let her go, she hadn't seen where they took her. Lyla smoothed the light wool stockings on and knotted the garters above her knees. "Grant told me the tower was for the very worst of prisoners."

"Aye." Besseta appeared pained, flinching as though wishing she were somewhere else. "Dungeon rooms and the worse sort of cells fill its base." She forced a smile. "But not up here where ye are."

"You lie worse than I do." Lyla resettled the shawl around her shoulders, grateful for its warmth as she returned to her ledge. "Let me guess. Those kept in this room are about to be executed. Right?"

Besseta didn't speak, but her eyes misted over with tears, providing answer enough. "Not a word has been said about any execution, m'lady. I swear it."

"It wouldn't be your fault if there were." She hugged her knees and leaned against the sill. "I have no one to blame but myself for destroying my happiness."

"I am sorry, m'lady. Are ye certain there is nothing I can do to make things better?"

She wanted to say, *make Grant love me enough to listen*, but that wouldn't be fair. "Tell my sister I am fine," she said, then managed a shaky smile. "And keep visiting me. It's nice to have someone to talk to."

Besseta rushed over and took hold of her hand. "They willna keep me from ye, m'lady. I swear it."

Lyla pulled her into a hug. "Thank you," she whispered, then took the maid by the shoulders and set her back. "But promise me you won't endanger yourself. I don't want you hurt because of me. Promise?"

"I am naught but a maid, m'lady." Besseta grinned. "No one pays me any mind. I am safe enough. I grant ye that."

Keys rattled in the latch, and the door creaked open. Geordie gave an apologetic dip of his chin. "Time, Besseta."

The maid squeezed Lyla's hand again. "I'll be back with yer shoes and that brazier. And a chamber pot. Dinna fash about that, aye?"

"The chieftain said I may see my sister." Abby's demand rang out with authority.

Geordie stiffened, then awkwardly shifted his tall, gangly frame around to face her. "Beg pardon, mistress. I didna hear ye come up. 'Twas busy getting Besseta out." Panic filled his face, then he jerked his head. "Please dinna tell Master Malcolm I didna hear ye. He will have me arse for certain."

"Geordie!" Besseta scolded. "Ye shouldna say *arse* when talking to the chieftain's sister."

He bobbed his head in another awkward bow. "Forgive me again. I beg ye."

"You better go save him," Lyla advised the maid.

"I'll return with yer shoes, pillows, blankets. Whatever I can carry." The maid scurried out, leaving the tray with the water pitcher and bread behind.

Abby marched inside, then turned and gave Geordie a stern shake of her finger. "I am staying here as long as I like or else my husband finds out I caught you sleeping on the job. Understand?"

"But I was nay asleep, mistress. Ye saw me with yer own eyes trying to get the maid to come out."

Abby glared at the poor man. Her mouth twisted into a malicious smirk. "Who do you think my husband will believe? You or me?"

He bobbed his head, backed out, and quietly closed the door behind him.

Lyla poured herself another cup of water. She lifted the linen and eyed the rest of the tray's contents. Bread. Cheese. A second small water pitcher. Nothing more. With a mocking toast of the cup toward Abby, she shrugged. "If you want a drink, we will have to share the cup."

"Are you serious? How can you be so flippant at a time like this?"

"It is called survival," she snapped. The last thing she needed right now was Abby. Where was Grant? Why had he not shown yet? She returned to her ledge and tipped her head toward the pile of straw. "I would offer you a chair, but I'm fresh out. The straw seems clean, though."

Abby closed her eyes, lifted her chin, and pulled in a deep breath. After a brief moment of holding it, she eased it out and opened her eyes. "What happened? The two of you seemed so happy at the banquet."

"We were happy except for one thing." Lyla dreaded telling Abby. It would only release one of her tirades. "He was obsessed with knowing the truth about my past."

Abby opened and closed her mouth like a fish out of water. "You didn't."

"I did. A few hours before dawn."

"What about all your talk of fitting in and playing to the era so we don't end up burning at the stake?" Abby shuffled closer, wringing her hands, teetering close to hysteria. "What about all of that?" She thumped a fist to her chest. "And what about me?" Tears filled her eyes. "What about my baby?"

Lyla turned and stared. "Your what?"

"I am pregnant." Abby pressed both fists to her mouth. Tears streamed down her face as she sniffled. "At least, I am fairly certain I am."

"So, that's the reason you and Malcolm rushed the nuptials." It all made sense now. Lyla pulled her twin close, offering a reassuring hug and a shoulder for crying. It appeared they both had a talent for complicating their lives. "Do you love him?"

"I think I could. Very much, in fact." Abby sniffed again, then shuddered. "But I am so afraid. Pregnant in this century? Especially after what you suffered."

"I know." How could her sister not be afraid? Even though they were fraternal twins, they could still share medical complications. The miscarriage had almost killed her. With another comforting pat, she tightened the hug and gently shook her. "We are so different. I'm sure you'll be fine with having the baby." She wasn't sure at all, but what harm would the kindness of a lie do?

Abby pulled away and gave her a tearful scowl. "But now this." She jerked a hand, motioning at the bleak surroundings. "Don't you know this endangers me, too? We are sisters. They found us together on that hill outside Edinburgh. Remember?"

"According to Besseta, he thinks me insane." She repressed a heavy sigh. "Wouldn't you? The only reason we accepted the time travel theory so quickly was because we had to survive it."

"But you didn't tell him anything about me?"

Lyla briefly closed her eyes, struggling to maintain control. "I told him I was the eldest. That is the only time you came into the conversation."

"I know I sound selfish. I'm sorry." Abby stared at the floor. "But I have a baby to worry about now." She lifted her gaze. "And an adoring man I think I could really love."

"Trust me. If I had it to do over again, I would've done it differently." Lyla stared out the window, fixing her gaze on a dark band of clouds in the distance. A storm was coming. In more ways than one. "There is nothing I can do now," she said without taking her gaze from the flickers of lightning dancing across the roiling cloud line. "I've ruined everything."

"Tell him you made it all up. Just take it all back. Make up a counter lie to pass off as the actual truth. Something disgusting like they forced you to work in a brothel while you were still a child or something." Abby walked in a circle, talking faster with every word. "That's it. Then you could tell him you were so ashamed of your past that you made up the story about traveling back in time." She jabbed the air, looking victorious. "Because you heard a story about a witch talking about time travel and thought it sounded interesting."

"Would you believe that line of rubbish you just spouted?"

"He will accept it because he *will want* to believe it. It will solve his insecurities about your sanity." Abby grabbed her by the shoulders. "Don't you see? It's human nature to believe what you find acceptable. We're hard-wired to accept as true those things we want or like. How do you think con artists manipulate people so easily? They tell them what they want to hear and easily convince them it's possible."

"But I promised him the truth, and that is what I gave him."

"Well, take it all back." Abby shoved her away, stomped to the pile of straw, and kicked it. "Or do you enjoy sleeping in a cage like some kind of animal?"

"I don't think there is any doubt you are pregnant." Lyla massaged her throbbing temples, wishing for the aspirin still tucked locked away in a trunk. She felt like proper shit.

"Why would you say that?"

"Because the hormones are already kicking in and making you more impossible than usual." She didn't care that it sounded cruel. It was the truth. She motioned toward the door. "Maybe you should just go before you get yourself so worked up you get sick." That should get her sister moving.

"We can still salvage this if you will just be reasonable and manage it." Abby fixed her with a hard glare. "You know I am right." The furrow in her brow deepened and more tears overflowed. "You said you loved him. If you won't do it for me, then do it for him—and yourself. Please?"

"I will consider it." Humoring her sister was the only way to make her go away. Lyla motioned toward the door again. "Go back to Malcolm. You'll get chilled up here. We are about to lose the daylight to a storm."

"How will you stay warm?"

"I will manage. Besseta's gone to fetch blankets for me."

Abby grabbed her into another hug and squeezed her tight. "I am so afraid for you," she whispered. "Please be careful about what else you say to anyone. For your own safety. Please." She pulled back and tugged at Lyla's heart with a teary-eyed stare. "I can't make it here without you. You have always been the strong one. Always. I need you, dear sister."

Lyla took hold of Abby's hand and walked her to the door. "I will be as safe as I can. Now, go get some rest."

The key immediately rattled as though Geordie had been eavesdropping. Lyla tensed, bracing herself for whatever he might say. Instincts honed from protecting her sister from childhood bullies made her shove Abby behind her back.

The door swung open, revealing Lady Katherine and a very distressed Geordie standing behind her. "Be ye ready to leave?" the unsmiling woman asked Abby.

Abby dipped a hurried curtsy. "Yes, m'lady."

Lady Katherine nodded. "Good. I would like to speak to Lady Lyla alone." She stepped aside and arched a brow, making it obvious that Abby was dismissed.

After an apologetic glance back, Abby hurried out.

Drawing the shawl tighter around her shoulders, Lyla retreated a step as Lady Katherine entered, and the door closed behind her. A cool, damp breeze gusted into the room, promising to bring rain with the next windy surge.

Lady Katherine crossed to the window and grabbed one side of the large wooden square meant as a shutter. "Help me with it, lass. Before the storm gets here. Lest ye wish to be soaked to yer bones."

Lyla went to the other side of the wide bit of wood, grabbed it by the iron rings bolted at the top and bottom, and helped set it in place across the window.

"Geordie! Bring a lantern, ye ken? And be quick about it." The matron dusted off her hands, marched to the door, and yanked it open. "Did ye hear me, man?"

"Aye, m'lady. Got it right here for ye. But the chieftain said—"

"I dinna care what my son said. My ailing daughter will not improve if left in the dark or the damp cold. Now see that a brazier ready with hot coals is brought here immediately."

"But I canna leave my post." Geordie rocked back and forth like an uncertain student caught between dueling schoolmasters.

"Ye will do it now and with haste. I shall wait here 'til ye return." She glared at him, daring him to disobey.

"Aye, m'lady." He bobbed a defeated bow and then took off.

The exchange made Lyla's heartache worse. Lady Katherine reminded her of Grant. "Now, I know where your son gets it."

Lady Katherine's stern scowl softened into a look of kindly thoughtfulness. "Half the battle with men is appearance and tone. Never let them sense uncertainty or fear." One of her fair brows arched higher, and her head tipped to the side. "Now what happened between my son and yerself? Why would he put ye here under lock and key rather than leave ye in yer bed if ye have suddenly taken ill?" She studied her with pursed lips. "Ye dinna look unwell to me."

"It has been brought to my attention that he fears I might take my own life if not put someplace where I cannot harm myself."

"I see." The older woman clasped her hands together as though about to pray. "And why would he fear that?"

"It's my understanding he thinks I am crazy, but I prefer you sort that with him." While she wanted Lady Katherine as an ally, she had to take care. If Grant couldn't accept time travel, how could his mother believe it to be real?

Her mother-in-law circled like a predator coming in for the kill. "Something had to have put that fear in his head." She halted and leaned in close. "Ye didna refuse him in the marriage bed, did ye?" Her tone held the same hushed warning Besseta's had.

Funny how everyone from this time thought refusing a man made him act irrationally. "Absolutely not." When Lady Katherine still seemed skeptical, Lyla realized she had to give the woman a reason, or she would never leave. Grant must have gotten his stubbornness from her, too. "You know I told him I had been married before. And about my miscarriage." She paused for effect. "But I shared more about the pain. Those dark, terrible days. And how I still struggle with the fact that I can't have any more children of my own." She let her gaze drop to the floor and managed a faint shrug. "Then he changed." A twinge of guilt pinched her conscience about the lie, but it couldn't be helped. Her life depended on it.

"Ye poor wee lamb." Lady Katherine rushed forward, caught hold of her hands, and squeezed. "And he thought ye mad because ye said nothing of the extent of yer darkness before?"

"He wanted the truth." Lyla maintained a mournful demeanor to cover the lie of omission. With a bowed head, she offered a deep sigh. "So, I told him." The words were true. Just not the reason he had locked her away.

Lady Katherine sputtered like a boiling teakettle. "'Tis the fault of his past, my poor lamb. Even though he never loved Fawna and Rory's mother, he blamed himself for her death." She reached out and gave Lyla's hand another reassuring squeeze. "We tried to convince him that while some of her sadness came from birthing the bairns, the rest was God's will. I feel certain when ye told him ye lost yer wee one, he feared it would somehow tear ye away from him, too." Her sad smile tugged at Lyla's heart. "He loves ye, lass. Please bear with him. We will get him set straight. I swear it."

Lyla didn't trust herself to speak, so she just gave a demure nod.

With a pensive look, Lady Katherine patted Lyla's hand once more before releasing it. "And ye are absolutely certain that is truly all that could have upset him?"

Inner alarm bells went off, making Lyla adopt a confused look. "I don't understand what you mean?"

"When ye arrived, lass. Yer manner of dress. The strangeness of everything about yerself and yer sister raised many questions." The matron's head tilted the slightest bit but her gaze sharpened. "I couldna help but wonder if that had something to do with what came to pass between you and my son."

The back of Lyla's neck tingled like on fire. Lady Katherine knew something. But what? "I explained our clothes to him. Did he not tell you?"

An unreadable expression settled across her mother-in-law's features. "Oh, aye. That he did. But I didna ken if there was aught ye might wish to add."

"No." Lyla rubbed the back of her neck, wishing her sixth sense would use words instead of tingles. "There's nothing at all to add."

"I see." Lady Katherine accepted the answer with a graceful nod.

Wind and rain slammed against the shutter, rattling the wood held in place by iron hooks through the rings. Lady Katherine turned and scowled at the door. "Where the devil is Geordie with that brazier?" She cast a look around the room, her scowl growing darker than the storm clouds. "And naught so much as a single blanket? I'll be boxing his ears for him!" She reached out and squeezed Lyla's forearm. "Take heart, lass. Ye willna be here long. I swear it." After another reassuring pat, she stormed out the door, shouting, "Geordie! Where be that brazier?"

Lyla lowered herself to the floor and sat beside the lantern. One by one, she set sticks of straw on fire and watched them burn. She had two allies. Besseta and Lady Katherine. She lifted the straw higher, mesmerized by its tiny flame. Allies were good. But would they remain her allies when they found out the truth?

CHAPTER FIFTEEN

EVERY STEP TOOK him higher. Brought him closer. The slow, plodding thud of his boots echoing up the tower's winding staircase matched the heaviness in his heart. He hadn't found the courage to visit her yesterday, but today, as soon as the sun rose, the yearning to see if she had improved hurried him to her. But now as he climbed the steps, an ominous dark dread filled him. What if she was no better? Or worse, what if she hated him for locking her away?

Grant paused halfway up and leaned back against the stone wall. He stared upward. The black iron sconces with their blazing torches filled the space with the unmistakable tang of pitch and smoke. "Please let her be better," he sent up in a desperate whisper. No answer came. Nor a sign from above. With any luck, he would see the prayer realized when he ordered her door opened. After a resolute roll of his shoulders, he resumed the climb.

"My chieftain." Geordie greeted him with the same bumbling awe that had been the lad's curse since becoming a guard. The young man thought so little of himself, that it impaired his duties.

Grant gave him a nod. "Has she had any visitors yet?"

"Only her maid, m'lord." Geordie rocked back and forth like

a nervous bairn, trying to soothe himself. "Already brought her food to break her fast." With a sad jerk of his head, he added, "The lady refused anything yesterday." His head shook faster. "We didna hurt her none bringing her up here, m'lord, but it sorely upset her."

"I am aware." The memory of Lyla's screams and shouts haunted him every waking hour and gave him nightmares when he managed to doze. He shook off their terrible echo. "Unlock the door."

Geordie hurried to obey, then stepped back without opening it.

Grant took hold of the latch, then stopped and braced himself for what might lie on the other side. He eased open the door, on the defensive, ready to react. His first wife had attacked him and her maids many times before ending herself. He stepped inside and halted. The starkness of the room blindsided him like the hit of a war hammer. He had forgotten the tower room's brutal meagerness. God forgive him. He should not have put her here. But he had been so afraid. This had been the safest place that came to mind.

She sat in the windowsill, still as a statue, and stunning as sunrise across a springtime glen. The morning's rays silhouetted her, surrounding her in the same brilliant ring of light as on their wedding day. She didn't turn to greet him. Just stared out the window.

"Lyla?"

"Grant." She repeated his name in a rasping voice that held no emotion or interest. The dullness of her tone cut him like a knife, renting his heart in two.

"How are ye today?" He noticed the brazier and blankets. He had ordered none of those. She might do herself harm with such things. "Lyla? Are ye better today?"

She turned and stared at him with red-rimmed eyes greener than an emerald. He remembered she said when she cried her eyes changed to their greenest green.

"How are ye?" he asked again, not knowing what else to say.

"How do you think I am?" She pulled a small bit of linen from her sleeve and pressed it to the corners of her eyes. "Sorry," she whispered. "I know I sound ratty, but I can't bear this…this…" She sniffed and flipped a hand. "Whatever this is between us. You've cut me to the bone."

"'Tis only for a little while. Until ye are better. I need ye safe, m'love."

She glared at him, her jaw working as though holding back a torrent of emotions. "The truth you so badly needed to hear landed me here. The bloody damn truth I was fool enough to tell you." She swung her feet down from the windowsill and stood. "I know what I told you seems unbelievable. But it is real." Her mouth trembled, but her narrow-eyed stare didn't soften. Instead, she lifted her chin higher. Defiance shouted from her. "Do you really love me? If you did, you would at least try to believe."

He didn't answer. How could she even ask that? Heart sinking to his gut, he realized his prayer had fallen on deaf ears. She still believed herself from the future. He refused to encourage her or entertain what she suggested. "Have ye eaten today?"

Confusion creased her brow. "What difference does that make?"

He took another step closer, fighting the urge to pull her into his arms and never let her go. "Ye must eat to heal. To live."

She turned away and propped her hands on the window ledge, staring outside. "Food won't heal what is wrong here. Only you can do that."

"Tell me how my dear one." He almost dropped to his knees, needing her to be whole.

She didn't turn and face him, just shrugged. "Believe what I tell you. Love me." She cast a glance back at him, a look that seemed quite sane. "I am not *tetched* in the head, addled, or barmy. I am a victim of some strange twist Mother Nature came up with to keep herself from getting bored." With a heavy sigh, she turned and leaned back against the ledge, bowed her head, and rubbed her forehead. "But if you keep me up here in this godforsaken room, I will lose my mind." She lifted her head. "I truly believed I loved you. Looked forward to loving you even more." She flipped a hand, motioning at the room. "But we need to get something straight. I am not your pet to be caged or crated for whenever you see fit to grace with me your presence. I will not, cannot, live like that." Her defiance increased, hardening her scowl. "I will find a way out of here. Mark my words."

He stabbed the air with a trembling finger. "And that is exactly why ye are here, m'love." He strode closer. "Because I command ye to live until God sees fit to take ye. I will not allow ye to die by yer own hand."

She pushed away from the ledge and closed in on him, shaking her own finger like rattling a sword. "When I say I will not live like that, I mean I'll bloody well escape this place and leave you." Resentment flashed in her eyes. "But I suppose I should thank you for the proper lesson in seventeenth-century etiquette. Now I know to keep the truth to myself no matter what." She poked his shoulder. "Why don't you do me the favor of letting me pack and relieve you from having to worry about me ever again? I promise to be gone from Eadar before noon."

"Enough!" He crushed her to his chest, tangled his fingers in the braid at the back of her head, and took her mouth with his. Possessiveness surged through him, pounded harder with every heartbeat. Her taste on his tongue. The scent of her filling his nostrils. Her soft curves molded against him. All were his. Forever. Even the sharp sting of her words belonged to no one else but him. Not ever. He lifted his head. "Ye are mine, woman. Get that through yer head. Ye are mine until the grave claims one or both of us."

"I will not live like a caged animal," she growled, her lips already swollen from the kiss. "I only stay where I am loved."

"I love ye more than ye will ever know," he rasped across her mouth, nuzzling the tempting suppleness of her lips. "And that is why I need ye safe. I refuse to lose ye."

She pushed away, wrenching herself from his grasp. "When you hold something too tightly, it dies. Is that what you want?"

"I want ye to be well," he whispered, aching for her to understand and heal. "I want ye to be the mother to my children, but I canna trust ye when speaking of wild imaginings that canna possibly be true." He shook his head. "Tales of fairies and monsters to entertain bairns is one thing, but what ye say happened to ye—I canna risk ye repeating it to anyone else, lest they think ye a danger or accuse ye of consorting with the devil."

Frustration seemed to leave her, and she perked with interest. "I will never speak of it again or say a word of it to Fawna and Rory. It can be our secret." She tipped an apologetic shrug. "But it is the truth of what happened to me, and how I came to be here. Me and Abby both."

His heart ached worse than before. She believed everything she said. He saw it in her eyes. The madness had well-rooted in her mind. He couldn't risk letting her out of this room. No matter what she promised. Not with her habit of misspeaking. She would soon reveal herself to someone else. He scrubbed a hand across his face and stared down at the floor. "I must go now. Try to rest, ye ken?"

"Grant?"

He turned away, strode to the door, and exited before she caught hold of him. As he slammed the door shut behind him, she hit it with a hard thud.

"Grant!"

"Lock it," he ordered. He charged down the steps, covering his ears to shut out her screaming shouts of his name over and over. Even outside he still heard her although common sense told him it wasn't possible. If she screamed out the window, it would be as faint as a bird in a far-off tree. Her loud, furious yelling of his name between curse words had sunk their claws into his mind, forbidding him to hear anything else. He had experienced this before. On the battlefield. Unable to escape the sound of his dying men.

He walked faster, putting as much distance between himself and the tower as he could. God Almighty, he longed to release her, welcome her back into his arms, return to the way they were before. But he dare not. Not while she believed herself and her sister to possess the ability to travel through the centuries. He huffed out a snort. Of all the ways he had seen madness tear into a soul, he had never heard such as this.

His pace slowed as he reached the front of the skirting wall protecting Eadar Keep. A wise Reddoch ancestor had constructed the tower at the very back of the fortification. The only way to enter it was from outside the wall. No doorway existed, leading directly into the keep. Thus protecting those of Eadar even more from prisoners housed in the tower.

"Da!"

Fawna's call both lifted his spirits and set him on edge. Ever since Lyla's move to the tower, the bairns had nattered him endlessly to let them visit her. He halted and turned, smiling at his two wee ones barreling his way.

"Can we visit Lyla today?" she called out while still running toward him.

"Not today," he said, bracing himself for what he knew came next.

"But why not, Da?" Fawna peered up at him, using every weapon in her arsenal to get what she wanted. Big eyes. A pitiful tremor in her voice. And to top it all, a quivering bottom lip that threatened to overpower him.

Grant stared down at her, wishing he knew the answer to all the *why*'s troubling him. He daren't share the truth of Lyla's ailment. "She is feeling poorly and needs her rest."

"But we can help get her better," Rory argued. His small fingers stained purple and blue, he showed the half-full basket of berries. "She likes these. We picked them just for her."

"And these, too." Fawna waved a bundle of pale yellow flow-ers she clutched so tightly they already drooped. "We havena seen her since ye wed. Did getting married make her sick?"

He wasn't up to dueling with his two beloved children. "Where is Nanny Greer? Why is she not watching ye rather than letting ye roam all over in search of flowers and berries?" He realized every living soul at Eadar helped guard his bairns, but that didn't excuse the maid assigned to keep up with them. They must be kept safe. "Did ye tell her ye were going to pick flowers and berries? Did she say ye may do so?"

Fawna eyed her brother. He eyed her back. Both displayed the same level of guilt and neither spoke.

"Where did ye tell her ye would be so she would neither worry nor come and fetch ye?" The wily pair outfoxed the poor woman repeatedly. While proud of their quick thinking and ability to pull off a well-laid plot, he feared their adventurous natures would someday bring them harm. "Fawna? I would appreciate an answer from ye. Now."

"We told her we would be wif Cook since today is baking day." She poked her bottom lip out even farther. "Why do ye always make me answer? 'Twas Rory's idea." She hitched a tiny shrug. "Leastways this time it was."

"Was it now?" Grant shifted his focus to his son, who was usually the follower rather than the leader. A trait he found somewhat disturbing since Rory would be the next chief of Clan Reddoch someday.

Rory stood taller and jutted out his chin. "I like Lyla, and so does Fawna. We need to see her. We willna be loud or worrisome and make her tired."

"Perhaps tomorrow," Grant said, knowing it untrue.

"Ye said that yesterday." Fawna flopped the wilted flowers into the berry basket and glared up at him. "Father Rubric says 'tis a sin to lie, Da."

"Father Rubric also says ye are to honor yer father, does he not?" Grant turned in a half-circle, scanning the grounds just outside the gate, searching for reinforcements. An uneasy mix of relief and concern filled him at the sight of his mother storming their way. The woman looked to have a purpose in mind, and he had a fair idea of what. He pointed at her. "There is yer grand-mam. Go and tell her what ye did to poor Nanny Greer yet again."

The children stood their ground.

"What about Lyla's flowers and berries?" Fawna asked.

He took the basket and tucked it under his arm. "I will see that she gets them and knows they are from the both of ye. With any hope, yer fine gift here will make her better."

They still didn't move, just stared up at him, more sullen than if he had told them no more sweets for an eternity.

"Why such unhappy faces?" Lady Katherine asked as she joined them.

"Da willna let us see Lyla," Rory said.

"We even promised to be quiet, so's not to tire her too much," Fawna added.

Grant aimed a steely-eyed glare at his mother, willing her to remain neutral in the battle.

She did not. "I shall take ye myself." She graced her grand-children with a loving smile, turned them both toward the keep, and gave their behinds a gentle swat. "After I speak with yer Da, I shall take ye for a short visit, but ye must promise to be quiet and good, ye ken?"

Both children reeled about and dove into her skirts, hugging her so tight it stirred Grant's jealousy.

"On wi' ye now," she gently urged, peeling them away and setting them on their path.

They scampered off, pausing long enough to shoot knowing smirks back at him, just as he expected they would.

"Turning my own bairns against me." He shoved the berry basket into her hands. "Here. They will ask to give this to her."

"I would nay have to turn them against ye if ye would use the good sense the Almighty gave ye." She moved closer, fisting a hand as though ready to strike him. "Just because the dear woman suffered the greatest loss a mother can bear, doesna mean she will fall to it as Merideth did." She paused, crossed herself, and muttered, "God rest her soul."

He ignored the mention of his first wife, but it told him all he needed to hear. "Ye went up there. Defied me and went up there." If not for the fact that he loved and respected his mother, he would order her locked in her rooms for such infuriating behavior. He clenched his teeth and turned away to keep from cursing at her.

"I did it for ye," she said softly. "I see how ye love her."

"It is because of that love that I protect her." He stared down at his boots, soaked with the heavy dew and mud from yesterday's storm. The weight of his mother's hand on his shoulder made him flinch and yank away. "I am not a child anymore, Mother. I am chieftain, and ye will do as I bid or be sent away. Is that understood?"

"Then ye might as well order my things packed now, because I willna stand by and watch my precious child make himself miserable for no reason." She pinched the tender spot underneath his arm.

He jerked away from the punishing sting he had often endured as a youth. "Dammit, Mother! I am not yer bairn anymore."

"Ye will always be my bairn," she snapped in a tone that sounded more like a growl. "No matter how old ye grow to be. Even when they put ye in yer grave. Ye will always be my precious bairn." She closed in on him, shaking a finger. "Yer Lyla is as sane as I am. End this foolishness and release her. Ye can know happiness with this woman, and I would see it so."

"If my Lyla is so verra sane, then why does she claim to have been born in the year 1989?"

"What?" She backed up a step, clutching the berry basket to her chest.

A sense of hollow victory filled him. Now she understood why he feared his precious Lyla so addled she might harm herself. "Aye, Mother. The year 1989. Far off into the future. She also said she and her sister found themselves tossed back to our time while watching stars on the hillside above Edinburgh. Tossed back from the year 2019."

Lady Katherine covered her mouth with one hand, paling as though about to be ill. Her nostrils flared as she pulled in several shuddering breaths. With a shake of her head, her hand fell away. "Is that all she told ye?"

"Is that not enough?" It was now his turn to shake a finger. "I accepted that she divorced her first husband because he never cared nor wanted the bairn she lost. I even told her ye would be a kindred spirit to her since ye lost two wee ones yerself. But I canna bear her imaginings of coming from the future." He shook his head, the knot in his chest making it hard to speak. "How could I believe such?"

"I am so sorry, my son," she whispered. "I did not know."

"Perhaps next time ye will listen to me when I bid ye to either do or not do something, aye?" He stared at her, concerned at her sudden trembling. "Mother? Are ye unwell?"

She jumped as though startled. "No, son. Just concerned. For the both of ye."

"As am I."

With a jerking nod, she backed up a step and appeared to take another deep breath. "I must keep my word to the bairns, but I swear I willna let them tarry long when they visit her." She stared at the ground, frowning. "And I will pray for guidance."

He dismissed her with a dip of his chin, not trusting himself to speak. At least now she understood and would cease her infernal meddling. His frustration with her cooled somewhat as he watched her walk away. Everything she did, she did out of love. He understood that, but God grant him patience when she didn't agree with his decisions.

"The rumors of Cromwell heading to Edinburgh are no longer rumors," Malcolm said.

Grant spun about, still amazed how a man so large could move with such stealth without even trying. "He is there?"

Malcolm shook his head. "Not yet. But the runner from the

Lowlands says he has entered Scotland with his New Model Army, as he calls it, of about sixteen thousand."

"I have heard it called God's Army. Since he only accepts those who share his faith." Grant stared up at the keep, then his gaze shifted to the tower. "We must ride out and lend our support to the cause. Stand against Cromwell." He needed this distraction to occupy his mind.

"It will take some days for the call to reach all in the clan." Malcolm scowled up at the sky, still overcast after yesterday's storms. "While it be a proper time of year for warring, this is a woeful time for the farmers to leave their land, what with crops just put in and the coming of the late lambs and calves."

"Be ye a war chief of fighting men or farmers?" Grant knew Malcolm spoke the truth, but he would be damned if he held Clan Reddoch back for the farmers' sake. To do so smacked of cowardice.

"I be loyal to my clan and also in reminding my chieftain that pride puts nothing in a bairn's belly during a long cold winter." Malcolm locked eyes with him. "I mean no disrespect, but we must choose our battles wisely. Starvation kills more cruelly than a blade. Let Cromwell come to us. I have my doubts he can make it past Stirling."

Even though Malcolm's reasoning seemed sound, Grant itched to join the fray for so many reasons. To avenge his uncle. Defend his country. But most importantly, this battle meant escaping the heartbreak of his new wife's madness for a little while. Selfish as it sounded, warring with the English was the diversion he needed more than anything right now. "Are ye refusing yer chief's wishes to gather our forces?"

Malcolm blew out a heavy sigh and bowed his head. "Nay, my chief. Yer wishes will be done." Disappointment clouded his dark eyes. "But as yer friend, I will say, ye are a damned fool for doing this."

"Ye would rather be a coward?"

"I would rather we guard Eadar and our land. If the fight

comes to us, then so be it." He glared southward. "Do ye think the Lowland clans would rush to our aid and condemn their women and children to a slow death?"

Guilt about playing to his own selfish needs filled Grant, making his gut clench. "It is my hope they would render us aid without hesitation." He turned away, gritting his teeth with his refusal to back down. He could not. Pride was all he had left. The order had been given. To take it back showed weakness.

"Is that all, then?"

He turned to stare down Malcolm's scowl. "Aye, that is all. Keep me apprised of yer progress."

After a curt nod, Malcolm strode away. Grant never doubted his friend would do as ordered, but that didn't mean he had to agree or be pleased with his chieftain's decision. The set of his shoulders and fisted hands as he marched toward the keep showed his disapproval.

Grant shifted his attention back to the tower. Everything in him ached to return to her, pull her into his arms, and beg her to be of sound mind once again. But he feared facing her again, knowing she wouldn't understand why he had done what had to be done. He prayed it hadn't made her worse. That was his reason for ordering no brazier, no lanterns, and no blankets. Crafty as she was, she could use those things to harm herself. He made a mental note to order them removed once he returned to the keep. With summer's warm days, the tower would be bearable enough. He prayed by winter she would be well. If not, he would order her bound in her chambers.

He turned away from the keep, flinching his eyes shut at that horrible possibility. How could he treat her like a mongrel, and yet, to save her life, how could he not?

CHAPTER SIXTEEN

A HEAVY SIGH escaped her. She should have remained calm and reasoned with him better. But his inability to accept what she told him hurt her heart. Made her wonder if he really loved her as much as she loved him. Lyla wiped her eyes and massaged her forehead. No more crying. All crying did was make her pounding headache worse.

The bruised stems of the wilted flowers made her smile. She pinched them off and floated the delicate yellow blossoms in her cup of water. The precious bouquet Fawna had loved to death meant more to her than a dozen long-stemmed roses.

She sat cross-legged on the blanket beside her improvised food tray bucket table. They had brought a chamber pot up along with the brazier, enabling her to leave the makeshift table intact. The slow-burning coals in the iron pan that squatted on all fours like a small sea turtle knocked the dampness from the room at night and when it rained. The rest of the time, she kept the window uncovered more to have contact with the outside world than anything else. She enjoyed the fresh air, too, but the warm breezes made her long to be outside playing with the children.

A subtle movement in the berry basket caught her eye. A tiny ladybird. An American she'd met in Edinburgh had called them ladybugs, but ladybird was so much nicer. She extended her finger and waited for the inquisitive beetle to climb aboard. "You'll starve to death here," she warned as she carried the red and black bug to the window. "I'd stay to the cracks between the blocks if I were you unless you want to end up as lunch for a passing bird." It crawled off her finger and disappeared over the edge.

"A busy day of visitors," she mused aloud while studying the overcast sky. Rain again today, but perhaps not too much. It looked like the sun was trying to break through the clouds here and there. She wished the children could have stayed longer. She missed them so. Their worried little faces made her want to cry. For Grant's sake, she had faked a cough and acted tired to convince Fawna and Rory their father knew what he was doing. It wouldn't be fair to drag them into this mess. They were much too young to understand. Lady Katherine had ushered them out after just a few minutes.

Keys rattling in the lock drew her attention away from the small bit of world outside the window. Her heartbeat increased to a fast pounding. She hoped Grant had returned, but also feared facing him. Breath held, she clenched her hands as the door slowly opened. She blew out a disappointed huff when Abby marched inside, then whirled about, poised for a rant.

Geordie cut her off with a surrendering flip of a hand as he backed out and pulled the door closed behind him. "I know. Long as ye like, m'lady. Long as ye like."

As soon as it shut with a hard thud, Abby whirled about, panic filling her face. "Grant plans on taking every able-bodied Reddoch to fight Cromwell." Wringing her hands, she rushed closer. "We must stop him. If they go there, who knows how many will die or be taken prisoner? We could lose them, Lyla. Both of them."

Her sister had always been far better at remembering historical dates and events. Lyla tried to recall anything she could about Oliver Cromwell other than the fact that after the man died of natural causes in 1658, they dug him back up in 1661, tried him, hung him, then cut off his head and placed it on a metal spike and raised it above Westminster Hall. It was so macabre to her that they went to the trouble of executing a dead man. She found those dates easy to remember. "Which battle is it they're headed for? How badly were the Scots beaten? Can you recall?"

"Dunbar, I think," Abby cried. "I'm not sure. All I can remember is that it's a night attack in September, the Scots are heavily defeated, and those who survive abandon Edinburgh and run to Stirling. Some are taken prisoner and treated so harshly that they die on the way to the prison in England. It's horrid, Lyla. The things I read about the battle and its aftermath are horrid."

Her sister's panic spread and wrapped icy fingers around Lyla, making it hard to breathe. She couldn't lose Grant. Not like this. They had to repair this rift between them and grow old together. "What's keeping Cromwell from coming here?"

"As I remember, it takes the English a year to cut off Stirling's supplies with the Battle of Inverkeithing next July." Abby pressed a fist to her mouth, muffling uncontrollable sobs.

Lyla dropped to the blanket, hugging herself as she huddled on the floor. "Eadar is only safe for a year? Then what?"

"Even after Scotland loses and is absorbed into the Commonwealth, there will be scads of infighting while Cromwell rules as Lord Protector. Charles II won't be crowned King of England until April 1661 even though the Scots crowned him in 1649." Abby dropped to the floor beside her. "I used to love history," she whimpered. "But now that I'm living it, I hate it."

"I agree," Lyla said. History books had always seemed so dry. Boring. Lists of dates, numbers, and a few names to be memorized long enough to score a passing grade on a meaningless exam. But knowing the people about to be maimed or killed, loving them, waiting for a catastrophe you knew would happen, made history a terrible beast with relentless, gnashing teeth. "Is there nothing we can do? You're the smart one. The one with the bloody degree. Think of something."

Abby gave her a bleak look of despair.

Lyla pushed herself up from the floor and returned to the window. The cold, rough surface of the stones beneath her hands mocked her, reminding her of reality's ability to change in the blink of an eye. There had to be something they could do to protect Grant, his children, Malcolm, and everyone they loved. She wondered if whatever they did would ripple through time and change something in the future? Make it better? Or make it worse? She didn't care. All she cared about was now. Her hands closed into fists, scraping her knuckles on the crude stone ledge. "We have to do something. Who can we convince that might change Grant's mind? We must have an ally here that would listen to us."

"Malcolm knows in his heart they should stay here. Protect Eadar with whoever volunteers to fight rather than go to Edinburgh." Abby clutched her hands to her chest. "But I fear if we told him all we know, he would be too shocked to help." She bowed her head, rocking back and forth on her knees. "He would think Grant was right about you and that it had spread to me."

"I doubt Besseta could help." Lyla paced around the room, still hugging herself. Instinct told her Besseta would believe, but the maid wouldn't be able to get anyone to believe her. They would merely think she had gone as daft as her mistress.

"Eufamie won't believe us." Abby shook her head. "And it would be dangerous to even try to convince her. I overheard her say her brother had gone to apprentice with the Witchfinder General in East Anglia."

"Eufamie must remain ignorant then." Lyla mentally crossed the maid off the much too shortlist. The last thing they needed was an accusation of witchcraft. Thankfully, Grant had gone with insanity instead of works of the devil. Both her heart and her hopes sank to the pit of her stomach and gurgled in despair. "That leaves us no one to convince Grant that no matter what, he must stay here and shore up Eadar for what lays ahead."

"There has to be something. Someone." Abby shuddered out a sniffling sob and buried her face in her hands. "I can't bear this. I've adapted to this bloody place and now it's going to kill off everyone I've come to love."

Lyla took hold of Abby's wrists, pulled her hands down from her face, and forced her sister to look at her. "Stop it. Panic helps nothing."

"Why shouldn't I?" Abby crumpled with another onslaught of tears. "It's lost. All of it."

Barely restraining the urge to shake her sister, Lyla let her go, rose to her feet, and returned to the window. "I need to talk to Grant. One way or another, I will convince him. Somehow." She latched hold of the rusty wire between the bars. "Maybe I can convince him that I just have visions and sometimes get them confused with what has already happened and what is about to happen." She gripped the wires tighter. "Of course, then I'll have to take back all the things I said about us coming from the future. I'm not sure he'll believe anything I say now."

Abby sniffed, pulled a square of linen out of her sleeve, and dabbed her nose. "But you think you can make it work?"

"I have to. What other choice have we?"

Noise on the other side of the door interrupted them.

With a hurried wiping of her face, Abby jumped up from the floor and joined Lyla at the window. "If I can't speak to Grant and get him up here, I'll get Malcolm to do it," she whispered as the door creaked open.

Lyla didn't answer. She backed up to the window ledge and gripped it with both hands. Lady Katherine had returned and didn't look to be in the best of moods. Something bad had either happened or was about to happen.

"I should go," Abby said and started toward the door.

Lady Katherine lifted a hand and hurried forward. "No. Please. I would speak to the both of ye." She cast a warning frown back at Geordie. "No interruptions, ye ken?"

"Aye, m'lady." Geordie backed out and closed the door, but

no key rattled in the lock.

Lyla gripped the stone of the ledge so hard it dug into her hands. She didn't care. Instinct told her this was no casual visit. The back of her neck tingled like set on fire.

Abby backed up beside her, wringing the small square of linen between her hands.

Lady Katherine moved closer, her light gray eyes fraught with unreadable shadows. Shoulders squared. Chin lifted. Regal strength and courage emanated from her. The woman looked ready to demand their execution.

Lyla straightened her spine and pushed away from the ledge. She refused to cower. "Lady Katherine?"

"I believe ye," the matron whispered, her unblinking stare pinning Lyla in place. "I believe everything ye told my son."

Uncertain as to what Grant had repeated, Lyla guarded her words. "What exactly did Grant tell you?"

The weary woman's disturbing stare shifted off to somewhere in the distance. "He said ye come from another time. From the future." She slipped a hand into the folds of her skirt and withdrew something shiny from a hidden pocket. "I believe ye," she repeated and held it out.

Lyla took hold of the large golden locket, then frowned at its weightiness. It wasn't a locket at all, but a fine pocket watch. "It's lovely," she said, amazed such a thing existed in 1650. She turned it over in her hand, admiring the workmanship. "I don't understand."

"Open it." Lady Katherine tipped a nod toward the watch, her tone almost reverent.

With a press of the ornate button at the top, the watch's lid popped open, and soft, tinny music filled the room. The white dial had yellowed, but the stark black numerals, the watchmaker, and the words *musical movement 1965* were still quite legible. Behind the delicate golden frame inside the lid was a black-and-white photograph of a smiling young woman in aviator sunglasses. She wore a flowered midriff shirt with matching shorts and leaned against a car. A chill raced across Lyla. She snapped the watch shut, silencing its song. "Where did you get this?"

"From the only woman my father ever ordered executed by crushing beneath the stones."

Lyla hurried to hand it back, fearing it a deadly omen. "So, what are you telling me, Lady Katherine? That I should have the same fate?"

The lady shook her head. Strands of gray in her blonde braid caught the sunlight and glinted like silver. "No, my child. Never." With a sad smile, she stared down at the watch, rubbing it like a wishing stone. "Rebecca was a bright light who came into my life when I was barely a woman grown and dreading the prospect of who my father would choose as my husband." She moved to the window, looking off into the distance at something only she could see. "I found her walking along the riverbank. Lost. Confused. Frightened." She shook her head. "Yet so kind and filled with wondrous stories of things I could not even imagine." Her smile disappeared, and she suddenly looked ready to weep. "Father ordered her executed because of me. Said she bewitched me. Filled my head with thoughts I should not entertain. Unholy things." She tucked the watch back into her pocket. "As they slowly piled stone upon stone on the board on top of her, she shouted she loved me and would see me on the other side." A tear trailed down her cheek. She swiped it aside as though ashamed.

"I am so sorry." Lyla clutched her fists to her churning middle. Terrified. Saddened. Ready to vomit. She and Abby could easily have met the same end had someone other than Grant and Malcolm found them. "You know she wasn't a witch or a demon—right?"

Lady Katherine faced her. "I know she was an amazing woman who traveled through time and met a terrible end." The faintest of smiles tugged at her mouth. "She even showed me what she called her air o' plane. It was how she got here." Her jaw tightened, and her brow furrowed with resentment. "My father had it mangled into smaller pieces and thrown into the sea." After clearing her throat, she stood taller. "Are there air o' planes in yer time as well?"

"Yes." Lyla didn't correct Lady Katherine's pronunciation. It didn't matter. Grant's mother had loved Rebecca and lost her in a horrendous way. "You should know that Grant must not take an army to Edinburgh." Since their truth was out, time to put it to use. It might be futile, but she had to try. "He should stay here and prepare Eadar. Cromwell decimates the Scots in the south. Many die." She willed the woman to listen and heed the warning. "We studied the battle in our history books. The Scots do not overcome Cromwell." With a shrug, she added, "The man dies at home in 1658, and they crown Charles II King of England in 1661. The Stuarts are restored. Such loss of life is unnecessary for Clan Reddoch. They should stay here and prepare for all that is yet to come. Protect their home."

"My son plans to leave as soon as Malcolm gathers enough men."

"Malcolm needs to drag his feet," Lyla told Abby. "Tell him."

"How can I tell him without telling him about us?" Abby twisted her handkerchief. "He will think me as daft as you."

"We can tell him together," Lady Katherine said. Then her gaze hardened as it shifted to Lyla. "But it will be up to ye to convince Grant to see sense and stop worrying about his pride."

"One goal at a time," Lyla said, tensing at the prospect. "Win Malcolm first. Then we conquer my hardheaded, unbelieving husband."

⇥⟫⟪⇤

"ABBY SAID MALCOLM already advised Grant not to take the men to Edinburgh, but Grant ignored him." Lyla sipped the wine Lady Katherine had ordered brought up, hoping the alcohol would fuel her dubious level of creativity in coming up with a proper plan.

"Are we certain bringing Malcolm into our little group is wise? Even though he didn't agree, he bowed to Grant's will and gathered the troops."

"That is because, first and foremost, Malcolm is loyal to his chieftain. The man has trailed after Grant since they were both weans pretending sticks were swords. But he has a wife now and a bairn on the way. That should aid us in convincing him to help us." Lady Katherine refilled both their glasses while wrinkling her nose at the meager offerings of cheese and bread on the platter. "Cook spared ye verra little. Does she mean to starve ye?"

Lyla ignored her mother-in-law's concerns about her diet. "I hope Abby can convince him to come up here. She can be a bit dodgy at times. Especially now with her emotions running away with her."

"If she fails, I shall fetch him myself." The matron peered out the window, then cut her gaze back at Lyla. "The grace with which ye have borne all this amazes me, child."

"What choice did I have?" Lyla paced back and forth across the room, tapping her fingers on her glass, keeping time with every step. "I couldn't bury my head in that straw and hope things would change."

"Many would have."

"I am not many." With a half-hearted shrug, she managed a faint smile. "And I don't know if that's good or bad."

Lady Katherine lifted her glass as if toasting. "I would say good."

"All I know for certain is I have to save Grant." Even though she hated her imprisonment, she had finally come to terms with it and understood Grant had done it because of his past. But this was no way to live, and it had to change.

Noise outside the door made them both turn. Lyla eased a step closer, straining to overhear. Her spirits lifted. She made out Malcolm's voice. Something about Geordie failing in his duties. Poor Geordie. She hated Abby had used the man as bait to get Malcolm to show. Somehow, they would smooth things out for the bumbling chap later.

Keys rattled, the door opened, and Malcolm stepped inside. As soon as he spotted Lady Katherine, he turned back and gave Abby a stern look.

"You will thank me later," she said, stepping up to his side and looping her arm through his.

"I doubt that, wife." He resettled his feet, offered Lady Katherine a proper bow, then managed a sympathetic tip of his head toward Lyla.

"We need you to drag your feet in gathering Eadar's forces." Lyla stepped forward, determined to bring Malcolm to their side. She hadn't asked to be the spokesperson. She had literally drawn the short straw. "Or if you gather them, somehow keep them here to protect Reddoch land and concentrate on preparing for what lies ahead."

Malcolm stared at her, his eyes flexing to narrow slits. "Such is not my place to d-decide."

"Cromwell wins," she said. "Many suffer and die. It would be in the clan's best interest to make a stand here. Not in the south."

He frowned at her for a long moment, then shifted his attention back to Abby. "Yer sister is not well, ye ken? We shouldna be here."

She didn't answer. Instead, she aimed a quick nod at Lyla.

"Abby and I know what happens because we read about it in history books." She sidled closer to Lady Katherine. It would probably take the timepiece to convince him. "We are from the future, Malcolm. From the year 2019."

He slowly shook his head, then turned Abby toward the door. "We m-must go."

Abby pulled away, hurried to the door, and backed up against it. "No. You need to listen. What she says is true. Lyla and I were born in 1989. She's the eldest by a few minutes. We're not sure how it happened. What sent us here. One minute we were enjoying the stars over Edinburgh in 2019 and the next, it's morning in 1650."

He strode to Lady Katherine and went down on one knee. "Dinna p-pay her any m-mind. I b-beg ye. Our bairn is on the way. She is overtired."

"She is telling the truth." With a sympathetic smile, Lady Katherine leaned forward and rested her hand on his shoulder. "I understand it is a lot to comprehend. But it is the truth. I believe her without question."

"It c-canna be," he whispered. "I b-beg ye, dinna think her a witch."

Lyla folded her arms. "Show him the pocket watch."

"Cover the window first," Lady Katherine ordered. "I dinna wish him to cast it out."

Pointing for her sister to stay at the door, Lyla shook her head. "Guard the door. I can manage it." As she pushed the wide panel of wood in place and settled the iron hooks into the rings, she sent up a quick prayer. The watch needed to work. If not, she had no clue how they would convince Malcolm to believe them. She took a stance in front of the brazier, in case he decided to throw it into the fire.

Lady Katherine pulled the timepiece from her pocket and opened the lid. The eerie music filled the room. "Another woman from the future gave this to me. I met her many years ago. Heed me, Malcolm, when I say that traveling back across the years is verra possible."

Malcolm rose and backed away, shaking his head as he refused to take the object.

Lady Katherine advanced on him, still holding the golden timepiece open. "Look inside. At the woman. Her clothing. The thing she stands beside. Have I ever lied to ye? Ever?"

"Nay, m'lady," he whispered, so awestruck he forgot to stutter.

"The only proof we can offer is the tags on our clothing or the label on the aspirin bottle," Lyla said. "And Grant has the key to wherever those are locked away." She moved to her mother-in-law's side. "We don't understand how it happened. We are as dumbfounded about all this as you are." She feared the man was about to collapse. Beads of sweat covered his dangerously red face, and he kept swallowing hard as if fighting to breathe or not vomit. "Would you like a cup of water?"

He bounced a trembling nod.

She hurried to get him a cup. As she placed it between his shaking hands, she adopted as soothing a tone as she could manage. "This is why Grant decided I am unwell. He is afraid I am unhinged." At Malcolm's confused frown, she tried again. "Not sane. He thinks the only reason I would say such things is because I am mad, and he fears I will take my life like his first wife did."

Malcolm nodded again, this time seeming more controlled.

"But since we come from the future, we can warn the clan." She searched for the words to convince him. "We're not trying to take over or have you take control away from Grant." She laced her fingers together and clasped her hands in a tight knot. "We're trying to save the people we love." When he still didn't answer she continued, "Grant is a good chieftain, but his mind is clouded by pride and by what I told him about traveling through time. You are right about taking a stand here where we are strongest. We're looking for a way to convince him to change his mind and do just that."

With a slow, cautious move, he eased the timepiece out of Lady Katherine's hand and studied it. His brows knotted as he brought it closer to his face and squinted at the photograph. "How can all this be?"

Abby hurried to him, hugging his arm. "We don't understand it either. We're simply trying to survive it."

He gently closed the golden lid and handed it back. "But Cromwell is not defeated in the battles to come?"

Lyla shook her head, giving him a chance to absorb all they had said.

He wrapped an arm around Abby and kissed the top of her head. "However it happened, I am glad ye are here," he whispered.

"Me, too." She smiled up at him. "But I am not glad about the danger. Please help us."

He scratched his jaw, scrubbing his fingertips through his beard. He shifted his gaze first to Lady Katherine, then Lyla. "I havena gathered any men. Not yet. But Grant will demand a reason why when next I see him. Once an order is given, the man never backs down."

"There is a first time for everything." Lyla removed the wood from the window. Her eyes burned from the smoke coming from the brazier. The cool breeze on her face strengthened her, cleared her head. Malcolm believed after seeing the watch. Wouldn't Grant do the same? "Do you think it would do any good to bring him to the three of us like we did you? Show him the pocket watch so he'll believe like you now do?"

"That might convince him ye be of sound mind, but that willna make him change his order. Too many have heard of his plans to join the fight in the south." Malcolm glanced at Lady Katherine, then frowned back at Lyla. "The man is prideful and stubborn. Both will be his downfall."

At least with the watch, there was hope of Grant accepting the truth. Now the problem was getting him to listen to their warning. "If he had an excuse not to go…" Lyla rested her hands on the window ledge, struggling to think of a proper snare. Preferably one that would get her out of this tower. Enough was enough. "What if I escaped and disappeared for a while? Do you think he would delay his plans until he found me?"

"And where would you go?" Abby asked. "You don't know your way around Scotland. Especially the wilderness of the Highlands."

Very true. She also knew nothing about surviving in the rough. "What would stop him from going to Edinburgh?" She looked from Malcolm to Lady Katherine and then back again. "I may be married to him, but you two know him better than I do."

Lady Katherine turned to Malcolm. "Well? Answer the woman. She is the lady of the keep."

"How should I know?" Malcolm stared down at the floor, stroking his beard. "If Eadar were under attack, we would stay and defend it. No one would judge him for countering his order because of that."

"That's it then." Lyla rubbed her hands together, the possibility making her heart beat faster. "Since we can't very well fake an actual attack, what would happen if we warned Grant about a pending attack? If someone from the south showed up and said Cromwell had broken through their defenses, he would believe them, wouldn't he?" Problem is, that didn't get her out of this tower. "Of course, the more people we involve in this, the more dangerous it becomes."

"The fewer who know the truth about the two of ye, the better," Lady Katherine advised. "Remember what happened to Rebecca?"

She would never forget what happened to Rebecca. "What then? What is something we could do that wouldn't involve anyone outside this room and still be effective?"

"A death," Lady Katherine said with a thoughtful look. "Or at least, a looming death."

"Whose?" Killing someone might be a bit extreme. Lyla edged back a step, eyeing Grant's mother with renewed leeriness.

The wily matron preened with a knowing smirk, resembling Fawna and Rory when they plotted mischief. "He put ye here to protect ye from yerself, aye?"

"Right." Lyla hoped whatever the woman had in mind wouldn't be painful. "And?"

"And how remorseful would he feel if an ague sent ye so close to death's door ye could feel the chill of the grave?" Her smile broadened even more. "And while ye lay in yer bed waiting to die, we three could speak with him. Offer him guidance. After all, it would only be natural for ye to confess to yer sister what ye told yer husband when ye feared yerself about to die." She wagged a finger at Malcolm. "And distraught as she was about losing her only sister, she would confess the truth of it to her husband, who came to me for advice since his own dear mother departed years ago. I could show him my proof, and then he could be warned."

"He wouldna leave with ye on yer deathbed," Malcolm said, looking both impressed and relieved.

"And once we've stalled him long enough," Abby added, "maybe the delay will give him the room he needs to be comfortable changing his mind."

Lyla hated lying to him. She had done it before, but to spare him emotional stress, not cause it. If it kept him alive, it was worth him being overwrought for a little while. At least, she hoped so. What other choice did she have? She agreed with a slow nod. "Shall we begin today?"

CHAPTER SEVENTEEN

Grant vaulted up the steps, taking them two at a time. How could she fall ill so quickly? She had seemed well enough this morning. Angry enough to kill him, but healthy.

"Open that door!" he bellowed up the winding stairwell. The speed of his long-legged stride increased as he hit the landing. He charged into the tower room and came to an abrupt halt, unable to breathe, not because of the run but because of the sight that met him.

Lyla lay in the straw, twitching and thrashing beneath a thin blanket. Long damp curls clung to her face and throat. Her cheeks glowed an alarming scarlet. His beloved wife surely burned with fever. Her sister and maid knelt at her side, trying in vain to calm her. His mother stood near, head bowed, eyes closed, and lips moving in silent prayer.

"Malcolm said—" Words left him as his dear one cried out and batted wildly at something only she could see.

Mother rushed to his side. "'Tis the dark fever, son." Her voice broke, cutting off her ability to speak. Eyes squeezed shut, she pressed a crumpled linen to her mouth and turned aside.

"The dark fever? What is that?" He tried to move closer, but she caught hold of his arm and held him back.

"It blinds those it sets on fire," she whispered. "She canna see. Knows nothing but burning darkness."

He yanked free of her hold and dropped to his knees beside his precious Lyla.

Besseta skittered to the side, knocked off balance as he pushed his way closer.

"I will tend to my wife," he said.

The maid dipped an obedient nod, picked up the basin of water, and rose. "I shall fetch fresh water with stronger herbs."

"Lyla, m'love. Can ye hear me?" He caught one of her clammy hands and held it to his cheek. "I am here, my own. I willna leave yer side, ye ken?"

She rolled back and forth, tossing her head. Eyes wild and filled with fear, she worked her mouth like trying to speak. Her poor lips were cracked and dry as though thirst bedeviled her.

"A cup for her." Her suffering tormented him. "She must have water now!"

"Not yet," Abby advised. "It will only choke her. The dark fever sometimes makes swallowing difficult." She caught Lyla's other hand and leaned over her. "Lyla, you must fight. Do not give up."

Lyla moaned and bucked harder.

"She's going to beat herself to death on this floor. We can't keep enough straw under her." Abby gave him a worried scowl. "Can we at least move her to a bed so her last hours on this earth won't be so painful?"

"Last hours?"

"Dark fever is almost always fatal."

"Like Hell it is." He scooped her up into his arms and stood. "She will fight. My Lyla will live." He clutched her to his chest and headed for the door. "Send for a healer. I dinna care if ye have to get one all the way from Edinburgh."

She sagged against him, so limp her head rolled against his shoulder.

"Ye will live, m'love," he promised in a rasping whisper. He edged sideways down the narrow, winding steps to keep his footing secure. "I will consider nothing less."

When he reached ground level, he shouldered open the door and charged around the skirting wall to the main gate. "Clear a path and open the doors," he shouted while striding across the courtyard. Onlookers hurried to comply. All conversation ceased. Even the animals quieted. An air of doom settled over Eadar. Grant ignored it. He had no time for such. Nay, the place would soon be filled with Lyla's laughter. He would see to it.

As he entered the keep, Mrs. Fintrie, tall and long-legged for a woman, trotted along beside him, easily keeping pace. "Besseta told me everything. Cook's preparing a broth and boiling extra water. I've sent the maids to ready yer lady wife's chambers."

Grant halted. "Her chambers?"

"Aye, m'lord." The housekeeper gave him an encouraging nod, as though trying to make him agree. "When ye moved her to the tower, all her things were returned to the chambers she shared with her sister when they first arrived."

"By whose order?" How dare they do such a thing without his permission.

Mrs. Fintrie bowed her head and bent her knees, cowering like a whipped dog. "Forgive me, m'lord. The fault is mine. I thought—"

"Ye will order my lady's things brought back to the chambers she and I share, ye ken?"

"Aye, m'lord." The woman bowed lower.

Lyla moaned again, turning her face to his chest and flailing a hand against him.

"I will address this later," he informed the housekeeper, then took off toward the stairwell. He slowed while climbing the steps, dismayed to discover himself growing a tad winded. A braw Highlander such as himself should be able to carry his lady love up and down endless tower steps and unto the ends of the earth without breaking a sweat. Leaning back against the wall, he concentrated on taking one step at a time. "Soon, m'love. Back where ye belong verra soon."

He noted her warmth didn't seem overly hot, and that brought him hope. Perhaps the fresh air had broken the fever. Aye, that had to be it. It had come on so fast, surely, it would leave her just as quick. And maybe this was what caused her madness. The more he thought about it, the stronger he believed it to be true. While the fever built and prepared to take control, it addled her senses. His heart soared.

Over halfway to the third floor and the comfort of their private solar, he paused to catch his breath. He hitched her higher against his chest and kissed her forehead. Cool skin met his lips. He closed his eyes and sank to sit on the steps. "Praise God Almighty. The fever is gone."

He sat there with her, his heart soaring. Eyes still closed, cheek pressed to her forehead, he gently rocked while humming a mindless tune. "I love ye, my own," he whispered. "Pray open yer eyes and return to me."

She didn't stir. But no matter. At least the fever was gone. "'Tis all right, my love." He gently brushed the hair back from her face. "I ken ye must be weary from fighting this malady. But dinna fash yerself. I shall not leave yer side 'till ye order me gone." He chuckled softly. "And even then, I shall stay, ye ken?" He traced the outline of her cheek, smiling at its cool softness. "The bairns are worried about ye. Ye shouldha seen their faces when they spied me running through the keep with ye in my arms. Their eyes went wide with fear." He cleared his throat, finding it hard to speak around the emotions knotting in his throat. "But dinna fash yerself about that either. Soon as I get ye settled, I'll bring them to ye so they can see ye're on the mend."

Lyla pushed upright and climbed out of his lap. "I can't do this any longer. I didn't think about how it would affect the little ones. So thoughtless!" She knelt on the next step down and took hold of both his hands. "Please forgive me. I am so sorry, but this was the only way we could think of to make you listen."

Shocked silent, he stared down at her, reading the guilt flooding her features. Her cringing expression spoke louder than words. The way she caught her bottom lip between her teeth, as she always did when fearing she had done wrong.

Jaw clenched, he fought to control his growing rage. "I feared ye dying," he forced out in an even tone he barely managed. "Feared ye were about to be stolen from me. Ye set my wee ones to weeping."

She didn't speak, just dropped her gaze.

"What game is this where ye play me for a fool?" He stood and backed up, putting another step between them. "Malcolm? And my mother? They are a part of this humiliation, too?"

Still kneeling, she looked up at him. "They believe me," she explained softly. "They accept Abby and I are from the future. Your mother understands because she knew of another woman who did the same. She has proof. Tangible proof you can hold in your hand. Talk to her. Please." She stretched and touched his leg as though trying to calm him. "They understand we are trying to protect you, protect the entire clan from what lies ahead. Please, Grant. There is so much danger in the coming months. Please listen to us and believe. Let us help you as much as we can."

He jerked to the side, recoiling from her touch. Her madness had spread to members of his own clan. How could she do this to him? Torture him with such ruthlessness? "How could ye be so cruel to me?"

"We shouldn't have handled it this way." Hands clasped as though begging, she didn't rise from her knees. "I am so sorry. We chose poorly, but we were desperate. Please. As I said before, your mother has proof about traveling through time. Talk with her. Abby and I..." She paused and gave a sheepish shrug. "If we can remember our history lessons well enough, we can help soften the blow of the troubles that lie ahead." She held up her clasped hands, pleading. "Please, Grant. I love you and don't want to see you imprisoned or...worse."

"Love me?" A snorting huff escaped him. The sting of betrayal churned his gut harder, stirring the bile of rage even more.

"Love me?" he repeated. "Is that just another of yer lies?"

She opened her mouth to speak, but he stopped her.

"Nay. I have heard all I wish to hear from ye." The sound of someone entering the stairwell below filled him with resolve and determination. "I shall leave for Edinburgh as soon as I can saddle my horse. The others can follow when they are ready or I will fight alone." He glared down at her, still amazed and hurt by the ease with which she had inflicted so much pain upon him. Nay, she did not love him. Not the way he loved her. But battle would help him overcome that weakness. "When I return, I will decide the fate of yerself and yer sister."

All that was left to do was get to the stable and ride. He made to push past her and descend the stairs.

"Grant, please." She grabbed hold of his arm, trying to stop him as she rose to her feet.

He yanked his arm away. "Leave me be, woman!"

"Grant!" She teetered and slipped, tumbling backward down the stone steps before he could catch her.

"Lyla!" Horror replaced his rage. He charged after her, flinching as she rolled and hit repeatedly. "God Almighty protect her!"

She came to stop on the second-floor landing, halted by his mother blocking her path. She lay in a crumpled heap. Too still. Bleeding. Her arm twisted to a nauseating angle. Lady Katherine crouched over her, weeping.

"Is she?" Grant knelt beside them both.

"Not yet," his mother whispered, then covered her mouth and closed her eyes as she sagged to the side, shaking with silent sobs.

Grant brushed Lyla's hair back from her face. "I am so sorry, m'love. So verra sorry. I am such a fool." He clenched his teeth at the bloody scrape across her chin and the purple knot swelling on her cheek. Rolling back on his heels, he sat beside her, straightening her shift, easing her arm into the position it should be. "I have killed her," he rasped. "God forgive me and take away this damnable pride of mine. Please dinna take away my precious Lyla because of my insolence!"

An anguished shriek made him lift his head.

"Lyla!" Abby shoved closer and pressed her fingers to her sister's neck. "Pulse is strong," she said in a quivering voice. "I hate to move her, but we have to get her to a bed where I can do what I can."

Her orders reminded him she was a healer. "Ye must save her. She must not die."

"What do you care?" she snapped. "You penned her up like a rabid dog and left her to rot." She stood and shouted down the stairwell. "Malcolm! I need you to carry Lyla! Hurry!"

"She is my wife. I shall carry her." Before the woman could protest further, Grant eased his beloved into his arms and curled her close. He hurried to the third floor, kicked the door open, and strode to the bedchamber. As gently as possible, he eased her onto the bed, flinching as her arm returned to the unnatural angle. "Her arm is broken, and more than likely her shoulder is out of the socket," he said. "I dinna ken what else plagues her."

"Get out of my way," Abby ordered. "Malcolm keep him away from my sister."

"She is my wife," Grant bellowed. "I willna leave her side."

"Sounds like a guilty conscience to me." Abby gave him a malicious glare, then turned to Lady Katherine. "Can you have Besseta fetch loads of boiling water, bandages, and some wooden slats to splint her arm?" She focused on him once again, her eyes glinting with hatred. "If you are going to stay here, stay out of my way. Understand?"

"Aye." He moved to the other side of the bed and sat on the edge. "I can help ye put her shoulder back in place. I have done it many times on the battlefield."

"Not until I get her arm stabilized." She eyed him, disgust on her face. "Did you push her? Is that what you did? She wasn't all that keen on trying to fool you. Knowing Lyla, she gave up and confessed. So, is that what happened? You flew into a rage and threw her down the stairs?"

"I did not throw or push her." He rubbed his brow, then scrubbed a hand across his eyes. "Ye know yer sister well, though. She revealed the trickery." The memory of it still rankled him, but a cold shudder shoved it aside as he recalled every detail of the horrifying accident. "Though I did not push her, I fear I caused the fall when I yanked my arm from her grasp." He bowed his head. "If my dear one dies, it is because I killed her."

"I hate you," Abby said. "And if she dies, I will kill you."

He accepted her vow, knowing it to be just. "I would expect no less, Mistress Abby." He deserved whatever punishment the woman meted out.

As she, Besseta, and his mother worked feverishly to check Lyla from head to toe, Abby called out every injury she found. "Broken arm. Dislocated shoulder. Possible broken knee cap. Several hits to the head, but at least the swelling is external for now. Hopefully, there are no bleeds. Broken toe. Multiple scrapes." She forced open her sister's mouth. "She bit the bloody hell out of her tongue and broke a tooth." Abby cleaned the blood out of her mouth with a rag and turned to Besseta. "I'll need some wax to seal that tooth until I can figure out what to do about it. Dentistry is not my wheelhouse."

"Wax, m'lady?" Besseta repeated, looking confused.

"Yes. You'll see once you bring it. And, also, any medicinal herbs kept here in the keep. Willow bark, pine, meadowsweet, and cloves would be good, but I'm really hoping you have comfrey, or you might it call it boneset for her broken bones and bruises." Abby dismissed her with a smile, then shot another baleful scowl at Grant.

He met it with a curt dip of his chin because he deserved it.

Besseta's efficiency at gathering everything Mistress Abby required both amazed and made him thankful. He had always thought her a flighty servant who spoke her mind entirely too much. But her diligent service to his lady love made him vow she would always have a home at Eadar.

While a questionable blessing, Lyla's unawareness enabled

the women to clean her wounds, push her shoulder back in place, and set her arm without her feeling the pain. After they secured her shoulder and arm against her side with bandages wrapped around her torso, they settled her in a supportive nest of clean pillows and gently pulled the bedclothes up to her bare shoulders.

Abby concocted an herbal salve and gently applied it to the scrapes and cuts. The sharp, acrid scent of the mix filled the room.

A soft pecking on the bedchamber door made them all turn as it eased open.

"I have some medicinals that might help our fine lady," Mrs. Fintrie said in a hushed voice. She held out a vial and two small cloth bags tightly closed with drawstrings. "My cousin visited the apothecary in Edinburgh and brought these to me. She knows how I sometimes ail with my breathing and suffer from aching in my bones."

"What are they?" Abby took them, opened the bags, and sniffed the contents.

"Thorn apple and sage." Mrs. Fintrie pointed at the darker bag. "Beware the thorn apple, though. 'Tis verra strong and deadly if not used sparingly." She held out the vial, its cork sealed with heavy wax. "Milk of the poppy. I have another already opened. Does wonders for any pain. But take care with it as well. Just a few drops, mind ye."

"Thank you, Mrs. Fintrie." Abby placed the bags on the table beside the bed but kept the vial in her hand. "I don't know if she has any broken ribs that might lead to pneumonia, but I appreciate your efforts."

"What is new mona?" Grant asked, another surge of dread pushing him round the bed to Abby's side.

She flinched as though regretting her words. "An infection she could get in her lungs if she doesn't breathe deeply enough because of broken ribs." She wiped her hands on her apron while eying her sister. "But I can use the opium to keep her pain-free and medically induce a coma to allow her brain time to heal."

"Do what to her?" Grant stepped closer. Milk of poppy could

be a dangerous thing. He had seen it misused before. "Are ye speaking of the milk there?"

"I know what I'm doing," she assured. "Never would I endanger my sister." Before he could stop her, she opened Lyla's mouth and dribbled in a scant amount of the powerful liquid.

"You should rest now, child," Lady Katherine said while taking hold of Abby's arm and turning her toward Malcolm. "I shall sit with her and have ye fetched if need be."

"Come, dear one," Malcolm urged. "Ye've got the wee one to think of. Ye ken yer sister would never forgive herself if aught were to happen to the bairn."

"I will be with her, too," Grant added, though he doubted that would bring her any ease. "And thank ye. For everything."

"I didn't do it for you." She cast another angry look at him. "I did it because I love my sister and need her to live."

"As do I, Mistress Abby." Grant pulled in a deep breath and released a heavy sigh. Without another word to any of them, he dragged a chair as close to the bed as he could get it and sat. He took her limp hand between his and warmed it. "Come back to me, dear one. Open yer eyes and fuss at me. Tell me the wildest stories ye can imagine. Anything. Just come back. I beg ye."

Her light brown lashes remained still on her pale cheeks, but her breathing held true with a steady rise and fall. Thank God Almighty for that. As long as there was life, there was hope.

"Yer Lyla nay felt right about the plot," his mother said. She rested a hand on his shoulder. "She loves ye verra much."

"I just need her to live." He had no time for plots, blame, or fantastical tales about traveling from one century to another. All he had time for was Lyla opening her eyes and gifting him with a smile.

Eerie music, as tinny as a nail tapping a thin sheet of iron, floated softly all around. Without releasing Lyla's hand, he turned his head to find the source.

In his mother's outstretched hand was a shining gold disk with its lid lifted open like a wee trunk. "What is that?" He turned to better see it.

"A pocket watch. A gift from a beloved friend I met before I married yer father." She took his hand and placed it in his palm. "Her name was Rebecca, and she was from the future."

With an irritated huff, he shoved it back at her. "I dinna have time for more foolish lies."

"Ye will make time," she said, sounding sterner and more unforgiving than she ever had before. "Many years ago, I found Rebecca wandering beside the river close to my birthplace. Lost. Confused. Completely disoriented. Much like yer lady wife and her sister. She shared the most wondrous tales. Even showed me her air o'plane that had brought her here from the year 1969." She bent and brought her face closer to his. "Yer grandsire ordered her executed. Had her crushed beneath the stones because he decided her a witch." She shoved his hand holding the watch closer and tapped on the lid. "She died because she trusted my family, and I could do nothing to save her. Look closely. At the wee portrait inside. Read the date on the dial. Open yer mind to one of this world's many mysteries and stop being such a stubborn fool."

"Musical movement 1965," he read aloud, then stopped. A chilling uneasiness stole across his flesh. The smiling woman in the portrait. Dark glasses on her face. Shamefully strange clothing. But most befuddling of all, the thing she leaned against. The oddest carriage he had ever seen. And then he recalled Lyla's words right before her fall. *Yer mother believes me. She has proof that time travel is real.*

He snapped the lid shut, silencing the annoying bauble of gold and tin. With his stare locked on Lyla, he tightened his jaw, clenching his teeth as he carefully selected his words. "Why?" He stopped, unable to speak through his raging frustration.

"Why?" Lady Katherine repeated, her brows drawing together.

He shoved the watch at her. "Why did ye not show me this before now?" He rose from the chair and faced her. "So much pain couldha been avoided. So much heartache." He smacked the trinket down on the table and pointed at Lyla. "My beloved wife would not be knocking on death's door!"

"Do not lay your failings on me." She snatched up the watch and returned it to her pocket. "I knew nothing of yer wife's origins before ye shared them this morning." She thumped him in the chest, poking hard against his breastbone. "'Twas yer stubbornness. Yer refusal to see sense rather than protect yer pride that did this. Lyla wished to try telling ye, hoping to veer ye from joining the conflict in the south, but Malcolm and I both knew the watch alone would not stop ye. Ye bear the bloodlust and pride of yer father and grandsire." She thumped him again. "We knew that, so we convinced her to go along with the ruse."

"If that be true, then the guilt of this accident is no longer mine alone." He cast a longing glance at Lyla's still form, then turned back to his mother. "All ye had to do was try. Speak with me. Show me yer damnable watch and explain. But rather than attempt one simple conversation, ye devised some foolish ploy meant to keep me from leaving." He advanced on her, backing her up a step. "And what then, Mother? Whilst Lyla acted as though she suffered from some mysterious fever, what was yer plan then?"

"Malcolm and I would convince ye Lyla and her sister told the truth and could warn ye of dangers only they would know."

"Never in all my days have I heard such lunacy." If not for his beloved wife about to die, he would laugh. "Ye could have avoided her accident by simply telling me about that feckin' watch, which ye planned to do anyway, while Lyla feigned sickness. Yer reasoning makes no sense."

"Yer stubbornness. Yer pride. How ye never back down," she shot back in a desperate hissing whisper. "Can ye honestly stand there and tell me ye wouldha listened and stayed at Eadar rather than insist on facing Cromwell?"

"I canna say, and now we will never know, will we?" He gave her his back, returned to his chair, and dropped his head into his hands. They were all such fools. All of them. Himself included. And now Lyla's life hung in the balance because of their poor choices.

Silence fell across the room. Grant lifted his head, braced his elbows on the bed, and propped his chin on his fists. He counted her breaths, willing her to take another and another. If she awakened, if she lived, he would be the man she deserved. He prayed for that chance.

His mother moved to a chair on the other side of the bed.

"Ye are free to leave," he told her without moving his gaze from his precious wife.

"I promised Abby I would stay," she said quietly.

"It was neither a suggestion nor a request, Mother." He slid a hard look her way. "It was an order."

"I see." She pushed up from the chair and dismissed herself with a nod.

The door closed with a soft click behind him, but Grant wasn't fooled. Without a doubt, Lady Katherine would stand watch from the sitting room. Once she gave her word, she never went back on it.

"Lyla," he whispered. He rose and settled on the edge of the bed where he could better cradle her hand to his chest. "I am so sorry ye landed in a nest of fools unable to manage something as simple as talking with one another." A bitter laugh snorted from him. "Of course, we two muddled that task ourselves, did we not? Or at least, I did." He kissed her fingers, frowning at their iciness. "So cold, my precious one." He yanked open the throat of his léine and cupped her hand to the warmth of his chest. "Come back to me, m'love, I beg ye."

With her hand still held against his chest, he leaned forward and brushed the soft curve of her cheek. "Give me a chance to start again. I swear ye willna regret it."

A light rapping hit the door, then it creaked open.

"I brought a tray, my chieftain," Besseta quietly called through the narrow opening.

"She sleeps still."

"I brought it for yerself. Mrs. Fintrie felt ye could use it."

He wished the girl would just go away but didn't wish to yell at her. Not after all she had done to make his Lyla happy. "Set it on the table, lass, then leave me in peace, aye?"

She eased in and unloaded the tray's two bottles of whisky, a glass, and a small plate of bread onto the table.

"Two whiskies?" He would drink nothing but water. The last thing he needed was to addle his senses further. He almost snorted a bitter laugh but scrubbed a hand across his face instead. His refusal to open his eyes and see, to attempt to understand Lyla's story had caused this mess. He wished he could blame the whisky for his shortsightedness, but he knew better. Perhaps a wee dram or two was in order after all. Maybe the drink would make things clearer.

"Mrs. Fintrie's order," Besseta said while hugging the tray. "Malcolm's gone to fetch Father Rubric, and Greer and the bairns lit candles in the chapel and are still there praying."

The thought of his wee ones praying for their beloved stepmother both touched his heart and shamed him. They had trusted Lyla fully. If only he had—he stopped the silent accusation and shook it aside. "Thank ye, Besseta. Ye may go. Now."

"M'lady looks right peaceful." Besseta eased closer instead of leaving. "She is young and strong, m'lord. All will be well."

"I pray so. Now go." He kissed his lady love's hand again and tucked it back against his heart.

The candles burned low, and daylight melted away from the window. Besseta brought fresh tapers, then crept back out without a word. Abby returned. Felt Lyla's forehead and lifted the bedclothes to touch the position of her splinted arm and shoulder. One drop at a time, she eased the milk of poppy onto Lyla's tongue, then massaged her throat until she swallowed.

"You should get some rest," she said as she recorked the vial. "I can sit with her a while."

Still seated on the bed, he shook his head. "I willna leave her."

She turned and eyed the untouched plate of bread and unopened bottles of whisky. "You should at least try to eat. Or drink some ale. That would be better than whisky. I can order some sent up if you like."

"I have no hunger or thirst." All he needed was for his dear one to open her eyes and forgive him.

She shrugged off his words, then moved to the door. "I will leave you to it, then. I'll be out here in the sitting room. Come get me at the first sign of any change."

"I will."

"Any change at all. Understand?"

With a heavy sigh, he offered her an obedient nod. "I will, Mistress Abby. I swear it."

Chapter Eighteen

"Bloody Hell," she whispered to the darkness behind her eyelids. Excruciating pain. Everywhere. Head pounding worse than any migraine. A beast was trying to dig its way out of her skull. Arm throbbed. Shoulder burned like buried in hot coals. Each breath scraped its way in, then tore its way out.

"God help me," she whispered again.

"Lyla? Lyla, open yer eyes, m'love."

That voice. So familiar. Maybe. So confused. Mainly just ready for this torture to stop.

A warm, calloused hand gripped hers. Something brushed her cheek. She wanted to scream, *Don't touch me! Everything hurts!* but couldn't get out the words.

"Lyla. It is me. Grant. Please, I beg ye. Try to open yer eyes."

Grant. She repeated the name in her mind, but the terrible throbbing made it so hard to focus. Bracing herself for even more agony, she forced her eyes open the barest bit. His voice somehow steadied her. If she saw him, hopefully, the rest would fall in place, and she would understand why.

"That's it, m'love. Open those lovely eyes of yers."

The memories cleared. Her heart remembered despite her head. She tried to smile but couldn't. Even that caused pain. But at least Grant seemed healthy and whole. "I know you." She cringed at the sound of her own voice splitting through her head. "Hurt so bad."

"I know, m'love." He looked ready to cry. "But at least ye live."

"Why are you sad?" She kept her voice as low as she could, but even that still echoed through her skull like a shout. When he didn't answer, she squeezed his hand, studying him, trying to remember. It seemed like some of her thoughts had gone dark or disappeared, like chunks of stone falling into an abyss. "What happened? Did we get attacked or something?" How had she gotten so beat up? Memories teased her like dancing shadows, fuzzy images she couldn't quite make out. She squeezed his hand again. "Are you all right? What about Fawna and Rory?" Belatedly, her sister came to mind, bringing a heady dose of guilt with it. "Is Abby all right?"

He eased closer, smiling as he gently brushed her hair back from her forehead. "All are well, my love. Ye fell down the stairs to our solar. Almost a full flight of stone steps beat ye without mercy. Can ye not remember any of it?"

She thought about it. Brief glimpses muddled their way out from the recesses of her mind. "We were arguing about something, but I can't quite remember what it was about?" A weary breath escaped her, making her cry out with the subtle shifting it left behind.

"Let me fetch yer sister," he said. "She has something for yer pain."

Not having the energy to stop him, she closed her eyes and tried to ease air in and out of her body with as little movement as possible.

"Lyla?"

"Abby." She forced her eyes open, then squinted them shut again. "No! Get that candle away." She swallowed hard, fighting the bile hitting the back of her throat. The last thing she needed was to wretch. "Too bright," she whispered.

"As soon as I see your pupils, I'll take it away. I promise."

A cool damp cloth dabbed her throat, her cheeks, then settled across her forehead.

"Please open them," Abby said. "I'll be as quick as I can."

Lyla forced her eyes open again, held them open as long as she dared, then batted her sister away while closing them. "Enough! I hurt too much to heave."

"I should say so. Both pupils reacted properly. Thank God for that."

The bedclothes shifted. Their touch raked across her, rough and painful as sandpaper. "Leave me alone," she told whoever was so determined to torment her. "Abby, if that's you. I'm going to give you a proper thrashing. Now sod off and leave me alone."

"Difficult as always, no slurred speech, and you recognize me. More pleasing news." The cool cloth returned to her forehead and over her eyes. "You have a broken arm. Your shoulder was dislocated, but I'm fairly certain we got it back in the socket. A broken toe, maybe a broken kneecap, and multiple scrapes and bruises. If your tongue hurts, it's because you nearly bit it off, and you also have a broken tooth."

"How far did I fall?"

"Almost far enough to kill you," Abby said. "I've some herbal tea ready that should help with the pain. Do you think you can manage a few sips? I'd rather hold off on giving you more opium for now."

The thought of moving at all nauseated her, much less attempting to push herself upright. "I can't sit up. Shame we didn't bring any of those bendy straws from the pub."

"I can lift ye enough to drink," Grant said. "I'll hold ye upright with the pillows so as not to pain ye."

She picked up on the tension in his voice and pushed the cloth up higher on her forehead. He sounded as though he was suffering, too. She risked opening her eyes. "You never said if you were all right. If *we* are all right. Our fight. Whatever it was about. Are you still angry with me?"

He leaned closer and gifted her with a smile, but it didn't reach his eyes. "I love ye, my own, and I thank God Almighty for giving me another chance to prove it to ye every day for the rest of our lives."

"I love you," she whispered. "The pain isn't as bad when you are here." She reached up and touched his cheek, rubbing her palm against the stubble. "What is wrong? I see it in your eyes."

Ever so gently, he adjusted the cloth on her forehead, then bent and kissed her nose. "It is my fault ye fell," he confessed in a hoarse whisper. "Can ye ever forgive me?"

"How can it be your fault? I may not remember, but I know in my heart you would never hurt me." She allowed herself a smile that made her cringe at the soreness in her jaw. "I know we've had our moments where you've hurt my feelings. I can't remember the details right now, but I get glimpses. But without a doubt, I know you would never physically hurt me."

"Ye had hold of my arm, trying to stop me from leaving, and I yanked it away." He closed his eyes and bowed his head. "'Twas then ye lost yer balance and fell."

She struggled to bring back the memory, concentrating on their argument. More snippets cleared away the fog and made it through to her consciousness. "You were leaving because I hurt you." Her palm still against his cheek, she brushed her thumb back and forth across it. "You were so angry; you were headed to Edinburgh to fight Cromwell all by yourself." The emotions as well as the memories flooded back to her. The anger and betrayal he felt had been written across his face. Then she remembered the start of the fall. Her feet tangled in her shift from where she'd knelt and stepped on the folds. "You did not cause my fall."

"I feel I did, my love," he said with so much pain she wanted to hug him.

"My feet got tangled in my shift. I promise you. That is why I fell." Her next smile didn't hurt nearly as bad. "I remember it. I promise I'm not lying." Before he could respond, she pressed a finger across his lips. "And I am so sorry for trying to trick you and hurting you in the process. I swear I will never do such a thing ever again. No more lies. No more tricks. I promise."

He eased the softest of kisses across her lips. "I love ye, my own, and if ye are willing, we two will heal and learn from this. Will ye give me the chance to make ye happy all the rest of yer days?"

"Absolutely." She combed her fingers deeper into his hair. "No more lies. No more towers. No more tricks. Nothing but love." She smiled. "And perhaps the occasional disagreement. Little spats."

"Aye, m'love," he said. This time his smile reached his eyes. "Wee spats and loving forevermore."

EPILOGUE

One year later, summer 1651
Eadar Keep
North of Stirling
Scottish Highlands

"A RE THEY TELLING tales about you? I don't believe you kept your mama up all night. Not a precious little nugget like you." Lyla snuggled and tickled her three-month-old niece under the chin until she gurgled and cooed.

"Wee Violet likes the garden," Fawna said from beside her on the bench. "If she's nay too squirmy now, might I hold her for a bit?"

A sudden queasiness of being off-balance made Lyla stiffen and move her feet farther apart. That dreadful falling sensation again. What the devil? She had been quite fit after recovering from her tumble down the stairs a year ago. Why had the nauseating dizziness returned?

"Ye've gone pale, Mama." Fawna caught hold of her arm, peering up at her with more concern than a six-year-old should ever feel. "Want I should run and fetch Da?"

"No, we don't want to worry him. I'm sure I'll be fine." She pulled in a slow deep inhale and blew it out, thankful the feeling passed as quickly as it came. Of course, any time the children called her *Mama,* it made everything better. "Let's spread the plaid over there on that grassy spot. We'll sit together, and you can hold Violet. I believe she's getting sleepy and won't be so squirmy."

With Fawna beside her, happy and chattering to the baby, Lyla made up her mind to concentrate on the lovely sunny day and ignore the ailment that had reared its ugly head repeatedly over the past month. Abby claimed it to be either a mild case of vertigo or scarring from the blows to the head she had received during the fall. Neither made any sense. Not a year later. But Lyla didn't dare tell her sister she thought her diagnosis was wrong. No. It was something else. But she hadn't quite figured out what.

"And what have we here?" Grant said as he joined them.

"Auntie Abby needed a nap, and we told Nanny Greer we'd watch Violet for a bit." Fawna gave her father a proud smile, then cut her eyes up at Lyla. "Mama had another dizzy spell."

"Fawna!"

"Da needs to know," the little girl said with the bossiness of her father.

"Is that true?" Grant knelt beside her, took her hand, and made her look him in the eyes.

"Yes, it is true, but I'm fine now." She arched a brow at Fawna. "Just as I said I would be when I told a certain someone there was no need to worry you."

"That would be me." Fawna beamed with protective defiance.

"And I am glad ye told me, my fine lass." Grant chucked her under the chin, then tugged one of her blonde curls.

"'Tis time for the wee one's nap," Nanny Greer called from the doorway.

"Aww." Fawna cuddled the babe closer. "She's happy right here."

"Aye, well, she'll be happy in the nursery, too, once her

mother feeds her." Nanny hurried over to them. She took the child, settled her in the crook of her arm, and held out a hand to Fawna. "Come. Ye can rock her to sleep in her cradle."

The little girl bounced to her feet and followed. She paused and waved when they reached the door, then went inside.

As soon as the door closed, Lyla turned and eyed Grant. "Did you plan that?"

"What?" But the look in his eyes betrayed him.

"You know what I'm talking about." Concern filled her, making the nausea return. It had been a year, and Cromwell and his army had done everything as Abby remembered it. "What is it? Did Cromwell make it past Stirling? Did we get that part wrong?"

"Nay, m'love. But he has cut off their supplies and reinforcements, as yer sister predicted." He kissed her hand, leaned in, and kissed her cheek. "However, that is not why I wished to be alone with my lovely wife here in the garden."

"Sounds promising." She snuggled closer and nipped his earlobe with her teeth. A pleasant afternoon snog in the garden would distract her from the lightheadedness. "But we should go deeper into the hedges so we won't be disturbed."

He gave her a devilish grin while sliding his hand from her ankle to her knee. He squeezed her calf. "Aye. We will do that. As soon as we discuss this dizziness ye've had over the past few weeks."

A trap and she had walked right into it. She removed his hand from her leg and placed it on the blanket with a loving pat. "We have already discussed it, and I told you I am fine."

"Yer maid, yer sister, and my own mother say otherwise." With a stern yet loving scowl, he looked down his nose at her. "Ye've wretched at least once a day for the past several days. All that allays the sickness is a crust of bread and a sip of that herbal concoction yer sister calls tea."

"It is a sorry day indeed when a person's confidence is betrayed." She had discussed her ailments with all three of the women, hoping to come up with a valid reason. Had to be some sort of influenza, food poisoning, or a food allergy. "Which one ratted me out?"

"*Ratted* you out?"

"Told you all these things?" She folded her arms and glared at him, plotting exactly what she would say to the traitors.

"It doesna matter." He pried her arms loose and held both her hands. "But it made me think."

"Well, I'm glad something makes you think. Men do entirely too little of that."

"I shall let that pass." Mischief twinkled in his eyes as he kissed one of her hands. "When was the last time yer courses came?"

"Courses?" she repeated, stalling while she tried to bring the date to mind. It should be easy enough to remember since it was such a royal pain, with uncomfortable rags knotted between her legs like a wadded diaper. Feminine hygiene products had turned out to be one of the things she missed most from the twenty-first century. And she really didn't bother keeping track of her menstrual cycle. Why should she? After all, she was infertile.

"The date, m'love."

"I do not remember," she finally confessed. "What with baby Violet's birth and trying to help the clan hunker down and prepare—I have been so busy. I just can't recall."

"Besseta said the last time ye bled was the sennight before Beltane." His gloating smile tempted her to shove him backward onto the blanket. "Tomorrow is the first day of August."

Her heart fell, weighed down by sadness and disappointment. She didn't wish to hurt him, but he had to understand; if her menstruating had ceased, it had to be for a reason other than pregnancy. "What you are suggesting, what you are hoping is not possible. The doctors said I could not have children. Not get with child. Remember?"

"Then how do ye explain this?" He pushed up to his feet, hurried to the door leading into the kitchens, and retrieved something just inside the doorway. Victory, pride, and a great deal of smugness shouted from him as he marched back with what looked like newly sprouted heads of wheat piled on a plate. "Well?"

"It is wheat." That's all she knew. How had they gone from talking about pregnancy to identifying wheat sprouts?

His smile widened. "That it is, m'love. Wheat that Besseta soaked in yer piss."

"That's disgusting."

"Maybe so, but when it sprouts as quickly as this did, it means ye are with child." He set the plate on the ground in front of her, then settled down beside her. He tipped his head toward the golden clusters of grain bursting with bits of green. "That paired with yer sickness and yer missed courses canna be wrong."

"But the doctor. He said…" She couldn't finish. Was it possible the man had been mistaken?

"Men err all the time," he argued softly. "Why could one of yer doctors not make a mistake?"

She stared at the plate, so afraid to believe what he suggested. She thought back to her first pregnancy. No illness, dizziness, or being overtired at all. But here, diet and lifestyle had changed drastically. And she was older.

"It can't be," she whispered. "It just can't." But even as she said it, the knowing settled in her heart as the truth. And it wasn't merely wishful thinking. She *knew* without a doubt she had somehow conceived Grant's child.

He pulled her close, curling her against him. "It can be, my own, and it is. I know it." He kissed the top of her head. "No more taking care of everyone else at any cost, ye ken? Ye must take care of yerself and our child."

So many fears, so many worries, and yet such an impossible blessing. She hugged him tighter, burying her face in his chest. "We shouldn't tell anyone else yet." Then she huffed a silly laugh. "Let me rephrase that—how many know of this?"

"Since yer maid knows, I am quite certain it has spread through the entire keep." His contented chuckling tickled against her cheek. "With any hopes, Fawna and Rory dinna ken, but I would not lay odds on it."

"I am so glad those stars, or whatever it was, sent me back in time to you." She lifted her face and nudged him. "A kiss would be nice right about now."

"Aye, my dear one. That it would." Then all talking stopped.

Spring 1652
Grant and Lyla's Solar

NOTHING BUT DEAFENING silence came from the other side of the bedchamber door. Grant glared at it, willing whatever saints, angels, or any other entities who watched over childbearing to protect Lyla and the wee one. It had been hours since she awakened him with a sharp elbow to the ribs while groaning, *it's time.*

The sitting room door eased open, and Malcolm stuck in his head. "The bairns and I thought to keep ye company. What say ye?"

He waved them in, praying his children would share in the joy of meeting their new sibling and not the sorrow of losing their mother or the babe.

Malcolm ushered them in and pointed to the small, cushioned bench beside the door. "Remember. Quiet." He arched a stern brow at each of them.

His toes already tapping against the floor, Rory studied the door. "Why's it take so long, Da?"

"I dinna ken, son." Men had asked that very question for an age or more. Grant patted the cushions beside him. "Ye can both sit here if ye like."

Rory started to move, but Fawna caught hold of his tunic and yanked him back. "Nay, Rory. Remember what Besseta said 'bout guarding the doors and windows so wicked spirits canna come and steal the bairn away?"

"Mama said that was rubbish." Rory assumed a superior look, jerked away from his sister, and marched across the room to join his father. "And Mama would never lie." He looked up at Grant. "Would she, Da?"

"Nay, my son." Grant smiled, remembering all the lies he and Lyla had waded through before finding their precious truth and laying claim to it. "She would never lie to either of ye."

The bedchamber door flew open. Besseta hurried out, pulled it shut, then ran out of the solar without a word or a nod. Grant stared after her, his hands closing into fists balanced atop his knees. "Damn her silence."

"I can catch her and find out!"

Rory jumped to his feet, but Grant caught him and sat him back down. "Nay, boy. She's fetching something yer Mama needs. We dinna wish to hamper her."

"I wish they would let me in," Fawna said. "Grandmam and Auntie Abby are at her side. I'm a lass. I could help."

Before he could answer an angry wail came from the bedroom. Then another joined it.

"Two," he whispered. Twins again. But he supposed that made sense since twins had been born on both sides of the family. He clasped his hands and pressed them to his brow as he bowed his head. "Please let all be well. Please."

"It'll be all right," Rory said while patting his shoulder.

"We'll help take care of the bairns," Fawna reassured him while patting his arm.

"Nanny Greer will need yer help with such a full nursery," Malcolm told them both while gently nudging them back a step. "Let yer father breathe. They'll soon be calling him inside."

Besseta burst back in from the hallway, a steaming kettle in each hand. Another maid followed her with two more. Once again, they crossed the room without a word or glance, only pausing long enough to open the bedchamber door and hurry inside.

He could stand it no longer. He jumped to his feet, strode to the door, and took hold of the latch. Then his hand dropped, as all courage left him. Nay. He should not enter until summoned. It would only interrupt them from tending to his precious Lyla and the babies. Unashamed at looking like an eavesdropping washerwoman, he pressed an ear to the door.

Footsteps. Hurried footsteps. Murmurs. He wished they would speak louder. A fretting babe growled like an angry pup. Laughter. Praise God Almighty. He exhaled in relief. No one would laugh if anything dire had happened.

The door opened, and he found himself nose to nose with his mother.

She smiled and pulled him inside. "Come. All is well."

From her nest of pillows and propped against the headboard, a wriggling bundle in each arm, Lyla gave him a weary smile. "Come meet your daughters."

He rushed to her side, elation making it impossible for him to speak.

"Sit beside us," she said. "They're both tiny, but lively."

"My precious wee lassies." He eased down and kissed Lyla's temple. "And ye are well? I ken well enough ye are weary, but ye are well?"

"Tired and sore," she confessed. "But happier than I can ever remember." She turned and lifted the red-faced babe in her left arm. "Here. Take her. She's more opinionated than her sister."

"Is she now?" He accepted the squirming infant and smiled down at her. "Such a busy one, ye are. Where are ye trying to go, my fine wee one?"

The baby growled, stretching and batting her fists that were still as red as her face.

He chuckled, then kissed her velvety head. "A fierce one like her mama." He leaned and looked at the other baby, content and sleeping in her mother's arms. "A fighter and a peacemaker, eh?"

Lyla softly laughed. "Yes." She rested her head against his shoulder. "If it's all right with you, I have names. At least, first names anyway."

"As hard as ye worked bringing them into this world, I believe the right of naming them belongs to ye, m'love." He repositioned the wiggly bundle in his arms, taking care to support her tiny head. "What names have ye chosen?"

She stroked the tiny fist of the baby she held, then gently folded back the blanket to reveal the pale yellow ribbon tied around the infant's wrist. "This is Hope." She smiled at the grumbling bundle in his arms. "And that is Joy, the eldest."

His heart swelled. "Hope and Joy," he repeated, his voice breaking with emotion.

"Yes. Hope and Joy," she said. "Because that is what you give me every day."

"I love ye, my own." He leaned in for a kiss, but little Joy stopped him with an angry squeal.

Lyla laughed and stretched up to gift him with the sweetest kiss he had ever tasted. "I love you, too. More than you will ever know."

About the Author

If you enjoyed CAPTURING HER HIGHLAND KEEPER, please consider leaving a review on the site where you purchased your copy, or a reader site such as Goodreads, or BookBub.

If you'd like to receive my newsletter, here's the link to sign up:
maevegreyson.com/contact.html#newsletter

I love to hear from readers! Drop me a line at
maevegreyson@gmail.com

Or visit me on Facebook:
facebook.com/AuthorMaeveGreyson

Join my Facebook Group – Maeve's Corner:
facebook.com/groups/MaevesCorner

I'm also on Instagram:
maevegreyson

My website:
https://maevegreyson.com

Feel free to ask questions or leave some Reader Buzz on
bingebooks.com/author/maeve-greyson

Goodreads:
goodreads.com/maevegreyson

Follow me on these sites to get notifications about new releases, sales, and special deals:

Amazon:
amazon.com/Maeve-Greyson/e/B004PE9T9U

BookBub:
bookbub.com/authors/maeve-greyson

Many thanks and may your life always be filled with good books!
Maeve